Relative Strangers

Relative Strangers

Paula Garner

CANDLEWICK PRESS

Copyright © 2018 by Paula Garner

First edition 2018

Library of Congress Catalog Card Number pending
ISBN 978-0-7636-9469-2

18 19 20 21 22 23 BVG 10 9 8 7 6 5 4 3 2 1

Printed in Berryville, VA, U.S.A.

This book was typeset in Minion Pro.

Candlewick Press
99 Dover Street
Somerville, Massachusetts 02144

visit us at www.candlewick.com

For Gabe

Chapter 1

*T*he best things in life always seemed to be doled out in limited portions. *Por ejemplo,* this Friday's curriculum-related Spanish treat, an orange and almond cake, was absolutely to die for, but split twenty-two ways, it was kind of tragic.

I pressed my finger into the last tender crumbs and sugar-dusted almonds as I watched the end-of-day announcements on the screen at the front of the class. Girls' basketball game today against Jefferson, which I already knew—my best friends had boarded a bus for it an hour ago. Rotary Club would be selling "scrumptious" pink-and-white cookies at lunch Monday to raise money for breast cancer. Last call for senior baby photos for the yearbook, which were due a week ago. Ugh. Though a lot of seniors hadn't turned in a baby photo, there was only one member of the yearbook staff who was remiss: me.

It wasn't my fault — I had no idea where Mom kept old photos, and so far I'd had no luck getting her to dig them up. Mementos and sentimentality were hardly her forte, and anything that took away from her painting time was an annoyance. Still, how long did it take to locate some photos in our tiny house?

When the bell rang, I gathered my things, tossed my plate into the trash, and headed out of the classroom. I pulled out my phone as a stream of noisy hallway traffic swept and bumped me along and tried to send Gab and Leila a "good luck at the game" message, but it was an extravagant fail:

FOOD FUCK TONIGHT!

I sighed. So close.

When I reached the south exit, I pushed open the doors and filled my lungs with fresh, cold air, my destination: Laroche's Parisian café.

The path was so familiar I could have forged it blindfolded. Not much ever changed in Maplebrook except the price of gas, posted in crooked numbers in front of Jolly Earl's Gas and Tire Shop. (Jolly Earl died years before I was even born, but why change a perfectly good sign?)

Icy water seeped into the cracks of my weathered boots as I walked past Morty's Kold Kutz, home of the town's most inexplicably beloved, boring sandwiches and my place of modest employment; past Tina's Thrifty Treasures, which was the source of most of my wardrobe (but also the occasional find: an antique medicine bottle or first edition of a classic novel); under the green awning of the vacuum cleaner repair shop, where dripping icicles hung like sparkling stalactites in the late winter sun. I reached out and knocked a few down with my fingers as I passed. They shattered like crystal on the wet sidewalk.

I crossed Second Street and slipped into the café — or almost into the café. The perennially defective door clamped shut on my backpack before I cleared the entrance and pinned me there like a butterfly on a board. Even better, this confounded the infernal *someone has entered the café* bell, which managed to get stuck and trill in rapid-fire like a burglar alarm. It took me two tries to yank myself free of the door, finally silencing the bell. I plowed resolutely ahead to the counter, my face burning.

Eli chortled from behind the espresso machine.

"Why don't you people get that damned door fixed?" I muttered as I slipped off my backpack.

He gave me his lopsided grin. "And miss an entrance like that? That was stunning."

Half of my friend's paltry weight derived from sarcasm, I was certain. Short and slight, he leaned on piercings, black hair dye, and a love of macabre subjects to give him substance, but the veneer was thin. Underneath he was as fragile as the antique china cups he served coffee in. I was not exactly bulletproof myself, but next to Eli I felt strangely solid — emotionally and also physically. Willowy I was not.

I stared into the glass case at the croissants, my Achilles' heel. Laroche's were a darker brown than I'd seen anywhere else, almost chestnut. They made an audible crackling sound when you bit into them, flakes of gold fluttering down like autumn leaves, and then the tender inner striations stretched seductively. The flavor was butter to the tenth power, and the ones I worshiped harbored in their depths a channel of intense bittersweet chocolate.

Eli came over and grabbed a pair of metal tongs in the pastry case, clamping down on a chocolate croissant with all the tenderness of an ax murderer. Several precious, buttery shards fell loose.

"Hey," I objected. "A little respect?"

He plunked the croissant onto a plate and shoved it toward me. "I'm an enabler. I'm feeding your addiction."

I gave him the steeliest gaze I could muster — not easy when you have the brown eyes of a Labrador puppy. Or when you actually love the object of your glare with all your heart.

I missed Eli. I missed the lit mag, missed being his assistant editor — or, as he called me, his "lit hag." I'd been at his side since my freshman year, when I'd meekly tiptoed in for a first recon and he announced, "Brown-nosers need not apply." I was intrigued by his individuality, his unapologetically dark outlook, his love of Sylvia Plath. I also felt sorry for him, because he was kind of a loner and people made fun of him and his "gay goth" style, not that he appeared to care. Motherless, he appealed to my maternal instincts, although our relationship was not exactly reciprocal. He was more like a pet cat: I fussed over him and he basically ignored me.

And then he graduated last year, and I left the lit mag, which was nothing without him, and joined the year-book staff instead — which was also nothing, but at least I had no expectations. Now Eli spent his nights writing his novel and his days pulling espressos and cleaning up after customers — "the Philistines," he called them, especially the ones who ordered complicated drinks with flavored syrups and never tipped.

For this he threw away a scholarship to Swarthmore. But it was a means to an end: he was only doing it to save enough money for a summer writing program in Iowa he hoped to get into — one he was convinced would connect him with people who would help him elevate his novel to Pulitzer levels and make publishing introductions for him.

I was eager to graduate and move on — probably to U of Illinois, which was hardly the private, lush Collegiate Gothic Utopia I longed for, but it required the least of the dollars we did not have.

I pulled some money out of my pocket, but he waved me off as he always did when no one was watching. "Thank you," I said. And I meant it. By my estimate, Eli's bad business practices were saving me in the neighborhood of fifty bucks a month — a substantial portion of my meager Kold Kutz earnings.

I pulled off a little bite of croissant, whose yeasty, chocolaty aroma was the culinary equivalent of a siren song, and laid it on my tongue. If they made communion wafers out of Laroche's croissants, I would be the most devoted Catholic in town.

Eli shook his head. "Is there anything in life you love more than those croissants, Drools?"

I ignored the nickname. "This is a bad time to ask," I said, closing my eyes as that familiar swoony feeling hit — a butter buzz. I knew it would be wise to exercise some restraint where these were concerned — but the flesh, it is weak. "They have it all," I told him. "The richness of the butter, and the sweet and bitter of the chocolate."

"So that's your trifecta. Rich and sweet and bitter."

"Stop analyzing me. Can I have some coffee?"

He took a cup — real antique china — from a hook on the wall. Its pattern was tiny flowers in shades of fuchsia and indigo, offset by splashes of green and yellow — slightly chipped and of English provenance. The saucer he laid it on was Austrian — scalloped edge, blackberry and rose design. No two items matched at Laroche's. It was one of the things I loved about the place. Where nothing matches, everything can belong.

Long hours spent examining the seemingly endless rotation of dishes at Laroche's had sparked in me an interest in antique china, leading me down endless rabbit holes of research. While other kids were binge-watching comedy and sci-fi shows, I was mainlining *Antiques Roadshow*, reading historical fiction, and fantasizing about eating my way through old European cities as I searched for treasures, perhaps as a higher-up for Sotheby's.

Eli poured coffee one shade past midnight into the cup and handed it to me. Then he pulled a book out from a shelf under the counter and laid it down in front of him. I leaned over to look at it. *Encyclopedia of Death and Dying.* Classic Eli. He opened it to an entry on decapitation, complete with a charming sketch of Marie Antoinette's liberated head.

What was this death obsession? Was it research for his novel? Or just a hobby? Or did it go deeper? Was it because of his mother? "Eli?" I hesitated. "How old were you when . . ." I trailed off. It was a hard sentence to finish. "When your mom . . ."

"When my mom died?" he said, without looking up from the book. "Five. Why?"

"I was just wondering if you have a lot of baby pictures. There aren't a lot of me. Do you think that's normal?"

Eli snorted. "You're asking me what's normal? I don't know. People are weird."

"But do you have a lot of baby pictures?"

He nodded. "Tons. My mom must have had the camera surgically attached to her. Me and my weirdo ears."

I smiled. They did stick out a bit.

"There aren't as many after she died, though." He went back to his book. "Maybe it's a mom thing."

Not all moms. Mine had hardly documented any-thing—sometimes it seemed like she didn't even care. "I'm glad you have all those pictures," I said, feeling bad. If I envied someone whose mother died when he was little, I probably had some rethinking to do.

He gave no indication of hearing me, but when I peeked over at his book, I saw what had captured his attention: diagrams of death by hanging. "Hey, Eli. Do you know why it's called 'bone china'?"

"Hm?"

"It's actually made out of bones."

It took him a second to register, but then he blinked and looked up. "Wait, what?"

I grinned. "Animal bones. Thirty to fifty percent."

His jaw dropped. "Get out."

"Swearsies." I held up my fingers in what I was pretty sure was some sort of Scout oath configuration.

His eyes widened. "How did I not know that? Oh my God, I am so putting that in my book."

As he turned to regard the now-interesting dishes on the wall, I took my croissant to the counter along the window. Made of scarred, waxy mahogany, the counter at Laroche's was reputedly salvaged from a nineteenth-century bar in Paris when it underwent renovations. Eli is convinced that this counter, having seen over a hundred years in a Parisian

8

bar, once held the drinks of all the greats: Hemingway, Fitzgerald, Camus . . . it was a piece of history.

Right now it was a piece of wood on which to place my croissant. I pulled out some homework, but I didn't get far. Pacing myself with croissants was kind of a challenge, and I liked my coffee piping hot, so I was quickly left with empty dishes and unsolved math problems.

I took my dishes to the counter, where Eli failed to register my presence. He was once again buried in his death book. "Well," I said, "I'm headed home to search for artifacts from my past."

He nodded absently, never lifting his eyes from the book.

"But I won't find them," I told him. "Because of the fire." Nothing. "Yes," I continued, more loudly, "the very terrible fire that took down my whole house last night."

Another nod.

"In fact, I died of smoke inhalation. This is just my ghost visiting you to say good-bye. Good-bye, Eli."

"Bye," he echoed.

I would have admired his concentration, except for the fact that I wasn't the most interesting thing — the story of my life. I pulled on my coat and left.

The sun was sinking as I headed home, and the temperature along with it. I huddled into my coat and stepped up my pace. Halfway there, my phone dinged with a message from Leila. *Halftime and we are down by 12, ugh. Meet us at*

Mario's after the game? Will text you on the bus on the way home. Pray for us.

I messaged back, *Prayer submitted to the patron saint of lost basketball causes. And yes to Mario's! You saved me from another night of gruel.* Probably Hamburger Helper; my mom stocked up on the stuff like the apocalypse was imminent. I could defrost ground beef with both hands tied behind my back. In desperation, I'd started adding things to spice it up: mango chutney, goat cheese, crushed potato chips . . . *I* was the true Hamburger Helper.

As I approached my house in the last violet gleam of daylight, I cringed at the peeling paint and splintered window frames. Our rented ranch house had benefited from no updating since it was built fifty-plus years ago. It was basically a teardown waiting for the housing market to rally.

My mom did her best — I knew that. But I was not so noble that I was grateful simply to have a roof over my head and the steady presence of a parent. No, I wanted more. Always more. Our house was a thing of sadness, and our dispassionate mother-daughter team wasn't exactly Disney Channel material. She worked a job she didn't care about to rent a house she didn't care about, and the rest of her time she spent painting, which was, as far as I could tell, the only thing she did care about. She was good at it, too — she'd actually sold a few. I had inherited none of this talent, but despite (or maybe because of) that, her work was a marvel to me.

There was Mom the mom and Mom the painter, and I had a hard time conflating the two.

Inside, I found a note from her waiting on the kitchen table: *Going to Harbach's, then meeting up with some people. Home around ten or so.*

The art store: her personal paradise. I could never feel such passion for a place that had no food.

I texted her, *I NEED A BABY PHOTO.*

I glanced at the clock — it was a few minutes before six. Gab and Leila would probably be back from the game around seven-something or eight. I went into the living room and gazed at the four photos of me on the bookshelves.

There was one of me as a newborn, looking like all babies look (too nondescript for the yearbook). One of me at about three, looking like a mini version of my current self (too old to use for the yearbook). My third-grade photo, which I despised but she liked. And my freshman-year photo. Kind of random, the collection. Or maybe a reflection of how often she had bothered to think about these things — i.e., almost never.

What she did have were photographs of other things. Unusual skies. Blurred reflections of trees in water. Weird things, like rusted-out old phone booths and bits of broken glass in dirt. I picked up an uncharacteristic photo — a sunrise over a lake. It stuck out from the rest because it seemed like a touristy, every-person kind of photo, not an artist photo. I slipped it out of the frame and turned it over. She had written something on the back in her tiny, perfect, font-like script. I walked closer to the lamp to read it.

It said *Day 50.* The date was inscribed underneath. It was about a year and a half after I was born.

I turned the photo back over. Where was this taken? We could never afford vacations. And if she was taking photos of lakes and sunrises when I was eighteen months old, wouldn't she also have taken pictures of me? Where were they?

A surge of nervousness fluttered through my belly as I considered the unthinkable: snooping. Trying to find the damn pictures myself. I had been bugging her for weeks, and this on top of the many times throughout childhood I had asked for baby albums. She had never produced any. Moreover, her excuses and reasons just did not add up.

My mom didn't care that much about "stuff" in general — that much I understood. She was always arguing with me over things I had wanted to save (she compromised by allotting me one box, which she actually labeled USE-LESS THINGS). I kept it in my closet — beloved items of outgrown clothing, shells and sea glass from the beach at Lake Michigan, toys or books I'd had a special attachment to. . . . Apart from papers I wrote or art projects I'd done — things I had made seemed to be an exception to her whole DUMP paradigm — I'd always had to lobby to preserve the pieces of my past I wanted to hold on to. And for whatever reason, I was as attached to "things" as she was keen to let them go.

I glanced at my phone to confirm that she still hadn't

responded to my text, then tiptoed to her studio and flipped on the wall switch. The bright track lighting made me squint. I moved carefully, peeking around the room. There was nothing in there that wasn't art or art-related. Even the closet was piled with supplies and canvases.

Next I ventured into her bedroom and approached her closet. I had never so much as snooped for Christmas presents before, and we didn't share any clothes, so the designation of "hers" vs. "mine" had always been a clear line. Breaching it was terrifying, and yet I pressed on, compelled by a need that went beyond yearbook staff obligations.

I slid the mirrored door open and peeked inside. There were a couple of boxes on the top shelf, and not much else. The boxes were labeled with spans of years too recent to be of interest except for one, which just had MILWAUKEE written on it in small letters.

Milwaukee was where my mother grew up. It was, as far as I knew, where we lived when I was a baby. Was it with her mother? I wasn't sure. She didn't talk about her parents — her mother had been dead for years and, from what I'd gathered, there was no love lost between her and the father she hadn't seen or heard from since she was small.

My heart pounded as I reached for the box, suddenly aware of every noise: Was there a sound from the entranceway? Was that her car outside? When I was convinced I was merely being paranoid, I slid the box out and set it on the floor, then pulled open the flaps.

Atop the contents was one of those orangey tie-string envelopes, unlabeled. Rolled in one corner of the box was my favorite scarf from childhood — one I thought she'd thrown away years ago, without pausing to consider that I might like to keep it with my other "useless things." It was sapphire blue with silver trim, soft as kitten's fur. I had adored it. I still did, actually. Dammit. I'd wear it now if I could reclaim it without revealing my transgression. I touched it longingly but left it tucked into its corner. Why had she kept it? Of all things?

I moved the envelope to see what was beneath it and immediately hit pay dirt: a photo album. I pulled it out carefully and lifted the cover. The first photo was a large full-page image of me as a newborn — the same one that sat on display in the living room.

I hesitated before turning the page, suddenly wishing for Gab and Leila. Just last week, the three of us had sat paging through Gab's enormous collection of baby books, photo albums, and scrapbooks. Every tiny event of Gab's life was clearly cause for documentation, probably the result of having parents who were shrinks. Leila's collection was famine, then feast. There were maybe a dozen pictures of her during her first three years at the orphanage in Ukraine, but from the time her parents adopted her, it seemed that nearly every blessed moment was chronicled.

Wasn't that how it should be?

Maybe if my friends were with me now, I would feel less unmoored, less set adrift in a sea of images that should have been familiar but instead were like trying to read a foreign language. On the second page of the album, there was a photo of me in my mother's arms in a hospital room, my face all red and scrunchy and indignant. Mom looked so much like me, it took my breath away. It occurred to me with a jolt that she was eighteen in this picture — exactly the age I was now. She could have been me — the resemblance was that strong.

My eye drifted to the next photo, where I was being held by a boy who must have been around the same age as my mom. He reminded me of Eli — a rail-thin waif with dark eyes and dark hair, skin as pale as moonlight. My heart caught as the familiar question came to me: Could this be my father? His eyes — didn't they look like mine? Or was I just projecting, the way I often did when I saw men in the world — wondering whether they could be my father, or an uncle, or a grandfather?

But it couldn't be. She didn't know who my father was — by her own admission, my mother was such a stellar teenage alcoholic that minor events like conception were hazy at best. So who was this guy who was close enough to her to be there when I was born, and what happened to him?

I turned the page. There were some photos of me in someone's living room, swaddled in a blanket, held by my mother or the boy. When I turned the page again, I was standing in a hallway, chewing on the ear of a well-loved bunny, a worried expression on my face.

Standing.

So I was, what, a year at least? Maybe a year and a half? I stared at the photo in confusion. That was quite a leap in the timeline.

The next photo was me in front of a birthday cake that had *Jules* spelled out in red icing. There were two candles on it.

My second birthday? I flipped back to see if pages were stuck together, then flipped forward to see if the album was out of order, but no. It went from a couple months old to a couple years old.

Where were the photos from all that time?

Where was I?

Chapter 2

Mario's was crowded and dark, the glowing red votives barely illuminating the tables. I could just make out Gab and Leila waving to me from their spot along the back wall. The smell of garlicky tomato sauce and pungent oregano and cheese was dizzying, and food as a distraction was always my best and most reliable coping mechanism. I needed a break from obsessing over the contents of that damned album. And what was missing from it.

"We ordered," Leila said as I scooted in next to her. "Hope you don't mind. We're starving." She leaned over and touched her head to mine — a Leila greeting, tender and sincere. I lingered there a moment, soaking up the love.

"So who won?" I asked, laying my napkin in my lap. I figured I'd get the formalities out of the way before launching into my personal drama.

"They creamed us." Leila shook her head. "It was humiliating."

"Next subject," Gab said, pulling a hair tie off her wrist and corralling her frizzy hair in a ponytail. Heeb hair, she called it. Jewfro. Moses mop. Slinging racial slurs at her mane was something of a hobby for her. "Oh, God," she said, craning her head to see around me. "Jason Godfrey is here. Isn't he the sexiest?"

I glanced at Leila and bit down on my lips. If you looked up the word "nerd" in the dictionary, you'd find a picture of Jason Godfrey, with cross-references to "Trekkie" and "virgin."

"He's with his Portal Guardians friends," Gab said in the same reverent, longing tone I reserved for phrases like *buttery caramel sauce*. "They must be having a gaming night."

Leila craned her head and looked at Jason. "Him? Really?"

Gab looked pointedly at Leila. "Yeah. Why not him?"

Their eyes met for a moment, then Leila looked away. "Guys are like toilets," she said, picking up her water. "The good ones are occupied and the rest are full of . . . poop."

Gab rolled her eyes at Leila. "Why can't you say 'shit'?"

Their bickering both amused me and made me envious. Even though I'd been friends with them since I was six — twelve years now — somehow their longer history could still leave me feeling like the odd man out. They were almost more like sisters than friends. Admittedly, people with histories were kind of a sore spot with me, owing to my 50 percent unknown provenance and my mother's abiding disinterest in chronicling the past — especially mine. But then I thought again of the photo of the boy who was there at my birth. Who would be there for my mom at that time if not the father of the baby? But if he really was my dad, why would she tell me she didn't know who the father was?

"Leila's right about guys," I said, just to contribute something, although this was hardly my area of expertise. My relationships seemed to blow by faster than a spring zephyr; it never took long to figure out that I'd suffered from a case of rose-colored glasses and to seek the escape hatch. In my experience, boys had been more interested in finding their way into my pants than into my heart.

I'd had two relationships, if you could call them that, each a sexual version of the Turtle and the Hare. I, of course, was the turtle — an even more fitting metaphor when factoring in how I wanted to crawl inside myself and disappear when a guy inched toward my breasts or my zipper and I knew he didn't *love* me. I was not proud of how hopelessly old-fashioned that might be, but I suppose in the back of my mind there was always the story of how I'd ended up here at all: some guy had paused only long enough to impregnate my mother before he went on his merry way. Sex might mean a good time to most people, but to me it was firmly and irrevocably imbued with the potential for doom.

It didn't help that I was possibly the world's most modest person. Since puberty had blown in, changing my body lavishly and seemingly overnight, I was too self-conscious to undress in front of anyone. Even Gab and Leila. Even my own mother. And the only thing worse than having to wear the assigned gym suit in PE was having to change into it and out of it in the locker room with a hundred eyeballs in the room, even though I doubted anyone was looking.

In any case, Leila certainly knew what she was talking about: her last boyfriend, Brett, despite having worshipped her for months (as one does with Leila, if one is lucky enough to claim her), had blown off the homecoming dance at the last minute when his brother scored tickets to a Blackhawks game, leaving Leila with a vintage Hepburn-esque black dress and nowhere to go. We ended up in Gab's basement, Leila in her beautiful dress, watching *Downton Abbey* and drinking a bottle of champagne from Gab's parents' wine cellar, which she insisted they'd never miss. The next day, the wine cellar got a lock and Gab got a bill for $85.

After the pizza arrived and the focus shifted, I told them about the photo album.

"Two years?" Leila said, her eyes so round and blue they reminded me of the Abbey 1790 saucer at Laroche's. Staffordshire. Circa very early 1900s.

Gab dove into the pizza, serving herself two fat wedges. "You think she lost them?" she said.

"No," I said, helping myself to a slice when she was finished. Pan pizza, praise be. Cheese was my friend, and for me it was not a case of less is more. "She does not lose things. She throws things out."

"She wouldn't throw out your baby pictures," Leila scolded, elbowing me. "Nobody throws out pictures of their kid. Besides, she has all the others." She finally picked up the serving spatula. This was a classic order of operations for us: Gab, confident and perfectly entitled, would serve herself first. I, desperate to get the food in my mouth but self-conscious and neurotically polite, would go second. And Leila, patient and unconcerned, would go last. You would think the former orphan would perhaps be the grabbiest, but no. When she served herself now, a glistening, oozy glob of cheese fell off and remained in the pan. I stared at it. Was she going to leave it there? I would never leave behind cheese that was rightfully mine.

"There are other pictures she took from during that time. Just not of me." I picked up the wad of cheese once I was sure she wasn't going to and popped it in my mouth.

"It's probably nothing," Gab said.

Easy for her to say. Gab, who'd never had a moment's doubt in her life — nor a reason for one.

She rattled the ice in her glass, glanced up for a busboy,

and then, giving up, set it back down and drank some of Leila's water.

See, she wouldn't do that with me. With me, she'd ask first. But with Leila, it was different. There were assumptions, unspokens, givens. I had some of that with them. But not as much as they did. Not as much as I longed for.

I broke off a piece of crust, blackened on its edge where the rich tomato sauce had caramelized against the pan, making it both sweet and bitter. *Rich and sweet and bitter.* Maybe Eli was on to something about me.

"People categorize information differently," Gab said. "Your mom is an artist. You can't expect her brain to process and file information like other people."

I figured Gab knew what she was talking about, since her parents were experts on humans, and a lot seemed to trickle down. They were the coolest parents I'd ever met — I loved and coveted them. And her brother, Daniel, was amazing, too, although I didn't know him well, since he was twelve years older than Gab and went away to college when we were six — the year we became friends. But somehow they were close despite the age difference. He called her Gumby. They messaged all the time. She confided in him. He teased her and adored her. I knew it couldn't be objectively true that she had everything, but it really seemed like she did.

Leila's family was equally wonderful — I'd spent enough time at her house to know that my envy there, too, was warranted. For an adopted kid, it seemed like she'd totally hit the jackpot. She had an at-home mom who used to be a chef, which meant the meals at the Hathaways' were amazing. Dinner chez Hathaway could mean seared guinea hen with caramelized oranges or a Malaysian noodle curry — there was nothing that woman couldn't cook, nothing that wasn't the most delicious thing you ever had. And then there was Leila's dad: a sports doctor with prematurely white hair and a roundish belly who was perennially in a cheerful mood. He was a physician for the Chicago Bulls, and more than once he'd invited famous players to dinner. Often Gab and I were included, and these meals usually ended with NBA players giving Leila and Gab some coaching out on the driveway while I stayed behind, helping with cleanup and nibbling at leftovers.

In addition to two perfect parents, Leila had an adorable baby brother, also adopted from Ukraine — born with kidney problems, now in perfect health, thank God. Leila also had a network of aunts and uncles and cousins as abundant as flowers in a meadow. I had bupkes. My mother was the only known link I had on the continent. And vice versa. And I didn't get the feeling I was any more satisfying to her than she was to me.

"Did you find one?"

I realized Leila had been talking. "One what?"

She regarded me with her *Jules!* look: head tilted, almost

exasperated, but warm, and so, so familiar. It was one of my favorite Leila faces. "Photo," she said mock-patiently. "For the yearbook."

"Not really. I guess I could bring a newborn picture, but those aren't even interesting. Newborn babies pretty much all look alike. Or I could bring the one from when I was two, and just hope my mom never finds out." It seemed stupid to take such a risk, though, especially since it was clearly me in that photo. But the fun of senior baby photos was the in-between zone, the trying to guess.

Leila smiled. "I'll bet you were adorable when you were two."

"She's still adorable," Gab said, bumping me lightly under the table with her foot.

I rolled my eyes. "Hardly."

"You are," Leila said. "You have the sweetest smile, and you know I'd kill for your hair —"

"And you're built like a fucking pinup girl," Gab added. "I'd kill for half your curves."

"You're welcome to half my curves," I grumbled. My exaggerated shape was a bequeathal from my mother. In that sense, I was her carbon copy.

In other aspects, though — a lot of other aspects — I hoped that I was not.

Mom was *not* home at ten. She messaged at some point saying she was out for the evening. Out where? She had said she was "meeting some people." What people? That was a lot of atypical behavior in a couple of short messages, now that I thought about it.

I tried to wait her out by starting to study for Monday's bio test, but cell cycles were less enthralling than one might think.

Or maybe I was just distracted. I kept finding my attention orienting itself like a periscope to my mother's closet. I wanted to see those pictures again, to study them for clues. I wanted to know what else might be in that box. It poked and pressed relentlessly into my mind, dangling the possibility of answers that would fill the holes in my mother's stories.

I picked up my phone and messaged, *Hey, when will you be home?* Maybe there was time for a second recon.

I waited nervously. If she was driving, she wouldn't reply — and she could be home any moment.

Exactly five minutes passed before I leapt into motion.

I flipped her ceiling light on and pulled the box onto the bed. I opened the album and turned the pages, my focus drawn to the boy. Except for the fact that my mother told me she didn't know who the father was, this would sure as hell look like a young couple and their new baby.

I set the album aside and pulled out the string-tie envelope I'd noticed last time. With impatient fingers, I unwound the string and pulled out the thin stack of papers inside. They carried the letterhead *Wisconsin Department of Children and Families.*

Confused, I flipped through them, deeply unsettled to see our names on the forms. Why would there be all this official paperwork from a social services agency?

I jumped about a mile when my phone dinged, but it was nothing — just a question from a girl in my English class about an assignment. Still, I quickly packed up the box and shoved it back in the closet, diving to flip the light switch off. My heart rate was well into the triple digits; I was not cut out for this kind of work.

But I was also not cut out for not knowing things about myself. So when my mother got home, I would confront her, and I would not back down.

I returned to my room and answered the girl's message — I took comfort that someone else in the world was also living the high life on a Friday night. I tried to study, but soon surrendered to Netflix, unable even to focus on that. Finally, at one, with no sign of my mother, I gave up and went to sleep.

Chapter 3

I woke to the sound of the shower — our ancient plumbing produced a sound that resembled a five-year-old's first shrieking effort at the violin. I lay there, hands pressed to my ears, waiting for my mom to finish. There was the faintest glow of light around my blinds. I squinted at the clock. Just after seven.

When she was finished, I used the bathroom and headed to the kitchen, nervous about the upcoming confrontation but even more anxious about the outcome.

The door to her studio was open. She stood in front of her easel in her blue robe, hair dripping, a paintbrush already in her hands. She had all six track lights directed on her painting. "I'm rounding the bell curve," she said. "Stop me."

"You shouldn't try to do this in artificial light," I said, leaning against the door frame. "Wait until the sun comes over." She was dinking with the sky, always her personal Moby Dick. She never seemed to capture what she was after, and "rounding the bell curve" was her expression for when she started to ruin something by not leaving it alone, not stopping when it was done.

"I can't wait on the sun." She laid her brush down, making a noise of disgust, or maybe despair. "I need coffee."

I followed her to the kitchen. "So you were out late," I said.

She rustled through the cabinets on tiptoe.

From this angle, her hourglass shape was even more exaggerated. I was built exactly like her, although her butt was bigger. This was my genetic fate: my ass would just continue to expand, like the universe.

She picked out a powdered creamer for her coffee — peppermint mocha this morning, gag. "I met some art people at Harbach's, and I hung out with them for a while after my meeting."

"What meeting?" I asked.

"AA."

AA? When was the last time she went to an AA meeting? Was she struggling with wanting to drink, for some reason?

"Want coffee?" she asked.

"No thanks." Her coffee tasted like weak tea compared to the coffee at Laroche's, which could put hair on your chest.

I poured some grapefruit juice and sat at the table, confused about her suddenly going to AA. "Is everything okay?" I asked.

"Yes," she said carefully, as if unsure why I was asking.

I mulled over how to approach her about what I'd found, desperate for answers but also nervous to confess about my snooping. I stared at the table and scratched at a jaundiced bit of Scotch tape that had been there forever. Our kitchen table was a relic from the 1950s — the owner had left it behind, and I didn't blame him. White-and-gray Formica with a chrome lip, it came with four metal-and-vinyl chairs, two of which had splits in the vinyl patched with duct tape. I thought it was awful, the whole thing, but my mom thought it was a score — because it was vintage, she said, but I suspected it had more to do with its being free. I had some pretty fierce vintage sensibilities, but they were almost entirely prewar, not post-.

"So what are you doing today?" she asked. As the coffee maker began to gurgle and hiss, she pulled a Chinese food container out of the fridge. She opened it, sniffed it, and then started eating out of it with a fork. Mu shu pork. Little did she know I had eaten all the black mushrooms out of it.

I picked the bit of chipped tape off with my fingernail. "I have to work at four. I might go to Laroche's first — say hi to Eli, maybe do some homework . . ."

I was about to segue into the yearbook photo thing when

a look of annoyance crossed her face. "How much money do you spend at that place?"

"Not that much," I said defensively. "I just usually have coffee, and the refills are free." There were an awful lot of chocolate croissants omitted from that account, but since I didn't pay for many of them, it made for some slippery math.

"Are you going to be home tonight?" She tossed the rest of the mu shu in the garbage and poured coffee into her favorite mug. NO SOUP FOR YOU, it read, with a picture of a mustached guy on it.

She headed toward her studio with her coffee, so I followed. "I don't know," I said. "I work until eight. Not sure about after that."

"Okay, well . . . Let me know." She set down her mug and picked up her palette. Translation: *Get lost.* She jabbed the brush into a blob of periwinkle. She was going to wreck the sky — there was no stopping her.

"Mom?"

"Yeah?"

I stood in the doorway, chewing on my lip. "Is everything really okay? I mean . . . you don't usually go to AA meetings. Right?"

She hesitated. "No, not very often."

"You didn't . . ."

She turned to me and met my eyes. "No. I just thought it was a good time for a check-in."

That sounded reassuring, and yet . . . if she never went,

why did she need a check-in now? "I don't understand it, how it even helps you. Don't you have to believe in a higher power and all that?"

"That is sort of a flaw," she said, giving me a wry smile. "I'm not a model AA-er. That's one of the reasons I'm not great about going."

As much as I sometimes envied the Wassermans' Jewish festivals and rituals (and had been flat-out awed by Gab's bat mitzvah, where it was like she was speaking in tongues and owning the entire giant synagogue), and as much as the Hathaways' decorations and traditions at Christmas tugged at my heart in a way I couldn't quite explain, I kind of admired my mother's unambivalent atheism. "Well," I said. "I want to talk about the baby picture thing."

Her demeanor changed on a dime. "Okay, but not now." She turned toward her painting.

"Yes, now," I said, turning her to face me. "I found the pictures."

She stared at me uncomprehendingly, and I lowered my eyes, crossing my arms in front of me. "The ones in your closet. I snooped, okay? I'm sorry."

"What?" Her voice was sharper than I expected.

"I gave up on you," I said, my tone more defensive than I intended. "The deadline has passed. I'm on the *yearbook staff*, Mom. I asked you over and over. So, yes. I went looking. And I found your box."

She seemed to pale. "What box?"

"With the pictures. And the paperwork."

She lowered her eyes, and I waited tensely to see what she'd do. After what seemed like eons, she said, "Okay, then." She took a deep breath, then pushed past me and headed down the hall.

I followed her into her bedroom, where she went straight for the closet and pulled out the box. She set it down on her neatly made bed and then sat beside it, glancing up at me. "I don't know how to tell you this."

I sat down gingerly, suddenly feeling shaky.

She stared into her lap. "There are some things I've never told you. Because they were hard for me. And because for a long time, I didn't think it mattered."

A chill ran through me. She'd never said anything like that to me, ever.

"You know I haven't had a drink in a long time," she said, glancing up at me over the box.

I nodded. "Since before I was born."

She looked away. "Not exactly. I went through a rough patch after you were born. It was the hardest time of my life, Jules. I relapsed."

My heart hammered inside me. "What happened?"

Her eyes stayed trained to a spot on the floor. "I just . . . I needed help for a while. And I needed help taking care of you."

"What . . . what kind of help?" I clutched my arms to

myself, suddenly cold. "Who took care of me? Was it the boy in the pictures?"

She turned to me suddenly. "What?"

"The boy who was there when I was born. Who was he?"

She turned away. "He was a friend. He was . . . my best friend."

"Well, is he the one who took care of me?"

After a pause, she said, "No."

"So who did?"

"A family," she said without looking up.

A family? It was such a simple phrase, but I couldn't wrap my mind around what she was saying. "Who?"

She shook her head. "I don't know their name. It was . . . it was foster care."

I sat, stunned. *Foster care?* I was in actual foster care? I recalled the DCF paperwork and the gap in photos. What in the world had happened? "How long?" I finally asked.

There was a pause before she spoke, her voice so soft it was almost a whisper. "Nineteen months."

"Nineteen months?" I stared at her. That whole gap. Yes. The whole time.

She pulled the flaps back on the box and pulled out the photo album. "Here are the pictures I have of you. But . . ." She slid the envelope out and set it aside. "I also have a handful of photos from the agency. From the foster family."

The words "foster family" echoed in my head as she

rummaged through the box and pulled out a small, weathered envelope from the bottom. She glanced nervously at me, then held it out. I accepted it with trembling hands.

Baby pictures. Ones I'd never seen before. They were labeled in a neat slanted penmanship. *Jules at four months. Jules at five months.* One for each month. By six months I was smiling. And each month thereafter. When I lifted away the eleven-month photo to see the next one, something tightened in my chest. *Jules's 1st birthday!!!!!*

"You weren't there for my first birthday?" I asked. I didn't mean to sound accusatory; I was trying to process.

"No." She got up to get a tissue from her bedside table. She blew her nose, then took another tissue and wiped her eyes. She was crying? That was a phenomenon I had rarely seen. "I missed it," she said. "Just that one. I had you back before you were two. And I was okay after that. I've been sober all these years. I just . . . I had a hard time for a while. It happens."

I turned back to the photos, watching myself grow from a baby into a toddler. Me, standing on my own two feet at thirteen months. Me at fourteen months, on a piano bench, in the lap of a little boy. . . . Who? He was skinny and wore rocket ship pajamas. But his face was blocked out in the photo.

"Who is this?" I asked her.

She sank down next to me on the bed. "They had a son.

They can't include images of the foster family for legal reasons, so . . ."

My mind reeled. "You mean, I had a brother?"

Her brow furrowed. "Well, not really. I mean, sort of, temporarily. I guess."

I flipped the last picture to the back and looked at the four-month picture again.

Mom turned away. "I can't —" Her voice broke. "I can't look at that one."

I could see why. I looked scared to death, my lower lip curved into a pout that suggested I might cry. And I almost cried now, looking at it, except it was surreal. Trying to bridge the gap in my head between the baby in the picture and myself. . . . That was me, feeling that way — feeling whatever that baby was feeling. How traumatic must that have been? Being taken away from my mother and handed over to strangers?

"I probably should have told you." She sighed and wiped her nose again. "I just never knew when to do it. Or how."

I stared at the photo in my hands, thinking I should feel something, but too struck dumb to know what it was. Anger? I had a feeling that might be coming, but I was sort of stuck spinning in place. "Why is my scarf in there?" I asked. "You never keep anything."

She lifted it out and held it both hands. "It was from them. They wanted you to have it."

I stared at it. "It was from them? I wore that scarf for years! You never told me?"

She looked at me like the question was unreasonable. "How could I?"

I snatched it away from her. "What else have you been keeping from me?"

She looked as though I'd slapped her, but then she gestured at the box. "This is everything."

I stuck the photos, the envelope, the album, and the scarf inside the box and stormed out, slamming her door behind me.

Chapter 4

*M*orty and I worked at opposite ends of the stainless steel prep table, lost in our own tasks and thoughts, not that we could talk over the racket of the meat slicer. Today's special was the Gobbler, which meant Morty would be slicing pounds upon pounds of turkey, and I would be opening cans of cranberry jelly and washing more than the usual amount of iceberg lettuce. Despite the lavish schmear of Miracle Whip (which lacked anything even remotely resembling a miracle), I found the sandwich to be a total snore. But somehow it sold like crazy. My idea of a turkey sandwich worth eating would involve some runny, stinky cheese, or maybe a spicy sauce. Buffalo-style turkey sandwich, maybe — with blue cheese and chopped celery and a buttery hot sauce. *Something.* But I had learned long ago that my suggestions were of little interest to Morty. And maybe that was reasonable — twenty years of an unchanging menu, and business was as good as ever.

The relative solitude of our routines did at least give me space to think. Trying to comprehend having had a foster family (for more than five hundred days!) was, it turned out, a slow and consuming exercise. The last twenty-four hours had seemed like a year, so what would five hundred of those be like? Five hundred days of knowing people, of trusting them, of being fed and held. Five hundred days during which I'd cut my first teeth, learned to walk, probably uttered my first words. I was overcome with a need not just to know who they were, but to say thank you. Thank you for caring for me, thank you for making it possible for me to survive when I was completely helpless, thank you for saving my life. Wasn't that just good manners?

And what the hell had happened to cost my mom her sobriety? With a baby depending on her!

The phone jangled. I wiped my hands off and walked over to the tiny front room and picked up the wall phone — old school, complete with spiral cord, straight out of nineteen-whatever. "Kold Kutz, can I help you?"

I took the order — four Gobblers and one Horsey Moo (roast beef with horseradish sauce and sharp cheddar). I went back and called the order to Morty, who nodded without comment. The man used words as if they were priced by the unit.

I put on plastic gloves, applied the condiments to the rolls, and slid them over to him for the meats and cheese.

Before things got busy, Morty asked me the usual question: "What can I get you?"

"Um, could I have the Mount Etna?" I don't know why I always answered in a question. A meal was part of my meager compensation package, but I still felt like I was asking a favor, especially when I asked for a combination not on the menu (possibly insulting) or a hot sandwich (extra work). I wondered how having been tossed around by the currents of an unstable early life might have affected me. Subconsciously, did I feel like an imposition, unentitled to what others took for granted?

He nodded wordlessly and set to work. I would have been happy to make it myself — preferred it, even — but sometimes he had to slice something, and I wouldn't touch that horror movie meat slicer with a ten-foot pole. I'd probably lose a limb. Anyway, it was established from the start that Morty made my sandwich, and, like everything else at Kold Kutz, it didn't seem subject to negotiation. Fortunately, the Mount Etna, the most flavorful thing on the menu, was pretty good as is: salty cured Italian meats, pizza sauce, melted provolone, and spicy giardiniera.

The rush started not long after I finished eating my sandwich. I barely had time to think about my mother, about my days as a foster child, about anything, really, until close to eight, when things slowed down and we could clean up for closing. I vacuumed up the front room with the archaic carpet sweeper that picked up exactly nothing, but it was part of the job description, so I went through the motions.

When Morty gave me my paycheck, I thanked him profusely as I always did, as if he were doing me some extravagant favor by paying me for my labor. I pulled my coat on and wrapped myself in my reclaimed blue scarf, still stunned to think it came from my foster family. *My foster family.* The term seemed ludicrous, something made-up. Where were they now? Did they ever think of me? Was I just one in a long stream of foster children? And what about the boy? He looked a lot older than I was. If he was even a few years older — about five or six years old at the time I left — he might remember me.

The thought nearly laid me flat. What if he still thought of me?

The fresh night air was a welcome reprieve from the meaty smells of Morty's. A fine silvery mist swirled in the columns of streetlamp light. I pulled my coat tighter around me as I headed past Laroche's, which was now closed, past the familiar landscape of Maplebrook, the only place in my life I could remember. It boggled my mind that I'd once lived somewhere else — in a whole other town, with a whole other family. I racked my brain for memories of those early months, which of course was ridiculous. All I came up with were a few rogue snippets of the apartment we had lived in before this house — an old building in Chicago with high ceilings and peeling paint. I remembered the radiators, dangerously hot to the touch in winter, and the odd southwestern cactus and cowboy tiles on the kitchen backsplash. I remembered a neighbor — an old Polish lady named Mrs. Borski — who sometimes brought over tiny nut cookies or soft little parcels of meat- and rice-stuffed cabbage in a sweet and tart tomato sauce.

I wondered what memories were swimming in the soup of my head from just a couple years before that, and if they were, at this point, too far lost ever to recover.

As I walked, I played with the tassels of my scarf, fine silver threads sparkling among the blue in the light of the streetlamps. Above the knots of the tassels, the name of the designer, Luke Margolis, was neatly stitched. I was so happy to have the scarf back — and amazed my mother hadn't gotten rid of it. It occurred to me to wonder why she'd stashed it in her box of secrets. Why not let me keep wearing it, or throw it away if she'd gotten sick of seeing it? But I'd never had much luck making sense of her secrets and motivations, and this was no different.

At home, I zoomed past her studio without pausing. Nothing said "Do Not Disturb" like Stravinsky blaring from behind her closed door, and at the moment that suited me fine. I shut myself in my room, pulled off my clothes, which were spattered with mustard and oil, and put on sweats.

I settled on my bed with my precious box in front of me.

I wished I had someone to talk to, now that I felt ready to confront my past head-on. But Gab and Leila were in the city at a Bulls game, and Eli would probably cringe and eye the exit doors if I reached out to him in my time of emotional need.

How strange to think that none of them knew I had been a foster child yet. What would Leila think of that? Leila, who spent her first three years in an orphanage? For about half the time she was cared for by strangers, so was I. She and I shared something that Gab was not in on. The thought was a guilty tantalization. I treasured my friendship with Gab and Leila more than anything, but I was not above sometimes wishing they knew what it was like to be the one looking in from the outside. Especially Gab, whose brash self-assurance I sometimes resented.

But my friendship with both of them was more important than that. I needed their support. I needed Leila's compassion and Gab's knowledge and lack of judgment. I was at once desperate to tell them and also feeling a need to sit and process. And it didn't feel like the kind of news I wanted to text — especially when they were in the racket and pandemonium of United Center during a Bulls-Cavs game.

I pulled out the photos that documented my lost nineteen months, wondering if the family had taken more, if somewhere in the world there were dozens more photos of me that a family had held on to. I couldn't let go of the idea, the hope, that they still thought of me. I remembered my mother's words, her reasoning for not telling me — *I didn't think it mattered* — and something twisted inside me.

I turned to a photo of me sitting on a bed with a blue comforter. I was holding a toy car in my chubby fingers, and there was someone else there, too — a knee and elbow were visible in the shot. Was it the little boy? I squinted at the photo, wishing I could see more, find some clue about the family's identity. There were some things on a display shelf behind us, but I couldn't make them out. They were too small.

In a sudden burst of what I hoped would prove genius, I grabbed my phone and took a picture of the photo. I expanded the photo on my phone screen, which made things a little grainier, but still, I could see them better. There was a stuffed bear. A truck. A trophy of some sort. And a toy train, which, on closer examination, proved to be lettered wood blocks, one for each train car. I could make out an L and a U, and then there was something too blurry to make out, and then an E. I played with the sizing of the photo on my phone, looking for the sweet spot between big enough and clear enough. Slightly smaller, the letter looked to be a K. L-U-K-E.

Luke. I froze. *Luke?*

It only took a moment to realize why the name rang a bell: my scarf. I'd always assumed Luke Margolis was the designer. But — what if he wasn't? What if it was this boy's name? But why would someone sew his name into the scarf? And then give it to me?

I scrambled for my laptop and logged in. I typed *Luke Margolis designer* into a browser window.

Nothing. Not one thing.

I deleted "designer" and suddenly there were scores of hits. My heart pounded as I hovered over the trackpad, ready to click one of them. But suddenly I was terrified. I might be one motion away from finding the boy who at one time was my brother, the family that had, for a time, been mine. Was I ready for that?

I pulled out my phone and messaged Gab and Leila: *SOS. Can we get together tomorrow? I have a situation.*

I sat on my bed, wringing my hands. Tomorrow was a long time away. Maybe I should just do this on my own. But if I found possible matches, what then? What if I found e-mail addresses? Would I just message every Luke Margolis with UM, DID YOU ONCE HAVE A SORT-OF SISTER NAMED JULES? IF SO, ANY INTEREST IN MEETING HER? NO PRESSURE OR ANYTHING. IT'S NOT LIKE SHE WILL PERISH OF COMPLETE HEARTBREAK IF YOU DON'T, NOPE.

My stomach tightened at the thought of the stupid impulsive things I might do. I closed my laptop, and at the same moment, Leila messaged: *Are you okay?*

I wrote, *Yes. Just a thing I want to tell you guys about. Are you both free tomorrow?*

She replied, *Yes, tomorrow is fine. Come at lunchtime? My mom made your favorite — that butternut squash lasagna.*

I felt that warm but sharp-edged sensation — envy laced with jealousy. They were so lucky with their families, Gab and Leila. Did they even know?

I wrote back to Leila: *SOLD. See you then.*

I looked back to the pile of pictures, flipping until I found the one with the little boy in it. We were facing a piano, sheet music laid out above the keyboard. Did he play? Did his mother? His father?

His father . . . Was there a man who was like a dad to me? Who carried me around and played with me and took care of me? For five hundred and some days? The idea of a father was incomprehensible; "fatherless" had always been a primary aspect of my identity. But then I thought of the guy in my mother's photos, the one who visited her in the hospital and at least a few times after that. The one who wasn't in any of the post–foster family photos. My mother didn't say what happened to him, and I had gotten too tangled up wanting to know about that lost year and a half to press her about it.

I churned with outrage that I didn't know any of this. *She should have told me.*

I closed my laptop. I would start my search tomorrow, with my friends by my side. They would understand what my mother apparently didn't: I had a right to find the people who had met my every need when my own mother hadn't. I had a right to know my own fucking history.

Chapter 5

$\mathcal{W}$alking into Leila's house was like walking into a *House Beautiful* photo shoot. Fresh flowers, designer furniture, and a total dearth of taped-together vinyl crap. The sunroom, annex to the glorious kitchen, featured walls of windows, a cozy banquette, and plush stuffed chairs strewn with soft throw blankets. It wasn't a prewar home (it had been custom built by the Hathaways), but apart from that, it was hard to find fault.

"Back around three or four," Leila's mom said, kissing Leila. She was as beautiful as her daughter, despite the absence of genetic connection — lithe and elegant and sweet. In her early fifties, she looked easily ten years younger. "Garrett's already down for his nap. Bye, girls!" she called to Gab and me.

Dr. Hathaway put some money down on the table. "Pizza money, in case you're still hungry after you've eaten us out of house and home. Gotta keep those tapeworms thriving." He winked at us. I glanced at the cash on the table, thinking how many hours of work a few twenties represented for me and how they were nothing to the Hathaways, and the Wassermans, too. I cringed at myself for the money envy on top of the family envy, but apparently my coveting knew no bounds. When Leila's dad gave her a kiss on the temple, I wanted to crawl under the kitchen island with the copper-bottomed pots and fancy appliances and cry.

We sat in the banquette, a celery-green glass vase of calla lilies in the center of the table. Leila had already heated up the lasagna, and it was mind-numbingly delicious: layers of pasta filled with oozing cheeses, caramelized onions, creamy butternut squash, and fresh herbs. I daydreamed of someday traveling to Italy, where I could eat things like this with beautiful views of hilly olive groves or sunlit vineyards and a bottomless decanter of local wine and people who loved food as much as I did.

As we ate, I told them about my confrontation with my mother and showed them the photos. By the time I revealed my mother's confession, they were both staring at me, not even chewing.

"You were in foster care?" Leila stared at the photos from the DCF envelope. "I can't believe it."

I couldn't really believe it either. On some level, being

an orphan must be part of Leila's identity, as well-adjusted as she seemed. I was just a regular boring person with nothing interesting about me at all. How could I suddenly be a former foster kid?

Gab leaned over Leila's shoulder and looked at the pictures. "God, you were cute. You look good, Jules. I mean, you look happy and okay."

"They must have taken good care of me," I said, my chest tightening with feeling. How lucky I was. Given everything.

"Do you think you'll . . ." Gab hesitated, glancing at Leila, and I knew she was worrying about how this conversation might affect her. "Do you think you'll look for them? Maybe there's something in the DCF paperwork that could lead you to them."

I helped myself to a sliver more lasagna. "I can't even imagine the fallout if I told my mom I was going to do that." Although, what was she going to do? Ground me? I was eighteen and leaving for college in a handful of months. I hadn't experimented enough with flouting authority to know the likely outcomes.

"If I had a way to know something," Leila said slowly, "I wouldn't hesitate."

I lifted my eyes to meet hers.

She shrugged. "I'll never know anything. I was left there, with no information about where I came from. I didn't even have a name. I don't even know my real birthday."

"Oh my God." I felt helpless — and incredibly selfish. "So," I said, wringing my hands in my lap, "your birthday . . ."

"It's an estimate," Leila said. "It's probably accurate within a few weeks."

I considered the idea of such a simple thing — one's birthday — being forever unknowable. My own story suddenly felt much smaller. "How old were you when . . ." I couldn't finish the sentence.

"A few months old," Leila said.

Here I'd been reveling in my connection to Leila, and her reality was so much worse than mine. "I'm so sorry," I finally said. I wanted to hug her, but she was already leaning toward Gab, who reached out an arm, an anxious expression on her face.

They were a proton and a neutron in the center of an atom, and I was the electron that orbited them. It was always like this. So how did it keep hurting?

My eyes met Gab's, and to my surprise hers were damp. She was not normally one to cry, but the depth of her feeling for Leila was an exception. Emotions swirled in me: sadness, jealousy, love. So much love. I loved them more than anything. Even if I had to love them like an electron. I did. I just did.

"Seriously, though, Jules," Gab said, nudging me under the table with her foot. "Weigh pissing off your mom against never finding out your history."

49

"Did you ask her who that boy was in the pictures?" Leila asked. "The one from the hospital? Maybe he knows something."

"She says he was her best friend."

"So what happened to him?" Gab asked.

"I don't know," I said. "He's not in any of the photos once Mom had me back. Maybe they had a falling-out when she fell off the wagon? I don't even know his name, so even if he did know what happened to me back then, I have no way of finding him. Also, there's this." I got up and went to the foyer to get my scarf, then brought it back to the table.

"I remember that scarf," Leila said, reaching for it. "You wore that all through grade school."

"And junior high," I said. "But there is a tag on it that I'd always assumed was the name of the designer."

Leila found the tag at the end of the scarf. "Luke Margolis?" Her brow furrowed. "Never heard of him."

"Right. And I couldn't find anything online. But then there's this." I picked up my phone and showed them the photo with the toy train spelling out L-U-K-E.

Gab stared at the photo, then at me. "Did you google him?"

"I started to, but then I panicked. I wanted to do it with you guys."

Gab picked up her phone and started typing.

"Wait!" My heart rate doubled just thinking about what she might find. "Hang on."

"Slow down, Gab, jeez," Leila said. She scooted closer to me and put an arm around my shoulders. "What are you afraid of?"

I took a breath. "I don't know what I'll do about whatever I find. Should I have a plan?"

"There are too many possibilities here to see around all the corners," Gab objected. "Let's just find the results and we'll go from there. We're right here, Jules. You won't have to figure it out alone." When I nodded, she told Leila to get her laptop so we could all look.

We sat at the table together. As Leila typed in "Luke Margolis," I held my hands up in front of me, watching them shake. "Is he a pedophile?" I asked. "A serial killer?" I craned my head to look out the window and avoid watching the screen, listening to her fingers clicking away. I heard Gab murmur, "there," and out of the corner of my eye I could see her pointing at the screen.

"Ohhh," Leila said softly. "Do you think?"

"Jules," Gab said. "How old do you think he is?"

"I don't know," I said. "Judging from the picture, I would guess he was around six when I was one? Or maybe just tall for his age? All I have to go on are limbs and pajamas, basically."

"Well, there is a Luke Margolis who is a senior at Lawrence University. He's a student of the conservatory. A pianist."

"What?" I clutched my heart, still not turning around.

51

Lawrence was in Wisconsin. "We were sitting at a piano in the other picture. The one with his face blocked out." This suddenly seemed entirely possible. This could really be him.

"Jules, it says he's from Milwaukee."

"Oh my God." I was shaking all over now.

"We should probably warn you he's hot," Gab said.

"He's hot?" I squeaked. "You mean, like, Jason Godfrey hot? Or . . ."

"Just look, Jules," Leila said. I felt her hand on my back.

I turned slowly to the screen.

It was a portrait shot — head and shoulders — and Gab was right. He was objectively very, very cute. He had dark blond hair, long enough to reveal it had a loose curl but short enough not to be a mop. His eyes were my very favorite color — hazel — and they were the exact hazel I loved best: river green, speckled with brown. I was jarred with the thought that maybe they were my favorite color eyes because they were his — because somewhere in the recesses of my memory, I knew them. He wore a soft-looking charcoal sweater with a bright white shirt underneath. And although he was only smiling slightly, his expression was very warm, very approachable.

"Jules?" Leila's voice was almost a whisper. "You don't remember him, do you?"

"She was too young," Gab said. "Not even two."

"Sometimes people remember things from earlier than that," Leila said.

"That's pretty rare," Gab said. She reached out and turned the computer toward her. "He must be really good, Jules. It says here that he just won second prize in something called the MTNA Division Young Artist Competition. He also was a finalist in the Schubert Club competition, and he has a whole bunch of honorable mentions. Jesus. He seems pretty epic."

"Wow," Leila whispered.

Gab pecked away at the keyboard. Suddenly, she gasped.

"What?" I said. "What is it?" I leaned over to see the screen.

It was Luke's Facebook page.

"Jules," Gab said softly. "You could message him right now."

"What?" I stood up. "No!"

Gab laughed. "Why not? Oh my God, just do it."

"Gab." Leila gave her a warning look. "Stop it. Don't rush her."

I expected Gab to have some snippy comeback, but she surprised me by nodding and looking abashed. "No, you're right. Sorry, Jules."

Leila put her hand on my shoulder. "You don't have to do anything you don't want to do. Maybe you should sleep on it."

"I want to talk to him," I said. "I just — I didn't know it would be this easy to find him. What would I even say?"

"Well," Gab said, glancing at his page. "You *could* just

say, 'Hey, did you happen to have a foster child in your family sixteen years ago?' And then you aren't really saying very much, just maybe opening a dialogue?"

I wrung my hands. "But what if he doesn't write back?" The thought was devastating but quickly followed by a flash of annoyance at myself. Was I going to give up on finding out about my past out of fear of rejection? I needed to stop being such a fucking sissy.

I sat at the table and gestured for Gab to pass me the computer. I logged in to my account and took a deep breath. *Hi, I'm wondering if you are the Luke Margolis who had a foster sister sixteen, seventeen years ago? If so, I would love to hear from you.*

"Is that okay?" I turned the screen to face them.

"Perfect," Gab said. Leila nodded.

I hesitated for a moment, my finger hovering over the keyboard. "Is my profile photo okay?" It wasn't the worst picture, but I was laughing. I looked kind of silly.

Gab rolled her eyes. "Oh my God, he's not going to care. You were his sister."

"I love that picture of you," Leila said. "And not just because I took it."

I smiled. "Okay." I took a deep breath, then clicked Send. A rush of adrenaline coursed through me. "Close it," I said to Leila. "Please. I can't just wait and watch. I'll look later. In fact, I should get home. I have to work soon."

"I'll give you a ride," Gab said.

Gab drove me home and offered to keep me company for a while, knowing how anxious I was. Inside, I found a note from my mom that said simply "Harbach's." She should have worked at that place instead of the community college's library. She'd probably break even if they had an employee discount on art supplies.

In my room, Gab busied herself on her phone while I opened my laptop, then tried to avoid looking at it. I let my gaze wander around my bedroom, and it occurred to me that I didn't even really *see* my room anymore. The walls were the same purple we'd painted it when I was little, only a little muted and faded now, and dinged and scraped in places. I still had the crappy white dresser of my youth, too, with peeling stickers all over it and drawers that squealed their objections at being disturbed. My bedspread was once white but now not quite, and bleaching was no match for some of the stains I'd managed to inflict on it over the years. Each thing my eyes lighted upon left me in a deeper funk than the last. I thought about Leila's beautiful house. Her bedroom was a dream. And then I felt like shit, because she didn't even know her birthday, and she'd never know where she came from. I might never know who my dad was, but at least I knew my mother. And when I was born.

"How is Leila so well-adjusted?" I asked Gab.

"I don't know — great parenting and probably some luck. Although . . ." She trailed off coyly.

I glanced at her. "What?"

She grinned. "She did suck her thumb until she was eight."

"What? Really?"

"Well, not when people were looking."

People. Gab wasn't people. I was.

"Don't tell her I told you."

"No, I won't." I tried to smile, but I couldn't. For one thing, it was another in the string of endless reminders of the private things they shared. For another, it was a lot to process about Leila. To me, her adoption was always a simple fact, a story with a happy ending. But I realized that it didn't have an ending. I hadn't thought about the phantom pains it must have left her with. Things that never could be fixed, things she would never know . . . "I feel bad," I said. "I didn't know about any of that."

Gab shrugged. "It's not your fault you don't know, if she didn't tell you."

"Well, I still feel bad." And it didn't make me feel better to know that Gab *did* know all those things.

"Come on, cheer up. Want to see something funny?" Gab got up and grabbed my computer from the desk. She settled back on my bed, and I scooted next to her as she opened a browser page and typed. Then she grinned and turned the laptop to face me.

It was a photo gallery of men in kilts. With nothing underneath. Exposing the, um, goods.

I stared, mesmerized by all those man-parts, by the

56

vast array of shapes and colors and configurations. One picture — a good-looking strawberry blond with one leg propped up on a bench (not exactly subtle) — particularly fascinated me. I knew from personal experience that this kilt-wearer was uncircumcised. In an unfortunate careless move last summer, I walked into my mom's studio without knocking when, as it turned out, she had a model in there, which is how I learned that an uncircumcised penis looks like a cross between a yam and an anteater.

This guy's yam/anteater was quite small, and it nestled into a blushing, generous package of balls. The whole visual reminded me of the new litter of mice we had in fourth-grade science: so pink and tender and soft-looking.

"Do they really go naked under those things?"

Gab nodded. "Real Scotsmen do. God, I'd like to be in Scotland."

"On a windy day!"

Gab tilted the computer so she could see the screen better. "Hey," she said without looking my way. "Have you ever touched one?"

My face grew warm. "No — whose would I have touched?"

She shrugged. "I don't know."

"Have you?" I asked. Gab hadn't had a boyfriend since junior high, and that was sort of in name only. She seemed to have more curiosity about sex than interest in relationships.

"Maybe."

My jaw dropped. "Whose? When?"

She clicked at the computer, avoiding my eyes. "My cousin's. We were playing doctor."

"Which cousin? The one you set me up with?"

"Oh, God, no," Gab said, laughing. "My cousin from Connecticut. We were kids."

I must have looked shocked, because she rolled her eyes and said, "Sexual exploration is a normal part of childhood development."

No point arguing with Dr. Shrink Jr.

"What was it like?" I asked.

She tilted her head and thought. "Well, it was small, and when it got hard, it was kind of long and skinny."

"It got hard?" I squealed.

"Yeah, when I touched his balls. Which were pretty cool. Very soft."

"Oh my God." I drew my hands up to cover my face. "I can't believe you never told me! Why?"

She lifted a shoulder. "You weren't ready."

I was speechless for a moment. "Does Leila know?"

Gab's eyes went round. "No, and she never will." She gripped my arm. "Swear you'll never tell her. Oh my God — she'd think I'm even more of a pervert than she already does."

I laughed at the thought of how horrified Leila might be.

"I'm serious, Jules!" She squeezed my arm harder.

"Okay, okay!" I said, pulling my arm free and rubbing it. Of course I wouldn't say anything — and not just because

Gab had asked me not to. I liked the idea of sharing something private with one of them, something that the other wouldn't be privy to.

"Wait," I said. "Your cousin. Did he touch you, too?"

She nodded. She might even have been blushing.

"You mean, *there*? Naked?"

"Yup."

"Oh my God." I laughed. "So what happened?"

"Well, he looked at it very closely, then told me I had cancer and I needed an operation. And then we put our clothes back on and went outside to play."

I let my breath out. "Have you two ever talked about it since then?"

She made a face. "God, no."

I had little comprehension of familial relationships — cousins, siblings . . . It seemed mysterious to me, mysterious and wondrous. My thoughts went back to Luke — and the idea that I'd once had something like that. It was beyond my ability to imagine.

"What if he doesn't answer?" I said. "What if he's not interested in me? I should have taken down my profile picture."

"Oh my God, you are so clueless sometimes," she said. She typed a new search in, a sly smile on her face. "Check this out."

She brought up a screen full of vintage pictures and posters of pinup girls, curvy and scantily clad.

"These are so you, Jules," Gab said. "I swear, if you curled your hair and put on red lipstick and a vintage outfit, you'd look exactly like them." She stared at the page, shaking her head. "How do you not love your body? All that tits and ass."

I skimmed the images. "They all look better than me."

"No, they don't! Get out of your head. Anyway, Daniel loves big asses."

I regarded her curiously. "You talk about that?"

She rolled her eyes. "You know what it's like at my house."

True, I did. No subject was verboten. I remembered nearly dying of embarrassment once, when I was about eight, when her parents had argued at the dinner table about sodomy laws. I was like, *What's sodomy?*

It was years before I ever hazarded another question at their house.

"Do you tell Daniel everything?" I asked her.

She tilted her head, thinking. "Almost." Her brow furrowed and she went silent for a moment. Then she turned to me. "Wouldn't this be weird? If you and Luke get to know each other? We'd all have brothers, sort of."

As if that hadn't already occurred to me. The idea of having something they both had, something I'd envied so much, was so dear I almost couldn't bear to contemplate it.

"If I ever have kids," Gab said, sliding my computer away and folding her legs up, "I'm going to have them close together. Daniel moved out when I was six. Garrett will be four when Leila leaves. I want my kids to grow up together."

"Why were you and Daniel so far apart?" I asked, hoping I wasn't crossing a line. Then again, the Wassermans seemed pretty lineless.

"My parents were going to stop at one, but they got hammered on my mom's fortieth birthday and they decided to play roulette." She gestured at herself. "Voilà!"

That made her mom fifty-eight. She was twenty-two years older than my mom — old enough to be my mother's mother. The differences between my upbringing and Gab's (and Leila's, too) fell into sharp relief. I was raised by a girl who was herself still trying to grow up. When Mrs. Wasserman had Gab (and Daniel, too), she was an actual adult with a career and financial stability and life experience (and a loving partner). My mother was the age I am now — and all on her own. If I had a child today, I would have no idea what I was doing. And even as I felt compassion for the girl my mother was, I also couldn't help feeling sorry for the child she was bumbling along with: me.

My phone dinged, alerting me to a message. I picked up my phone from my bedside table, and Jesus — it was right there, a message from Luke B. Margolis. "Oh my God! It's him!" I grabbed at Gab and caught a handful of her kinky hair.

"What did he say?" Gab asked, extricating my fingers.

I showed her his message: *Please tell me this isn't a joke. Is this really Jules??*

She yelped in excitement.

"That means he remembers me, right?"

"Well, duh! It sounds like he's been hoping to hear from you. Write back!"

My stomach felt like a cage full of drunk birds. Yes — I had to write back now, while he might be waiting. What to say? Having Gab over my shoulder was making me even more nervous.

"Call Leila," I suggested. "Let her know what's happening."

As Gab paced my room, narrating to Leila what was happening, I tried to think what to write back. Finally, I settled on, *Hi! Yes, it's really me! I would have looked for you sooner but I only found out this weekend that I was ever in foster care.*

He wrote back immediately: *You're kidding! I always wondered if you would remember anything about us. Are you still with your mother? Are you okay?*

Somehow I hadn't considered how much he might know about my situation. Obviously they must have known something — you don't foster kids from healthy, functioning families.

Yes, I wrote, *I'm fine! Well, as fine as a person can be when they discover they were once a foster child.*

Gab jumped onto the bed, scaring the bejeezus out of me. "What's he saying?" She peered over my shoulder, still holding the phone to her ear.

Luke had written: *I've thought about this moment for years. How did you find me?*

I typed, *I found your name in my scarf.* ☺

HOLY SHIT. ARE YOU KIDDING? His all-caps-ing at me made me flutter all over. *I switched our scarves when they took you away. On purpose.*

I stared. This was unreal. *You left me a clue?*

I tried, yes! I can't believe it worked! All these years later.

I jumped as Gab gasped in my ear. She proceeded to read Luke's message aloud to Leila, which I tried to block out — I wanted to be able to focus on Luke.

My mind spiraled with the meaning of everything he'd told me. He'd thought of me all these years. He'd wanted me to find him!

I wrote, *I thought my mom had gotten rid of the scarf years ago, but it just turned up. I thought "Luke Margolis" was a designer label!*

He replied, *Ha-ha no, just the kid whose heart was blown to dust when they took you away. God, I can't believe I'm really talking to you!*

My heart swelled. He *did* care about me. He *did* miss me. I could hardly process that this was really happening.

Gab read his lines aloud to Leila, and I hit a wall. I took a breath and gave Gab a gentle smile. "Gab. I love you. But I think I'm good. Thanks for staying with me."

"Seriously? You're kicking me out now? Just when it's getting good?"

I nodded solemnly.

She rolled her eyes and got up. "She's kicking me out,"

she said into the phone. "I'm coming back over." She gave me a look. "You *better* call us later."

"I promise."

She left, grumbling, and I switched to the computer for faster typing. I wrote, *You were sad when I left?*

You don't even want to know. You were my sister! When we lost you, it was one of the worst things that ever happened to us.

I stared at his words. Since unlocking the secrets of my past, I had thought a great deal of the generosity of a family who fosters a child, but I'd never considered how hard it might be for the family to say good-bye. The idea that I'd been the reason a family had gone through something terrible was nearly beyond my grasp.

He wrote, *You're really okay? Your mom's all right?*

Yes, I managed to type. *Clean and sober this whole time.*

God, that's a relief. Listen, this is terrible timing, but I have to run — I have to rehearse for an audition. Do you live in Wisconsin still?

No. Illinois. North of Chicago.

Really? I'm going to be in Evanston next Saturday!

Evanston? It was barely half an hour away! I typed, *No way!*

I have an audition at NU for grad school. Maybe we could meet up before I head back to WI? Probably early- or midafternoon?

My stomach did a 360, possibly a 720, who knows. *I would love that.*

He sent back a smiley and gave me his cell phone number. *Where should I meet you?*

I frantically scrolled through town in my head. *How about Laroche's Café in downtown Maplebrook? On Second Street.*

Perfect. See you then! ☺

And then he was gone, leaving me warm and trembling. I reread our entire conversation, lingering over the lines about how devastated he and his parents were to lose me. What if I'd finally found someone to whom I might matter more than anything?

The thing I had always longed for most.

Chapter 6

*T*he week crawled by. I avoided my mother — not that it was necessary, since she seemed to be staying out of my way, too. Fine with me. There were countless things I could have demanded information or apologies about, but for now my focus was singular: Luke. And I was not remotely inclined to confide in her about him just yet.

Saturday morning, she was sequestered in her studio. While I waited for Luke's text to alert me that he was finished at NU and on his way north, I tried on everything I owned, not that such an activity took very long. I went with layered lilac and white thermal tops and my favorite jeans. I wanted to look good, but not like I was trying too hard. Not that it should matter, as Gab pointed out. He was coming to connect with a onetime sister that he had always cared about, so how I looked was hardly the main point. Still, he was awfully attractive in his photo, and I figured it could only help my cause if I didn't look like a total slob.

His text came just after noon. I hurried out the door without so much as a word to my mom. I wanted to arrive first so I could be calm, collected, and ready for him. I certainly didn't want the awkwardness of his possibly passing me in his car on the street and maybe recognizing me.

Stepping outside was like receiving a hug from a benevolent deity. The sky beamed a blue of impossible vibrancy, and the air smelled of rain soaked earth and budding green life. Spudly, the Powells' basset hound, barked joyously at me through the fence as I passed by. Sun flashed in the water rushing along the drainage ditches on Elm Street. As I made my way through the neighborhood and into town, I buzzed with excitement and hope. Downtown, the streets bustled with people and cars. I hoped Luke would find a parking space without too much trouble.

I entered Laroche's with very deliberate attention to the door, just in case Luke had somehow beaten me there and was watching. I went to the counter and told Eli everything that had happened, periodically eyeing the window with a belly full of knots.

"So you're telling me that your former foster brother is on his way here to meet you?" He poured coffee into my cup. "That seems improbable."

"And yet!" I picked up the saucer with shaky hands and sipped from the cup.

He gave me that trouble-making grin of his. "Did you ever watch *Game of Thrones*?"

I glared at him. Figures he'd go straight to incest.

He shrugged, his skinny shoulders nearly touching his ears. "Hey, you're not even related. I'm just sayin' . . ."

"It's not like that. Jesus."

"Dude, you need to lay off the caffeine," Eli said, eyeing my cup, which was rattling frantically on the saucer. My pulse hadn't dipped below 200 bpm since Luke texted me, I was pretty sure.

"Shit," I muttered. I needed to calm down. I glanced into the pastry window. "Hey, could you set aside two of the chocolate croissants?" I asked. "It would be sad if Luke didn't get to taste them."

He smirked at me, his lip ring glinting. "Right, that's what would be sad. Poor Luke."

I huffed at him. "Shut up. I really want him to try one."

He reached in with tongs and, with exaggerated care, set two on a fluted pink depression glass plate I coveted half to death and had talked myself out of slipping into my purse more times than I cared to admit. He moved it up to a shelf next to the water glasses. "There," he said. "Safe unless Madame V. sees, and then all bets are off."

"Thanks."

My cup and I clattered our way to a table near the window. The counter — and the people sitting at it — obstructed much of my view, but I hoped I'd spot his approach. I fiddled with my hair about a billion times as I waited, keeping tabs on the availability of parking spaces.

At precisely four minutes to one, I spotted a little blue car easing into a space across the street. I leaned as far as I could to see around a customer. After a long minute, the car door opened and the driver unfolded himself from the front seat and — oh, lord — was that him? He was tall, and lean enough in his faded jeans and pea coat to give me a complex. His hair was a little longer than in the picture I'd seen, but he had that expression that looked so open, so sweet. As he crossed the street, his scarf caught my eye. It was an exact replica of my scarf!

He pulled open the door with such effortless grace, I seriously worried for myself (what was *with* me and that door?). Once inside, he tossed his hair out of his eyes and scanned the room. I watched, immobilized, waiting for him to see me.

And then he did. As his expression changed to one of stunned but certain recognition, he pressed a hand to his chest.

I lifted my hand, a small *hi*, giving him a tiny smile. I lowered my hand quickly because it was shaking so badly.

He took a few steps toward me. "Jules?"

I nodded, not trusting my voice. Should I stand up? Was it unfriendly and impolite if I didn't? But if I stood up, should I hug him? Offer a handshake?

He paused when he reached me, shaking his head slightly. "It's really you," he said, breaking into a smile. "Can I give you a hug?"

Relief. I stood and he squeezed me so hard it made me squeak.

"Sorry," he said, pulling back with a smile that warmed me to my marrow. His eyes were even more river-y and fleck-y in person. "I've been wanting to do that for — well, years." He unbuttoned his coat and slipped out of it. He wore a soft and faded long-sleeved shirt. He was slim, but he had shoulders and pecs, and the kind of nearly concave stomach that would normally make my mind wander so far into the forest of fantasy, I'd need a map and flares to get back out. I blushed, remembering Eli's lewd insinuations. I reminded myself that this person was a pseudo-brother, not a potential love interest — and to him I was certainly a sister figure.

He slid into the chair across from me, never taking his eyes off me, so I sat back down, too.

"I'm so glad you found me," he said. "I always wanted to look for you, but my mom wouldn't let me. She was worried it would disrupt your life, and maybe you didn't even know you were in foster care."

70

"And I didn't!"

"Mother knows best." He grinned. "Do you need another coffee? I'm gonna grab one."

My internal organs were already vibrating under their fascia. "I'm good. But, hey — do you like chocolate croissants?"

His raised his eyebrows so they disappeared under his hair. "Uh, more than most things. Do they have good ones here?"

"The best." I got up. "I'll come with you."

There was a short line at the counter, and we stood awkwardly, smiling and trying not to stare at each other. He had left his scarf on, and I waited for the chance to comment on it. When the people in front of us stepped away, Luke ordered a coffee, and then asked if there were any chocolate croissants.

"That depends on Drools," Eli said, giving me a lazy, evil grin. "She causes some supply-and-demand problems."

I'd kill him.

Luke gave me a puzzled glance.

"She thought ahead, though," Eli said, reaching for the plate.

As he poured Luke's coffee, I wondered how I had failed to consider how embarrassing it would be for Luke to know I'd reserved two chocolate croissants for us. My cheeks burned.

Eli put Luke's coffee on the counter by the plate of crois-sants, eyeing Luke up and down and giving me a *not bad* nod that made me want to kick him.

I grabbed the plate to be sure I didn't end up carrying Luke's coffee with my shaking hands. His hands, I saw when we sat back down and he picked up his coffee, were steady. He had pianist's fingers, too, long and lovely.

"A friend of yours, I take it?" he asked, nodding toward Eli.

"Something like that," I mumbled. A friend I'd like to karate kick in the tenders at the moment . . . "Nice scarf," I said to Luke, smiling. I twisted around to pull mine out of my coat, which was hanging on the back of my chair.

His mouth curved into a smile.

That smile . . . I had never seen a more adorable smile on any human, ever. And he had dimples, the left one a little deeper than the right.

He unwound the scarf around his neck and found its tag, then held it out to me.

JULES, it said. That's all. "Did you know my last name?" I asked.

He nodded. "I think my mom was thinking about the possibility that your last name could change . . ." He draped the scarf over the back of his chair. "Okay, let's see if these measure up to the hype," he said, picking up a croissant and pulling a piece off, golden flakes scattering. He lifted the bite to smell it, then gave me an *oh, come on* look. When he popped it in his mouth, he rolled his eyes. "Butter! So much butter."

"Right? I'm kind of obsessed with them." I pulled a little piece off of mine and put it in my mouth, trying not to get pastry shards stuck in my lip gloss. "So, um. Your parents. What are they like?"

He glanced up at me, then turned his eyes to his plate. Had I done something wrong? "They're the best," he said softly.

"Oh," I said weakly. I mean, I could have guessed that they were great people, taking in a foster child, but it still hit me, somehow, hearing him affirm how good they were. "That's great."

"Your mom is really okay?" Luke's voice stayed soft. "We never stopped worrying."

I nodded, feeling suddenly uncomfortable. How much did he know about my mother? Apart from Leila and Gab, no one knew my mother was a recovering addict. It was strange to meet someone with whom information about my private life was not entirely in my control. "Yeah, she's fine. Really."

His relief was clear to see, and it made my heart swell, despite my confused feelings. This guy, this family, had been worrying about me for sixteen years! And I might never have known. I guess if it were up to my mother, I *wouldn't* have ever known.

He sat back and watched me for a moment, till I ducked my head in embarrassment. "Sorry for staring. It's just . . .

man. I'd know you anywhere," he said, shaking his head. "Those big brown eyes. That angelic face."

A thrill ran through me. Before I could come up with a response, the door made its racket and a pack of tweens crashed in, their volume dials set on "clueless." Poor Eli. But now Susan-the-flaky-part-timer had returned from her break, so in theory he'd have some help.

The kids argued about what the best drinks were, their voices crowding the place. Luke went back to his croissant, and I scrambled for something to say. "How did your audition go?"

"Good, I think." He wiped his fingers on a napkin. "I did about as well as I could have hoped. You know — there's always something you could have done better."

"So you're graduating this year?" When he nodded, I said, "How old are you? Twenty-two?" I played with a bit of croissant. That I still had some on my plate after this length of time was a testament to just how nervous and over-whelmed I was.

"Twenty-three. I took a gap year after high school. And you," he said with a gleam in his eye, "are eighteen as of New Year's Day."

My eyes widened. "You remember my birthday?"

He laughed. "It's not a hard one to remember, but yes, of course I do. I helped make your first birthday cake."

I blinked, struggling for words. "You did?"

"Well," he said, pulling off another bit of croissant,

"mostly I licked the bowls, but you know. It's important work."

I smiled. "The most important. What kind was it?"

He regarded me as if I'd asked something ridiculous. "Chocolate. We're not heathens."

I laughed. I wondered if that's why I loved chocolate so much. That would have been the first time I had tasted it — with Luke and his family.

"So what about you?" he said. "What are you into? What are your college plans?"

The part of small-talk conversations I hated most: *Tell me about yourself.* There was nothing to tell. I was uninteresting, limited in talent, and even more limited in experience.

I skipped straight to the college stuff, which was only marginally easier to answer. "I'd like to go to small liberal arts school, but . . . have to see how financial aid and scholarships pan out."

"What are you thinking of studying?" he asked.

I shrugged. "I don't know. I like English."

He nodded encouragingly. "Do you like to write?"

"I like to read. And I like history, but not, like, politics and war and stuff. I like small-life history. What the furniture looked like. What the kitchens were like. What people were cooking." I shrugged again.

"That's really cool. How did you get interested in that?" He did the cutest mini–head toss when his hair tickled his eyes.

I tilted my head, thinking. "I've always liked old

things — antiques and stuff like that. But I think the real spark was probably the Thorne miniatures at the Art Institute. Have you seen them?"

His face lit up. "The little models of rooms? Downstairs?"

"Yes! I love those. My mom took me to the Art Institute when I was a kid, and I couldn't tear myself away from the Thorne miniatures."

That was a pretty whitewashed version of what was actually not the happiest memory. Yes, my mother took me to the AIC, but instead of enjoying the miniatures with me, she lost her patience because all she wanted to see were the painting exhibitions, and I wasn't old enough that she'd leave me alone and come back for me, so I didn't even get to see them all. I was barely through eighteenth-century England when she dragged me off to stare at twentieth-century paintings of flowers that looked like psychedelic exploding vaginas. It was years before I was able to go back and take my time with the miniatures. And that was with the Wassermans, not my mother.

"What did you love about them?" he asked, leaning forward and propping his chin on his hand.

"Everything." I struggled to articulate the magic of the little rooms. "The way they capture a place and time. The light pouring in from outside. The views of gardens out the windows. Staircases that lead somewhere you can't see. All the tiny details — copper pots, crockery, place settings.

Just imagining life in those rooms, pretending I'm there. Everything."

He looked absolutely riveted. I wanted more of that like I wanted air.

I gestured at our dishes. "And then this. The china at Laroche's."

He glanced down at his cup and saucer. "These don't match," he observed, picking up the cup.

"Nothing here matches." I looked at my own duo — English cup with a pastel cottage scene, Lenox saucer with a gold border. "It's sort of a theme." I hesitated. I wanted to show off a little. "I probably can identify every piece of china they have here."

He made an *I'm impressed* face. "Okay," he said, sitting back and gesturing at his cup. "Let's hear it."

"Okay," I said, tossing my hair back over my shoulders. "Your cup is English — Royal Albert. It's the Snowdrops one from the Flower of the Month series, introduced in the nineteen fifties."

He squinted at me, skeptical. "So how do I know you're not making this up?"

"Check the bottom." Obviously I wouldn't have named this as a skill if I didn't have a good handle on the china on our table. Madame V. was shuttling in new pieces all the time — their fragility meant a high rate of attrition — so I couldn't always bat a thousand.

He held the cup aloft so he could see. He smiled and mouthed, "Holy shit." His teeth were pretty. Straight on top and slightly crooked on bottom. And his eyelashes were ridiculous.

"The saucer," I continued, "is also English, but older. Royal Crown Derby. The pattern is called 'Vine.'"

He checked my work, shaking his head. "Okay, do yours."

I complied, loving the intensity in his expression as he verified my answers.

"Okay," he said, folding his fingers together, "so you're a china savant. I'm not sure there's a major in that."

I laughed. "I wish."

He pushed the cup and saucer aside and leaned toward me. "What else do you like?"

I dared to mirror his position, putting our faces about a foot apart. "Food."

At this he smiled, hypnotizing me with his dimples and his lips and his teeth. "You always did."

I blushed. "Oh, God. Was I a pig?"

"No!" He gave me a chastising look. "You were adorable, and you just . . ." He considered, obviously struggling for diplomacy. "You were enthusiastic about all things edible." He smiled. "All right, what else?"

"Am I good at? Um . . . cooking."

This was a wee stretch.

He raised his eyebrows. "That's awesome. What do you like to cook?"

I wanted to name classic French recipes, dishes suggestive of complexity and sophistication, but I was way over my depth. "I have bastardized ramen noodles a hundred ways to Tuesday."

That laugh again. "Okay, let's hear your top ramen perversion."

I thought for a moment. "My ultimate ramen dirty pleasure is probably *cacio e pepe*. It's a Roman dish — pasta with lots of Romano cheese and black pepper. It's really sharp and creamy and intense. I like to make it with ramen. Faster that way."

His eyes were wide. "That sounds awesome."

"I could tell you how to make it." I shrugged. "It's easy. Takes like five minutes."

"It takes *you* five minutes. I'm a disaster in the kitchen."

I couldn't help smiling. Even his flaws were charming. "I'm telling you, a trained chimp could do it."

"Trained chimps are pretty high level," he objected. "Opposable thumbs? Plus training?"

I laughed. He was so funny! "You could do it. Sometimes I throw a fried egg on top. With a runny yolk."

"Okay, now you're making me drool."

Eli suddenly appeared with coffee. "That's why they call her Drools."

I glared at him as he refilled our cups. How had he handled all those kids already? "Nobody calls me Drools," I told Luke after Eli walked away. "Except Eli."

"You used to call me Duke." He laughed kind of sadly.

"I did?"

He nodded. "You couldn't say your *l*'s. You'd say, like, *wight* for *light*. You mixed up letters a lot. You called pancakes *tanpakes.*"

Good God. So many things about myself that I might never have known, so many specific details. He held keys to my past — keys nobody else had. Not even my own mother.

"We still call them that at home," he said. "And we still call cookies *tookies.*"

The idea that I had added permanent vocabulary words to a family I didn't even know about was more than I could get my mind around.

"I'm sorry." He reached forward as if to touch my hand but stopped short. "You know, we've thought of you all these years, but for you, it's new and probably overwhelming. Is it too much?"

"No, it's okay." I tried to give him a reassuring smile. "I mean, yes, it's overwhelming, but . . . it's good. I just can't believe there are people out there who have been thinking about me my whole life, and I never even knew. And if I hadn't found my baby album, and if you hadn't left me your scarf, I might still never know."

He nodded. "Actually, your timing is . . ." He trailed off and glanced down. After a pause, he took a deep breath. "Look, there's something you should know. And I don't want to pressure you or anything, but . . ." He looked at me. "The thing is . . . my mom is sick."

My stomach dropped. "Sick?"

He nodded, his brow furrowed. "Yeah, she . . . she has cancer."

"Oh," I said in a tiny voice. "Is she . . ." I couldn't finish the sentence.

"It's not great." He scooted his chair in closer so he didn't have to shout over the increasing din of customers. "She's just had another round of chemo, so she's pretty weak right now, but we'll see if it makes a difference."

I took a breath, stunned. This woman I didn't even know about until now, this woman who had been an actual mother to me, might be dying. And my God, poor Luke. To face losing a mother like that?

"Jules," he said softly. "My mom's always hoped to see you again. Do you think you'd want to . . ."

"Of course!" I said. "Of course I want to meet her. My God."

He tried to smile. "Let's hope she rallies. I have a recital next Saturday and . . . well, I hope she can be there. She's had to miss too many of them already, and . . ." He lifted a shoulder. "She's the kind of mom who always is there for everything, you know?"

I nodded. I knew what that was like, but only because Leila had a mom like that and Gab had a mom like that.

He glanced at his watch. "Shoot, I have to hit the road." He gave me a regretful look. "I have a lesson. Now I wish I'd canceled it."

I did, too. It seemed like he'd just gotten there.

"I'm so glad this happened," he said. "Seeing you again . . . It's literally a dream come true."

A bright, warm ache filled my chest. That someone felt this way about me . . . it was everything. "It's like a dream for me, too," I said.

He grinned and shook his head. "I still can't believe it's you." He stood up and pulled on his coat. "Hey! Should we get a picture together?"

"Oh! Okay. Sure."

He put an arm around me and aimed his phone at us. I hoped I'd look good in it. What if it came out badly and he kept looking at it, thinking, *Meh*? I smiled shyly and he took the picture.

"Here, I'll send it to you, too," he said, poking at his phone. When he finished, he grinned and said, "I'll text you later, okay? Maybe you can walk me through making your Roman ramen."

"I'd be happy to! But yeah . . ." I trailed off with a sad shrug. "Yeah, let me know how your mom is doing. I hope . . ."

He nodded. "I will." He smiled and reached for me.

The hug. It was warm and safe, unhurried and amazing. Plus, I couldn't help noticing, he smelled good. Not

82

like men's cologne or anything obvious, but fresh and shampoo-y and something a little new age-y — sort of like a clean-smelling kind of incense or a high-priced natural soap from Whole Foods. I didn't want to let go. When we pulled away, he reached behind me for his scarf, the one with his name sewn on it.

"Oh," I said, surprised.

"You want to keep each other's?" He laughed at my surprise that he knew exactly what I was thinking.

We traded and I held his close to my chest.

His gaze held mine for a long moment. "Man, those eyes." He took a few steps backward. "See you, Jules."

"See you," I said, although what I wanted was to stop him. I wanted to talk all day. I wanted another hug. I wanted him to not go away.

As he left, he turned to glance at me one more time. He smiled and shook his head as he pushed the door open. And my stomach flipped over.

It was such a thrill, this whole Luke thing. Having something like a brother would be amazing — an impossible gift falling out of nowhere.

But, man . . . if I met him under any other circumstances, I was pretty sure it would be me doing the falling.

Chapter 7

*B*ack at home, I googled the drive time from Laroche's to Appleton, Wisconsin, so I would know when to reasonably start hoping to hear from him. While I waited, I had a long call with Gab and Leila, telling them every last detail I could remember. Their excitement meant the world to me — as did their admiration of the photo I'd forwarded them. "That is one happy dude," Gab said. And Leila had chimed in, "Well, sure. He's waited her whole life to find her."

But there was a wistful tone to her voice, if I wasn't imagining it, that gave me a pang. Something wonderful was happening to me that would probably never happen to Leila. And I ached over it.

They invited me to come over for a movie at Gab's that night, but I passed. If I ended up talking to Luke later, as I hoped, I wanted my evening clear.

While I waited to hear from him, I made my ramen *cacio e pepe* to make sure my instructions would be perfect, in case he actually tried to make it. I devoured it, not worrying about spoiling my appetite for dinner, since my mom was out for the evening yet again. More meetings, more friends . . . I wasn't sure whether to be relieved she was getting support and had a social network, or worried she was struggling with wanting to drink and hanging out where people might be doing just that.

Apart from that, I stared a lot at the picture Luke took of us. We looked pretty sweet together — Luke nearly a head taller than me, and smiling so big, eyebrows up as if to say, *Can you believe this?*

He did look happy. And it filled me up.

But by well into the evening, hours past any reasonable drive time, I still hadn't heard from him. I was tempted to text something like *Hope you're out buying ramen and Romano,* but I didn't want to seem like a pest. Still, it seemed reasonable to message him that I was happy to meet him. So I sent a message to that effect, then watched my phone obsessively for about half an hour, at which point it stopped seeming likely that a response was about to arrive any second.

As the evening wore on and I tried in vain to amuse myself with TV and homework, I wished I had accepted

Gab's invitation to watch a movie at her house. All I had wanted to do was to talk to Luke, but here I was with nothing to do but fret and pine and stare at our picture.

Finally, at eleven, my mom returned. I was lying on the sofa, gnawing on an apple and half watching Anthony Bourdain buy a duck press in Paris — it operated like an instrument of torture, and I thought maybe Eli would like one just for decor.

She glanced up at me as she slipped her shoes off by the door. "Hey," she said.

I ignored her. I didn't want to share anything with her. Luke was a secret she had kept from me, and now he was a secret I wanted to keep from her. At some point the compulsion to interrogate her might eclipse my need to distance her, but I wasn't there yet.

"Is there anything to eat?" she asked on her way to the kitchen.

A question I'm pretty sure Leila's or Gab's parents never asked them . . .

"I didn't make you anything, if that's what you're asking." I heard the refrigerator opening and closing, then the cabinet, then the utensils drawer. She was eating peanut butter out of the jar with a spoon. It was her go-to maneuver for impatient hunger. Suddenly it grated on me. She didn't shop and cook something amazing, like Leila's mom would. She didn't order in sushi or deep-dish pizza, like Gab's mom would. She ate peanut butter from the jar and left me to my own devices.

I flicked off the TV and went to bed without saying good night. I read a book, periodically eyeing my phone, until 1:00, when I couldn't hold my eyes open anymore. Nothing from Luke. Why? Not one tiny message? No *Hey, great seeing you, too?*

Nothing.

In the morning I found out why. His messages were stamped at nearly 2:00 a.m.

Jules, it was amazing meeting you, too. It still feels surreal. I keep staring at the picture of us.

I'm in Milwaukee — never made it to Lawrence. Bad news: my mom took a turn for the worse. ☹ She's been in the ICU all afternoon and evening. She's breathing better now, and when her oncologist comes by for morning rounds, we'll know more. I hope she can be discharged soon. She hates the hospital.

Going to try to get a few zzz's at the house before heading out early for Appleton. I have lessons in the morning and a rehearsal in the afternoon.

More soon!

I felt like my insides were caving in. Why did such terrible things have to happen? My heart went out to Luke, and to his mother and father, and, yes, to myself, too. Because I wanted a chance to know her. And I wanted to enjoy Luke, enjoy getting to know him, and now everything was terrible.

I wrote back, *Oh Luke. I'm so sorry. My thoughts are with you all. Please let me know if there's anything I can do. And please keep in touch.*

I wondered if he'd told his parents about me. I mean, I could understand if he didn't — they had actual life-and-death issues going on, after all. But if he *had* told them, how had they reacted? Were they happy? Did the news make his mom smile, even in the midst of everything? Even though I couldn't remember them, I felt a strong urge to do whatever I could to make these people's lives a little bit better. After everything they'd done for me, it felt like the very least I could do.

I didn't hear back from him the rest of Sunday. Or Monday. I fretted about him — and his mother. What if she wasn't okay? Would he tell me?

At lunch on Tuesday — Valentine's Day — I sat with Gab, since Leila had a different lunch period, and felt sorry for myself out loud. We sat at the corner of a long table, heads close so we didn't have to yell over the racket.

"Just message him again," Gab said, pulling off her hoodie and letting it hang off the back of her chair. "What do you have to lose?"

"I don't want to be a pest. He said he'd write more when he could." I stared out the long bank of windows that overlooked the football field. I wondered if Luke played any sports. I guessed he had to protect his hands. Running, maybe? He could be a runner with that lean build. There was so much I didn't know about him. And oh, how I longed to know *everything*.

Gab scooped a pita wedge through a little Tupperware of hummus, sending an invisible plume of cumin and garlic into the air — a pungent contrast to the greasy burger-and-spaghetti smell in the cafeteria. "Here, eat something." She pushed her food at me, but I held up my hand to stop her. She leaned down and rummaged through her backpack. "I bought a Valentine cookie from the GSA fund-raiser." She offered a cellophane-wrapped neon-pink monstrosity.

I shook my head. "I can't. I feel sick. And I can't message him. I'd just feel so pathetic. He has important things going on. His mom might be dying!"

She set the cookie on the table. "Then ask him about that! Ask how she's doing."

"I can't. What if he feels like I'm intruding?"

"See, that's your problem," she said, shaking a carrot stick at me. "You're too self-conscious, and you always assume the worst. You should take more chances, do things that scare you."

Spoken like a person with a dependable safety net at home. If I had Gab's parents, I might be bold and fearless, too. All I had was my mom, and if I fucked up — or if she fell off the wagon — then what? Who would I have then? Every move I made in life was analyzed and calculated for its safety rating.

After school, I endured a yearbook meeting, where I

turned in a copy of one of the baby photos from the social services file. Fifteen months old, I stood laughing in front of the piano, one dimpled hand on the bench, my pajama'd feet planted in a pair of men's dress shoes. I looked silly and happy — and just enough like myself to make it interesting. No doubt my mother would be upset that I used a foster care picture, if she knew. But my mother paging through my yearbook? Slim odds.

After the meeting, I trudged to Laroche's for some dubious comfort of the Eli variety — and some sure comfort of the chocolate-and-butter variety.

No scarf or mittens today. In the sun it almost felt warm. February in Chicago was a lot like me: a study in yearning and hope. Whether the temperatures have been brutal or mild, the snowfall massive or meager, the one abiding truth about Chicago winters is that they are long. When the northern hemisphere reaches for the sun, signaling the end of another icy era, it's like a meteorological lifeline.

Banks of snow melted along the sides of the street, unveiling last fall's leaves, twigs, and spruce needles. The crisp smell of wet stone and the rush of water down the street gutters seemed to promise a spring at last.

Nearing Laroche's, I noticed a new window display at Tina's, featuring a mannequin wearing the most incredible hat — a pillbox style with a velvet ribbon and a black netted veil, probably from the forties? I had to see it up close.

Tina glanced up from the register as I came in. "Jules!"

she called, looking over her bejeweled horn-rimmed glasses. She was wrapping something in white tissue. "I've been hoping you'd come in. I've got something for you. Give me a minute."

"Sure," I said. She knew my tastes really well, owing to the years of my ogling special items in her store, only to walk out with a couple of four-dollar sweaters or a like-new jacket for a song. I just hoped that whatever she found this time wouldn't be more than I should (or could) spend.

I made my way to the mannequin to examine the hat. It was breathtaking. I slipped it on and stepped over to the mirror for a peek. Why didn't women wear hats anymore? They were so incredibly flattering. Regretfully, I placed it back on the mannequin's head. Even if the price tag weren't a bit rich for my secondhand blood, where would I wear it?

I turned away from the mannequin and flipped through some ancient issues of *Ladies' Home Journal*, full of flapper style and adorable hairdos. Then I spotted a weathered spiral-bound cookbook. *Charleston Receipts*. I knew that "receipts" was an old word for "recipes," so I picked it up and paged through it. It was put out by the Junior League in the 1950s, and it looked like it. There was a lot of focus on serving the lord, the church, and the men. The women's names were all "Mrs." followed by her husband's name. The book was filled with recipes for shrimp, oysters, punches . . . I tried to envision a version of a Thorne miniature of a 1950s South Carolina home. A coastal town in the South, postwar, during desegregation . . . What would that be like?

"Jules." I turned as Tina bustled past racks of Mason jars and vinyl albums, her overgrown gray curls springing from her head. She held an old cookie tin.

"Oh, look at that!" I took it from her. "Is it American? Or English?" I turned it over and the contents shifted.

"English. Came from an attic at an estate sale," she said. "Coated in about a quarter inch of dust. I don't think it's been touched since the nineteen seventies — maybe earlier. Open it."

I set it down and prized the lid off, then drew in my breath.

Buttons.

"Now those are old," she told me, shaking a pen at the tin. "Aren't they beautiful?"

I stared into the tin, overwhelmed by the hundreds of pieces of history inside. "They're incredible," I whispered. Metal buttons, glass buttons, ceramic buttons, enameled buttons . . . Flowers, words, birds, shells. Uniform buttons! All of the people whose hands had touched these, all of the places they'd been!

When I glanced up at her, she was grinning at me. "I thought you'd like it," she said.

"How much?" I asked, hoping she'd say anything even remotely reasonable.

"It's yours," she said, her eyes twinkling. "You're the one it belongs with."

I set the tin down and hugged her. "Thank you, Tina."

She pulled away, looking pleased. "I wanted to ask you, too . . . what are your plans for the summer?"

Summer seemed a million years away. I would be going away to school and I didn't even know where yet, so summer was beyond my ability to consider. "I don't know," I said. "Nothing so far."

The door to the shop opened, and she turned and called a hello to the customer. Then she stepped closer to me. "Listen, Anne's daughter in Boston is expecting a baby in June, and Anne wants to spend a few months with them, you know, helping out. I'll need someone to fill in while she's gone, and of course I thought of you."

I warmed inside, pleased she'd thought of me — and excited. The idea of handling pieces of history every day instead of Miracle Whip and meat was appealing. "I would love that," I said. "Thank you so much!"

"Don't thank me yet," she said, her eyes crinkling. "It only pays ten dollars an hour, but you'll get first pick of everything I bring in, and I'll give it to you at my cost."

"That sounds great." Ten bucks an hour wasn't bad, and old and special things for cheap? Yes, please.

"Let me give you an application. It's just a formality — mostly so I have your contact information." She turned to head back to the counter. "Hope you're not allergic to dust!"

"Nope!" I called back to her. "I love dust!" Ugh. *I love dust.* What an idiot.

I headed out with my treasure in tow, spirits lifted by the job offer and the promising clatter of the buttons in the tin. At Laroche's, I managed to get myself in the café door with only a single, civilized ding of the bell. The smell of peppermint hovered under the heavy coffee aroma — someone must have ordered one of those disgusting holiday lattes, with the peppermint syrup and crushed candy over the whipped cream topping. Fucking Valentine's Day. "Hey, you," I called, approaching the counter where Eli had his head in a book, his black hair falling over his face.

He said without glancing up, "Did you know that in New York City, more people die by suicide than by murder?"

I tilted my head at him fondly. "You are just a ray of sunshine, you know that? God, I miss you at school." I leaned over and gazed through the glass. Two chocolate croissants left. I thought of Luke with a stab of longing. "Where's the boss?" I asked.

"Bank, I think. Here." He grabbed the tongs and put a croissant on a plate.

"Bless you."

"What's that?" he said, nodding at my tin.

"Buttons. From Tina's. She offered me a summer job."

"Awesome — you'd love that, right?"

"It's perfect."

"Want coffee?" He poured some into an English Yuletide cup without waiting for an answer. I took a big bite of the croissant. My nervous stomach made an easy exception for this item.

"So." Eli gave me a *not sure I should even ask* look. "What's going on with Hottie McPianofingers?"

I shook my head. "Eli, no. His mom — she's really sick. She might be dying."

His expression morphed into something raw and unguarded. "Man. That's harsh."

I could have kicked myself for not thinking about what I was saying. Eli knew better than anyone how "harsh" it was.

Suddenly Madame V. appeared from the back. She screeched at Eli in French, her expertly lined eyes flashing with fury. She pointed to a cup left at the counter by the window, to the fingerprints on the display case, to some napkins on the floor by the garbage receptacle. My heart went out to Eli as he took his lashing and jumped into action. I skulked off to the counter.

As I ate, I gazed out the window at downtown Maplebrook. People filled up their gas tanks. Withdrew money from the ATM. Emerged from Lou's Quikmart with sodas the size of silos. No one went into or came out of the vacuum cleaner repair shop, per usual. Could there possibly be enough malfunctioning vacuum cleaners in the Maplebrook area to keep a store in business? It seemed implausible. Maybe it was a mafia front.

I opened up my tin and sifted through the buttons,

dreaming. I wished there were some way to ask each one about its past, some way to know the mysteries locked inside old objects. What could I study in college that would set me up for a career in antiques? Something sort of like an archaeologist, only less science-y.

When I was finished with my croissant and coffee, I brought my dishes over to the counter. "Hey, what time do you get off?" I asked Eli softly.

He wiped down the espresso machines. "I'm closing, if I'm not fired first."

I leaned across the counter "Eli? Honey?"

He looked over at me.

"You should really think about college. You're too good for this stupid job."

"Truman Capote said the only reason to go to college is if you want to be a doctor or a lawyer or something." He sprayed the counter with blue glass cleaner. "If you want to be a writer, and you can write and spell, there's no need to go to college."

"You'd only be a year behind," I said softly. On impulse, I pulled his head across the counter and kissed him on his lily-white cheek. He made a face, but I could swear I saw a trace of a smile underneath.

"Hey," he said. "Old man's out of town. You wanna get drunk tonight?"

I hesitated. Avoiding my mom appealed to me, and a distraction from obsessing about Luke for a while sounded kind of lifesaving. But there was always my personal neon skull-and-crossbones hanging over the entire subject of drugs and alcohol. Was there some kink in my DNA strand that would suck me over to the dark side and make an addict of me? Would getting drunk once lead to *becoming* a drunk?

No. I'd had champagne with Gab and Leila last October, and I hadn't had (or wanted) anything since. It didn't even interest me, the idea of frequent boozing or drugs. I wasn't that kind of person — I was too worried about being in control and playing it safe. But today a drink or two did not sound like a terrible idea. I didn't know if it would distract me or just numb me, but at this point, with everything I had going on, I'd welcome either.

"Earth to Jules." Eli waved his hand in front of my face.

I nodded. *I was not my mother.* "Let's do it," I said.

"Cool. See you later."

I headed out for the walk home. The sky had darkened to a deep indigo glow, a few streaks of pinkish-peach lingering at the horizon. With each step I took, I considered the buttons rattling in the tin and how many thousands of sunsets they'd seen on untold hundreds of people. I thought again of uniform buttons and war years and letters and Red Cross girls and USO dances. I lost myself in fantasies of times past, wondering what book or movie might carry me away to the times and places I imagined.

As I approached my house, the lights in my mom's studio glowed brightly through the closed blinds. She was home.

Inside, I dropped my backpack and left my coat and shoes in the foyer, breathing in the smell of paint and peppermint tea. As I passed her studio, she said, "Hey, how was your day?"

"Fine." I took a step back and paused in the doorway. She was fucking up the sky. She stepped back and looked at her work, head tilted, then turned to me. "What's that?" she said, eyeing the cookie tin.

"Buttons from Tina's. Don't worry, they were free."

She squinted at me. "What are you going to do with buttons?"

I sighed. More useless things — that was clearly her thought. "I am going to love them," I told her. I thought about telling her about my summer job, but I wasn't feeling very share-y where she was concerned. "I'm going to Eli's in a while," I said.

"Eli's?" Her lips drew into a thin line. "Jules? Does Eli do drugs?" She picked up her NO SOUP mug of tea, her expression tense.

I was a little alarmed that she might actually have some Spidey sense about my plans. I overcompensated by being defensive. "No. Why do you think that? Because he *looks* different? He does not do drugs. *I* don't do drugs. I'm not you, Mom." I turned and headed for my room, ignoring the guilt I felt for dealing an unnecessary blow. And then I bristled at the guilt, because wasn't my response warranted?

I lay on my bed and thought about Luke, staring at our

photo and replaying moments from our meeting at Laroche's for the thousandth time. I could still see his fleck-y eyes, his warm smile and pretty teeth. I thought about things he said, ways he reacted to things I said. I hoped he thought I was interesting and smart. I wondered what I'd be like if they hadn't taken care of me, if I had ended up with a less-loving family for those nineteen months — months I'm sure Gab would say are critical. Maybe I'd be different today. How much of my personality was the result of my early childhood experiences?

Thinking about my mysterious history led to thoughts about the tin of buttons. I opened them at my desk and pored through them, googling antique button websites. I was thrilled to identify one as being from a British Army General Service Corps uniform from World War I. From there, I fell into videos about the home front in England during the First World War, shocked at the ways it affected the lives of children, many of whom had to take on the duties of their departed fathers. And the women, flocking to work in munitions factories and to operate the railways. The rationing, the brothers and fathers and sons who never came home . . .

Before I knew it, it was evening and time to go to Eli's for some respite of the liquid variety.

"You want to take the car?" my mom asked as I came into the kitchen. "You can."

An olive branch. *I trust you,* she was saying.

"I'm sorry," I mumbled, staring at the floor. "About what I said."

"It's okay." She pulled a frozen meal out of the microwave. "I have that coming."

I glanced up, but there was no sarcasm there.

She shrugged and pulled the plastic cover off her meal. Tuna noodle casserole, by the smell of it. "I'm an addict. That's my reality."

"I'm still sorry," I said.

We stood there for a minute, marinating in the awkward silence. Finally, I said, "You've been going to a lot of meetings. Should I be worried?"

She took a breath and rubbed her forehead with her fingertips. "I don't think there's any point to your worrying," she finally said.

"Maybe if I knew what made you relapse, I would know what to watch for, when to worry."

She blanched, then reached for the pepper on the table.

"Seriously?" I leaned in front of her, forcing her to look at me. "You're just going to ignore me?"

"I'm not ignoring you." Her tone was quiet, measured.

"What happened to that boy in the picture? Your so-called best friend."

She paled, then glanced down at the pepper shaker. "That's . . . it's hard to talk about."

And that was it — I snapped. "It's been eighteen fucking years! Why can't you talk about it? He held me! He was there

100

when I was born, and it's not like I had a village of other people. I want to know who he was and what happened to him. Why won't you tell me?"

She set her hand on the counter and held very still. "It's hard," she repeated, her voice tense as she enunciated each word. "I'm working on it."

"Fine, you work on it." I strode to the door and grabbed my coat. "While you're working on it, though, you might be interested to know that I found my foster family."

Her head snapped up. "What?"

I held up my scarf, then wrapped it around my neck. "You should have thrown this out like you throw out everything else! My foster brother's name is sewn inside it. I met him Saturday! His whole family has missed me, all these years, and I never even knew they existed." I opened the door, then turned back. "I can't wait to meet them." I watched her stunned face with satisfaction for just a brief moment before I whirled and slammed the door behind me.

Chapter 8

*M*y heart pounded as I made my way to Eli's. *Don't think about it. Don't think about anything.* I was going to take an evening off of thinking. Less thinking, more drinking. That would be my motto for the night.

Eli's house, about a ten-minute walk if I pushed my pace, was in the oldest section of town — prewar two- and three-stories with the detail and craftsmanship lacking in later houses (e.g., mine). Eli's was a Victorian, complete with a turret. He greeted me at the door, and I followed him down to the crypt, his fond term for his chosen domain in the basement. It wasn't even a finished basement, really. The walls were sort of crumbly, and the place smelled every bit as musty as a century-plus could inflict.

As I slipped out of my scarf and coat, Eli demonstrated our libation choices, which he had set up on an old sewing table: cherry Heering, ouzo, and the kind of tequila with a worm in the bottle. Two giant plastic cups sat alongside.

He shrugged apologetically. "I had to pick things in the back that my dad never drinks. He'd notice if the gin or Scotch was missing."

A bare red light bulb was the sole source of illumination in the room, and it cast a horror-movie vibe on the punk rock posters on the wall. His computer glowed in one corner, and his desk was covered in papers and notebooks. Sloppy, sliding stacks of books lined the wall. I wrinkled my nose at a funky, ammoniac whiff in the air. "What's that smell?"

"Yeah, sorry." Eli unscrewed the cap on one of the bottles. "Jay and Daisy's cage needs cleaning."

I smiled, shaking my head. So Eli to name his rats after literary characters. Jay and Daisy were both boys, though (population control). I peered into the cage. This was the closest I'd ever gotten to his rats, because, truthfully, I was sort of freaked out by them. "Which is which, again?" The two rats slept in a cuddled heap under the ladder that ran up to the second level, but they opened their eyes, and the white one lifted his head.

"Jay is the black-hooded fatty with the adorable Dumbo ears, and Daisy's the pretty white one. You can take them out if you want."

"Um, that's okay." The rats peered out at me. Daisy's little pink nose twitched between the bars. "Do they bite?" I called to him.

"Don't be ridiculous. They're the sweetest creatures you'll ever meet."

He came over and opened the cage. Both rats jumped up and scurried to the door. He picked up Daisy and cuddled him to his face, and as he did, Jay jumped out.

"Watch out!" I pointed. "Jay's getting away."

Eli snorted. "He's not going anywhere. He panics if he's more than a foot from his cage. I could leave the door open all day and they wouldn't leave."

He held Daisy and stroked his head. Daisy closed his eyes, seemingly content, and made sort of a squirrelly chittering sound.

"What's that noise he's making?" I asked.

"He's bruxing." Eli scratched behind Daisy's ears. "It means he's happy. Feel him — he's vibrating."

"Kind of like a cat purring?" I asked, stepping closer and daring to stroke a finger down the rat's white back. "His fur is so smooth."

"Rats are the cleanest. They're obsessed with grooming. They even groom each other. It's so cute." And then he said in a baby-talk voice, "Aren't they just precious?"

He scooped up Jay, who had scurried back into the cage, and set him on his shoulder. I was endlessly fascinated by this aspect of Eli, this open, tender side that only seemed to exist for rats. I reached out and patted Jay's head, once I was sure he wouldn't bite me, although I did jerk away when he turned to sniff my finger.

Eli put Daisy back in the cage and picked up Jay in both hands. "Time for your medicine, sweetheart," Eli said in his baby-talk voice.

"Medicine?"

Eli pulled a tiny prescription bottle out of a small plastic storage container and shook it. "He has a respiratory infection," he said, picking up a syringe. "Watch how good he is." He held Jay in one hand and administered some pink stuff into his mouth with the other. Jay actually held the syringe in both hands and swallowed it down.

"It must taste good," I said.

More baby talk: "Or he's just the best wittle wattie ever, yes he is." He kissed Jay on the head and put him back.

"So is he all right?" I asked.

"Yeah, he seems better. Fingers crossed. He's over three years old."

"Is that old for rats?"

"Yeah," he said softly.

Eli set them down and gave them a few Cheerios out of a Ziploc bag. They ran off to separate corners with them, Jay managing to cram two into his mouth at once. He frantically buried them under some bedding and ran back out for more.

"That's all for now, sweethearts," Eli said, putting him away and closing the cage.

I did my best impression of a rat voice. "Clean our cage!"

"Ha-ha."

I sat on his unmade bed, which smelled a little like wet dog and had visible crumbs strewn about like ants — Oreos, possibly, judging by the color and texture. Eli returned to the bottles and started pouring from them into the two cups. Then he stepped over some dirty clothes and opened a door on the table that held the red light, which turned out to be a mini-fridge. "I have fruit punch and Dr Pepper. Let's just make an Attempted Suicide."

It figured that this would be the name of an Eli cocktail. "What's in it?" I asked, sweeping crumbs off the bed onto the floor. I was starting to itch.

"You just mix everything you have together. Kind of low-rent, but let's face it, our lives are more Tennessee Williams than F. Scott Fitzgerald."

Truer words had never been spoken.

"Can you go get some ice?" Eli asked.

I went, partly because I was dying to get out of the itchy crumbs and partly because I rarely got to see much of his house. I'd kill to have a house as old as his, a house with character and all sorts of unknowable history in its walls. Built in 1875, Eli's was one of the first houses to go up after the founding of Maplebrook. It had original woodwork and fixtures and claw-foot tubs. Eli said it was his mother's dream home, not at all what his dad wanted, but after she died, he couldn't bear to leave.

My heart sank as I thought again of Luke and his mother. I wondered what kind of house they had, and if it was the same one I'd lived in as a baby.

I tiptoed up the stairs, which creaked deliciously. The lights upstairs were off. A column of moonlight poured in through the front bay window and illuminated my path to the kitchen, but when I got there, I couldn't find the light switches. I found my way to the fridge and opened the door for light while I looked for something to put the ice in. There were old copper pots hanging from a rack on the wall, so I lifted one of those from its hook and filled it with ice.

When I got back downstairs, Eli was reciting some weird incantation while mixing the drink. I didn't ask for a translation; ignorance is bliss. I was just looking for a distraction, not an exercise in voodoo or Satanism or whatever other dark fun he might have been invoking.

He added ice and handed me a cup. "Cheers."

We clinked (more like clunked, owing to plastic acoustics) and took a slug. It was both disgusting and oddly intriguing — possibly from the black licorice flavor of the ouzo. I wasn't sure how to pace myself. Drink it like soda? Or was it more a sipping drink? I'd been tipsy a few times but never smashed — I was still sort of a rookie where drinking was concerned. I had always been an almost pathologically well-behaved child. I thought of Luke, and not hearing from him, and chugged half the glass.

Eli gave me a crooked grin. "Easy, girl." He took a sip and made a face. He sat on his bed and propped himself up on lumpy pillows.

I picked up something in a frame on his bedside table — or what passed for a bedside table. It was actually an overturned laundry basket. It was a framed newspaper article — small and kind of faded.

"My mom's obituary."

I nearly dropped it. "Eli! Why?" Why would he *frame* it? Why would he want that reminder so close by every day?

"I love obituaries!" He picked it up and hugged it to his concave chest. "They're this final tribute to a person, this way of immortalizing them. There is nothing like them in all the world."

I regarded him with worry, unable to think of anything to say.

"So where are your girls tonight?" Eli asked.

"Basketball game," I said guiltily. I brushed off the sheets as discreetly as I could and settled in next to him.

"Sportsball. What a waste of time."

I shrugged. "How's your novel coming?"

"Good. Mostly. There's one part that's kind of rough."

"Yeah?"

"I have this male character who's totally in love with a woman."

I gasped. "A woman! That's disgusting."

"Right?" He grinned. "She's going to end up pregnant, so . . ." He made a face. "Het sex. I might need some help."

I snorted. "Not exactly my field of expertise, either. Besides, didn't they cover everything you need to know in fifth grade?"

"Oh, so it should go something like, *Elmer inserted his penis into Annabelle's vagina, ejaculated, and impregnated her*? Ahh, so literary, so nuanced."

I laughed. "You're a shoo-in for that Iowa program."

"Don't joke!" he said, suddenly serious. "If I don't get in . . ."

"All is lost?" I suggested, hoping to preempt a more macabre threat.

My phone dinged. I sighed. It was only a matter of time before my mom had something to say in response to the bomb I dropped. Or maybe it was just Gab or Leila checking my pulse.

But it wasn't my mom, and it wasn't Gab or Leila. The display read *Luke.*

I opened the message, my stomach writhing like a pile of eels.

Hey, Jules! Greetings from your starving long-lost almost-brother. Behold:

After a moment, a photo came through of a package of ramen, a chunk of Romano cheese, and a container of ground pepper.

"What are you grinning at?" Eli said. "Don't tell me it's Hottie McPianofingers."

"Shhh!" I typed, *Luke! Are you okay? Is everything okay? I've been worried!*

He wrote: *We're okay. Good news is Mom is home. Tired, but home.*

I wrote, *That's good. She must be happy about that.*

He wrote. *Yes. Now help me feed myself before I chew my arm off. Which will wreck my piano career and it will all be your fault.*

I grinned, elbowing Eli away as he tried to peek at my screen. *It's so easy. Boil water. Cook ramen. Drain some of the water but leave a little. Throw in more pepper than you'd think advisable and an embarrassment of cheese. Stir. Enjoy. Praise the Ramen Queen.*

He wrote, *See, it's things like MORE pepper or pour off SOME of the water. And what unit of measure is an embarrassment?*

I quickly typed: *A LOT of pepper. More than you'd ever put on anything. Leave maybe a quarter cup of water. An embarrassment of cheese is the amount that you'd eat if no one was looking.*

He wrote: *What kind of cup? Coffee cup? And I'm from Wisconsin. There is no amount of cheese I would be unwilling to publicly eat.*

I laughed giddily.

Eli got up. "Fine. I'll clean the cage." He stopped and

poured himself some more drink and dumped more in my cup, too, splashing some on my thighs.

"Eli!"

"Sorry."

I typed: *Okay, cheesehead. Boy, you're clueless! Sure, a coffee cup, fine. Close enough.*

He wrote, *Okay, brb. STARVING.*

Eli came over and plopped the ratties right onto the bed. "Watch them, okay?"

"What?" I squealed as they landed inches from my legs. "What do I do?"

He tossed me a bag of Cheerios. "Here, you can give them a treat."

I yelped. "Eli! How long will this take?"

"Just a few minutes, calm down. I just have to change the bedding."

"You should think about changing your own bedding," I muttered.

I opened the bag nervously. Jay scampered right over to me, but Daisy held back. "What if he bites me when I give it to him?" I yelled to Eli, who was in the laundry room.

"Jesus fuck, Davis. You're not gonna get hurt. Give my babies a treat."

I positioned a Cheerio at the very tips of my fingernails and held it out. Jay snatched it so fast that I jerked away, scared half to death. Daisy inched closer. I glanced around for Eli, and when it was clear he couldn't see me, I tossed a few Cheerios onto the bed. Jay stopped eating to grab as many as he could. Daisy hopped over and grabbed one, then hopped away to eat it. I watched them for a few minutes, and it actually was sort of cute, the way they held the Cheerios in their tiny hands. "Hey, Eli," I called. "What keeps them from going to the bathroom on your bed?"

"Nothing," he called back.

"Oh gross!" I yelled, scooting back. I startled Jay, who moved away from me, then continued munching. I felt bad, so I slowly reached out, considering petting him. He ignored me, so I tried it, stroking him lightly with one finger. He held still for a moment, pausing in his mad munching, then continued.

Not wanting to play favorites, I reached out and petted Daisy, too. His coat was even softer than Jay's.

"What's going on with Hottie?" Eli called after a few minutes.

"His mother is home from the hospital. So that's good. Eli, your ratties are actually almost kind of cute."

"Well, duh! What's cuter than a rat?"

I checked my phone, realizing this was taking way too long. Ramen noodles cook in two minutes! I typed: *Getting worried . . .*

He responded: *I was eating. It was okay. But the cheese never melted in. It stayed in a big hard lump.*

I wrote: *Um . . . The cheese was grated, right?*

He wrote: *GRATED??*

I shrieked with laughter, which sent the rats scurrying.

"Hey, you scared the ratties!" Eli said. He came over and picked them up, crooning apologies at them.

I typed: *You just put a giant chunk of cheese in?*

He wrote: *You said an embarrassment! And nobody told me to grate the cheese! Jeez.*

I wrote: *So it wasn't creamy and luscious?*

He wrote: *No! It was watery, with a rubbery chunk of cheese.*

"What is so funny?" Eli asked, jumping onto the bed next to me, causing yet more drink to slosh onto my jeans. "You're not drinking my amazing creation. Snob."

I took a sip and made fake *mmmm* sounds. Eli snorted.

Luke wrote: *And it was way salty.*

I frowned, then gasped. *You didn't put the seasoning packet in, did you???*

He wrote: *YOU DID NOT SAY NOT TO PUT THE PACKET IN.*

I was horrified at how nasty it must have been, but that didn't stop me from laughing till I cried.

He wrote: *You are terrible at this! Next time give me a foolproof recipe. What else do you have?*

I started naming every halfway successful ramen experiment I could think of. He stopped me at ramen *Amatriciana* — another abuse of an Italian recipe.

He wrote: *Bacon??? You found a way to get bacon in ramen??*

I wrote: *I have two ramen dishes that use bacon. One with tomato sauce and one with eggs and cheese.*

Eli gave up on me and went over to his computer.

Luke wrote, *Okay, maybe I'll give you another chance one of these days.*

I wrote, *If I had known how hopeless in the kitchen you are, I would have given you much clearer instructions. Sheesh!*

He wrote, *I told you I was hopeless! Anyway, I learn by doing. You should show me sometime.*

My stomach flipped over. *I would love to.*

He wrote, *Let me get through this recital and then maybe we can make a plan?*

He added, *My mom is going to have to miss my recital, and my dad probably will, too. Which . . . It's okay, but it upsets her a lot, missing anything, and not being there to cheer me on. You know?*

Not really, I thought, my heart aching for everyone. Everyone except my mom. For Luke, for his devoted parents, and for myself. I had no idea what that kind of cherishing felt like. *I'm so sorry,* I wrote again. *If there's anything I can do . . .*

Thanks, he wrote. *My dad is super excited that you found me, by the way. We haven't told my mom yet — he thinks we should let her rebuild her strength first — but I know she'll be over the moon when she finds out. I think she might have missed you even more than I did, if that's possible.*

I was filled with a rush of warmth and wonder. To have

114

been loved that way — missed that way! How was it possible? As I struggled for words, Luke wrote again. *You've been on my mind a lot. FYI.*

I would have given anything to be with him. To be able to hug him. I wrote, *You've been on my mind a lot, too.* I took a gulp of my drink for courage. *Like, a LOT.*

He sent a smiley back, then wrote, *Oh, crap — I lost track of the time. I have to go.*

I frowned, disappointed that he was again leaving when I wasn't nearly ready to let him go. It felt like I could never get enough of him.

He wrote, *Take care of yourself, okay? I'll talk to you soon!*

Okay, I wrote. And then, before he disappeared, I started typing kind of desperately: *Good luck at your recital! And my thoughts will be with your mom. Keep in touch!* And then I stared at my phone until I became aware of Eli muttering dialogue to himself. "'You're just like your father.' No . . . 'You . . . You and your father are cut from the same cloth . . .'"

I set my half-full cup on the table and went over to Eli. "How goes the work?" I asked, touching his hair.

He leaned back into my touch, pushing his head into my hand for petting. He really was like my kitty. "Eh. Not great. How is Bromeo?" he asked.

I chortled. "Bromeo. You're so clever." I sighed, stroking his hair. "I used to call him Duke, apparently."

"Duke and Jules." He grinned, his lip ring glimmering. "Sounds like the title of a bodice ripper."

"Stop it," I said, giving his head a gentle shove. Then I sighed. "He's sad that his mom is going to miss his recital Saturday."

"You should go."

I blinked. "What?"

He spun his chair to face me. "You should go. Then he'd have someone there, and you could watch those magical fingers in action."

"Stop projecting."

He laughed. "Seriously, though. Why not go?"

I paused to consider. Why *not* go? If I could get there? The idea was hard to resist.

Eli's fingers flew on his keyboard, then he leaned back and turned the screen to me. "Here it is. It's Saturday at two. Be there or be square."

"I don't know," I said, but already I was thinking about it. Could I? Maybe I could! Gab had a car — maybe she'd take me. The more I thought of it, the more right it sounded.

By the end of the evening and another cup of voodoo juice, I had decided: if Luke's parents couldn't be at his recital to support him, his sort-of sister would be.

Chapter 9

Gab was jubilant that I was grabbing life by the proverbial balls. And she was more than happy to drive me.

I got up Saturday morning, showered, and made some tea and toast. As I pulled out my treasured jar of Oxford marmalade, I thought about the rationing in England during the war. I wondered what breakfast looked like during those years, with tea, sugar, bread, and milk rationed. Meat, too, of course, and even marmalade. How hard the women and cooks must have worked to produce meals in such lean times, depending on cleverness as well as frugality. Sometimes I imagined I could have done a decent job at that myself.

My mom padded in just as I was finishing my breakfast. We had exchanged few words since I took off for Eli's

Tuesday night. I kept expecting her to demand answers, but she mostly holed up in her studio. Perhaps she realized that demanding answers from me would set her up for the same in reverse. Apparently she was willing to forfeit one to spare herself the other.

"Hi," she said. She looked tired. She was still in her robe, and her hair hung in her face.

"Hi."

She leaned against the counter and crossed her arms. "Can we talk about what you said the other day?"

I stood. "I can't, it's too hard to talk about," I said, bitchily throwing her own words back in her face. I put my plate and cup by the sink and headed for my room. She didn't follow me. Frankly, I wouldn't have followed me, either.

When Gab arrived to pick me up, I called to my mom as I left that I was hanging out with Gab, then immediately closed the door behind me.

We headed north on 41 in Gab's Prius, music blaring. My palms were sweaty, and I kept feeling like I needed to pee even though I knew I didn't. I turned down the music and started spewing my worries so that Gab could talk me down, which she was good at. After a while, Leila messaged. *I hope your day is amazing. I'll be thinking about you. Wish I were there.* ☹

"Leila's sad she's not with us," I told Gab.

I watched Gab for a moment, observing, as I always did,

her sharp, aquiline nose in profile. It suited her. She was the most self-possessed, secure person I knew.

"Well, she had her cousins' brunch."

Ah, yes, the monthly gathering of the ten thousand cousins on her mom's side. "I know, but she feels left out." I bit my thumbnail, staring out at the road ahead, the gray, overcast sky.

"She'll get over it."

I thought that was kind of cold, but there was that Gab-and-Leila aspect that was hard for me to judge.

An hour into the trip, Gab spotted a frozen custard place and insisted on stopping. I was anxious to get to Lawrence, but the stop was probably a good thing, because toast wasn't much of a breakfast and who knew when I'd eat next. We sat at a tiny table by the window, my spoon dipping back and forth between my vanilla and my chocolate. I wondered which Luke preferred. Or if, like me, he just wanted it all.

We arrived at the campus early, despite the stop. Gab drove slowly around, looking for Harper Hall — the location of the concert, according to the website. We soon discovered that it had been moved to the chapel. The campus wasn't that big, so Gab just parked in the first spot she found.

"Oh my God," she said suddenly, staring out the window. "It's a sign, Jules."

I craned my neck around. "What is? Is it Luke?"

She pointed, and I started to laugh. Walking on the

sidewalk right across from us was a guy with blond dread-locks wearing a sweatshirt, Jesus sandals with socks, and . . . a *kilt.*

"Come on," she said, but she paused to take a quick look in her visor mirror. "Oh my God," she said, trying to flatten her hair on the sides. "Look at this latke lid. Hopeless." She snapped the visor shut, grabbed the keys, and opened the door, grinning. "Come on!"

"Gab, no!" I got out of the car and followed her. "What are you going to do?"

I had to skip to keep up with her — she was striding right toward him. *Oh, please God, don't let her ambush him with an under-kilt inspection.*

I glanced around — I liked the look of the campus, not that I'd seen many. It was small, a mix of old and new, and seemed like a cool place, judging by the wide array of dispa-rate student types I was spotting. It was sort of the Laroche's of colleges — nothing matched. And although it was windy, the sun was starting to peek out, which made the whole campus look prettier and happier.

Gab had stopped the guy, who was regarding her with a friendly expression. As I caught up, I could see Gab was dis-arming him with that down-to-earth, *we're all friends here* style she has. He was nodding and eating a muffin. Lemon-poppy seed, by the looks of it. He was probably stoned half-way to Tuesday.

"Hi," I said, out of breath.

"This is Jules," Gab told the guy.

"Byron," he said, switching hands with his muffin, wiping his hand on his shirt, and shaking my hand.

"So I have three questions for you," Gab said.

"All right," Byron said, his easy smile revealing huge teeth. "I'll give you three answers."

Gab smoothed down her hair, which was futile. "Okay. (A) Why are you wearing a kilt?"

He nodded. "That's easy. Comfort."

"That's it?" Gab said. "You just wear one because it's comfortable? Are you Scottish or anything?"

"Is that the second question?"

Gab smiled. "No."

He smiled back at her. "All right. Nope, not Scottish. I've got German and Viking blood." He took another bite of his muffin.

Some kids walking by across the street called out a greeting to Byron — only they called him "B-dog" — and he waved his muffin in response. He was built like a teddy bear: roundish belly, thick, solid limbs.

"So you just wear it?" Gab asked. "Anytime? Like, instead of pants?"

"Is *that* the second question?" he asked, squinting at Gab.

Gab laughed and shook her head.

There was flirting going on here.

"All right, I'll grant you another freebie." He tilted his

head and rubbed his bristly chin. "I'd say I wear a kilt four or five days a week. I try to keep my pants in the rotation so they don't feel forgotten."

Gab nodded. "I see. Next — and this is the second question, by the way — could we inquire as to what you wear under it?" She raised her eyebrows almost imperceptibly.

I would have liked to disappear into a hole in the ground. I pushed my hair over my shoulder — the wind kept blowing it in my face — and looked around impatiently.

"Ayup," he said, nodding. "People always want to know that. I could be coy and tell you to look for yourselves, but I'll just give you the straight answer: I wear boxers. Is that good or bad?"

"It's fine," I blurted out. When Gab turned to me, I tapped my wrist and gave her a *come on!* look.

Someone walked by in a giraffe costume. This place was a madhouse. I kind of liked it.

"Last question," Gab said. "Where's the chapel?"

"Ah, the easiest question yet," he said, turning toward a building across the street and down a little. "You just have to go around to the other side. Someone performing?"

"Luke Margolis," Gab said. "You know him?"

"Oh, sure. I had him in an art history class last year."

Do not invite him to come with us or I will kill you!

She heard my telepathic message. "Well, thanks for all the answers, freebies and all," Gab said. "We'd better get going."

"Hey, we're having a little get-together at my place later,"

he said, never taking his eyes off Gab. "I live in the building right over there —" He turned and pointed. "Plantz Hall.
Right next to the chapel." He turned back to Gab. "Little beer,
little tequila, little weed, some tunes . . . you should come."

"Maybe," Gab said, peering over at where he was
pointing.

Maybe not. I let out a breath and looked pointedly across
the street.

So Gab said good-bye to Byron, and we headed to the
chapel. My stomach was tying itself into knots that would
have stumped a sailor. Why hadn't I messaged Luke on the
drive over, to let him know I was coming? Was I really just
going to show up and surprise him? But it was too late to
text him now. He was about to perform and I didn't want to
do anything to distract him.

As we approached the chapel, my attention was momen-
tarily diverted. It was beautiful — large and white, with columns and a steeple. I wondered when it was built. It was not
a modern construction — I would have bet it was early twen-
tieth century, 1920s at the latest.

"Come on," Gab said softly, pulling me up the steps.

"I'm getting really nervous about running into him," I
said. "I should have told him I'm coming instead of ambush-
ing him like this. Why didn't I?"

Gab pulled the door open.

"This is gorgeous," Gab whispered. "Holy cats."

It was gorgeous, yes, but I was queasy and starting to

shake. Luke had to be here somewhere. What if he spotted me and it jarred him? What if I ruined his performance?

Right. I'm *that* important.

"Where do you want to sit?" Gab asked softly, pulling me out of the way as other people entered.

"Where he can't see me," I said, regretting that I wouldn't be able to sit up front where I could see him better.

"Oh, for fuck's sake," she grumbled.

We accepted a program from a pretty girl in a short retro plaid dress and cat glasses and found a seat in the back balcony. "Do you think he'll be able to see us?" I whispered to Gab. The place was so flooded with light from the windows that there was no chance of hiding.

"No way. Besides, he's not going to be staring into the audience when he plays."

Good point. I glanced down at the program. There were actually five performers — he was the last.

I took a deep breath and stared at the ceiling, which was coffered with huge octagons. It looked like the bottom of a giant snow boot.

By 2:00 the center seating area was mostly full, but the balcony areas were sparsely populated. When the performances began, I couldn't enjoy them. My mind raced in a million directions, and I kept looking at the program, trying to gauge how far we were from Luke's performance. I didn't even realize how frenetically my leg was jiggling until Gab laid a hand on my knee.

Was I going to just walk up to him afterward? *Surprise!* How did I expect him to react?

I wished I hadn't come. Why had this seemed like a good idea? Damn Eli and his voodoo juice and persuasion. When the concert ended, I would sneak out immediately, making sure Luke never saw me, and hit the pavement running.

Gab jabbed me with her elbow and gestured with her head toward the stage. A violin duet was wrapping up. It was Luke's turn.

When he walked out onto the stage, I slid down in my seat and let my hair fall forward, even though I knew he wasn't likely to spot me way in the back. He looked as perfect in a suit as he did in faded jeans. He gave a smile and a nod to the audience and then sat. He immediately got back up and started twisting the knob on the seat to lower it. Some shorty must have played before him, which I'd know if for the past half hour I'd had the attention span God gave a flea. I glanced at the program. The first piece was Chopin Étude op. 10, no. 12 in C minor, "Revolutionary."

He looked up with a grin as he finished adjusting the seat and took his place in front of the piano. A hush settled over the place. He sat stock-still for a long moment, then dove in.

I couldn't help tensing up. From the first notes, the piece was intense, fast, and furious. It sounded like there were about fifty-eight hands on those keys. He punctuated his playing with head movements that sent his hair flying. Gab was squeezing my hand so hard it hurt. She jabbed me and gave me an *oh my GOD are you freaking kidding me* look. Yes. Yes, he was that amazing.

When he finished the piece, my hands flew from my lap to applaud, but Gab stopped me just in time. I would have been the only sound in the place; clearly, applause was meant to be held to the end of his performance, and everyone knew that except me. I wished I had the faintest clue about music performances. I had missed so much in my life, and I felt so stupid.

His next piece was Schubert, Piano Sonata in A major, D. 959 Second Movement, which went on forever, and that was fine with me because it was one of the most beautiful things I had ever heard. There were moments where Luke's hands hovered over the keys, silent, still, taking his time. I glanced over at Gab at one point and she was transfixed. She was also practically breaking my fingers. My hands were wet with sweat, but she either didn't notice or didn't care.

The sound of his playing resonated inside me, filling my chest with feelings I barely understood. I slipped my hand free of Gab's and dug in my purse for a tissue when the piece ended. The music had moved me deeply, but also I despaired. I was a million miles from his world. I didn't know a sonata from a hole in the ground. I probably wasn't nearly interesting or cultured enough to hold his attention. What selling points did I even have? Knowledge of vintage china? Ramen noodle recipes? So stupid.

His last piece was J. S. Bach, Fantasia in C minor BWV 906. This one, too, sounded impossibly complex. I couldn't begin to fathom the brain and fingers that could finesse that. Hands crossing over each other, emotions changing on a dime . . . when he played the last note, he paused, hands above the keyboard, and then rested them in his lap.

The applause was fierce. He stood and smiled modestly. People started standing up in the front, and soon everyone else followed suit. He was the only performer to receive a standing ovation.

"I have to get out of here," I whispered to Gab, reaching for my purse.

She grabbed me. "What are you talking about? You have to see him."

"No. I changed my mind. Please. I want to go, Gab." The idea of his looking at me in confusion or maybe even annoyance was too much. He had friends, he had a life — and I was just a fawning pest. One who didn't even have the courtesy of checking with him before showing up at his recital.

"Jules Davis." She turned me toward her, and I could feel the tough love coming. "We came all this way to see him. He just gave an un-fucking-believable performance. You go talk to him."

I shook my head. "I can't, Gab. He's amazing and I'm just this idiot kid."

"This idiot kid he's cared about and missed and wished for all these years — almost your whole life!"

I shook my head, glancing up toward the front. At least a dozen people were waiting to talk to him. "He'll be mad. He didn't invite me. I didn't even tell him I was coming!"

"He'll be thrilled to see you." She held up her phone and wiggled it at me. "I am one text away. Talk to him."

I grabbed her arm. "No! Where are you going?" I didn't want to be left alone.

"Don't worry, I won't be far." Her smile had mischief in it.

"Plantz Hall?" I asked.

She shrugged. "I'm going to check it out." She reached over, gave me a quick hug, then turned and gave a pointed look in Luke's direction. "Go. Live your life, Jules."

And with that, she was gone.

I cowered in the back. Luke was accepting congratulations from people, if his humble demeanor was any indication. It amazed me that he could be that talented without one whit of arrogance.

I pulled out a compact and looked at myself. Not too bad, other than the slightly pink hue in my eyes. I put on some lip gloss and tiptoed up toward the front.

When the line had petered out and the place was almost empty, I crept closer. He was gesturing and laughing with a group of people — students, it looked like. He glanced up in my direction and did a double take. He stared for a moment, then looked back and forth between me and his friends. He held up a hand to them and walked my way.

"Jules?" He looked incredulous.

"I — I thought I'd surprise you." I started to shake, I was so worried that he wouldn't be happy I was there.

"Oh, I'm surprised all right." He ran a hand through his hair. "You saw the recital?"

I nodded. "Pardon my French, but you are fucking amazing."

That ridiculous, staggering smile — there it was. Relief rushed through me as I tumbled into his flecked, mossy eyes.

"Thanks. I screwed up a little on the Chopin, but . . ."

"If you did, I couldn't tell."

He stared at me, shaking his head, still apparently working on the fact of my presence. "Well, come here." He pulled me into a hug, and I let myself squeeze him back a little. He smelled the way I remembered, which, for better or worse, I liked an awful lot.

When he pulled back, he said, "So how did you get here? Did you come alone?"

"I came with Gab. She's here somewhere." I gestured vaguely.

He glanced around, perhaps assuming I meant more "here" than I actually did. "Well, do you have to rush off?"

"No!" I was so relieved and happy I couldn't help smiling. "No, I have time."

He chewed his lip, thinking. "We could go for some coffee or get something to eat, but . . ."

I started to deflate. Of course he probably had plans.

He gestured at his suit. "I'd kind of like to change. Is it okay if we stop by my apartment first?"

My heart lifted—he did want to spend time with me. "Sure."

"Just give me a second to grab my coat."

He turned back and ran almost headlong into a tall redhead who grabbed him in a tight hug. "You were brilliant," she said softly. I turned slightly away and busied myself pulling on my coat and zipping it.

"But you're always brilliant," I heard her say. And then I heard a kiss.

He thanked her and said that he had to run, but that he'd see her later. He'd see her later because . . . She was his roommate? His lab tutor? His boss? The idea that she might be his girlfriend brought a stab of something uncomfortable.

She passed me on her way out without even noticing me. She was tall enough to make me feel short, thin enough to make me feel fat, beautiful enough to make me feel plain, vibrant enough to make me feel dull.

Luke came back, pulling his coat on. "My apartment is off campus, just a few minutes from here. I have my car. Should we find your friend?"

"Oh—she's hanging out somewhere. She met some people."

His eyebrows rose as he smiled. "Great—so we can really catch up."

As he ushered me out the doors, I filled with the

excitement over this step into the past — and the future. A new world was opening its doors to me.

Luke's apartment was the finished attic of a beautiful old house in town. It was a little shabby and a little messy, but I couldn't help falling in love with it. It had slanty ceilings, leaded-glass windows, and a bathroom with a claw-foot tub, its exterior painted a seafoam green.

The floor in the living area was covered in a red Oriental rug, unraveling on one side. I imagined a family cat, decades ago, spending long afternoons playing with the tassels on the edge.

Off to the side sat a nubby brown love seat, and in front of it, a small trunk, covered in old travel stickers, served as a coffee table. An upright piano stood against the wall opposite the door. Sheet music covered nearly every surface in the room.

"Make yourself at home," he called out to me as he went to change.

His bedroom had just a curtain — no door. He slipped behind it, but I could hear everything: the unzipping of his pants, the crumple of fabric, the slide of a dresser drawer . . . My stomach fluttered at those sounds, just a few feet away. I was just nervous, I told myself — and excited about the idea of spending time with him, getting to know him better. I loved the way he made me feel — the way he was always excited to see me, always interested in everything I thought or said. Talking to him was so easy, and he was so sweet and talented and funny. I was silly to have worried he'd find me dull or immature. I sat down at the piano. "Are you going be, like, a concert pianist?" I asked, picking up a sheet of music.

"That's the dream," he said, coming back into the living room. He wore faded jeans and a lightweight hoodie in a washed-out shade of once-red, now almost a dusty mauve. He picked up a few mugs from the coffee table and moved them to the kitchen. "I'll probably end up teaching talentless six-year-olds and flipping burgers on the overnight shift at Wendy's."

"Ha-ha," I said, leaning so I could see him in the kitchen. "You have way too much talent not to be successful." I looked at the keys in front of me, thinking how many millions of times his hands had passed over them.

He grabbed a beer from the fridge. "You want something to drink?"

Did he mean a beer? I would take one if he was offering. But what if he just meant a soda or something? I took the safe way out and said, "No thanks, I'm fine."

He reappeared, sipping his beer. "You play?" he asked, nodding at the keys.

"Not a note," I said, turning toward him. His hair was sticking up. I wished I could smooth it into place. Maybe if we had been raised together, I could do something like that without it being weird. Would we ever develop that kind of easy closeness now? Or was that a ship that had sailed, never to return to port?

He sat down next to me, set his beer on a stack of music on the piano, and picked up one of my hands. "Look how small. You probably can't even reach an octave." He stretched my hand over the keyboard, pulling my thumb and pinkie as far as they could go, then laughed. "Barely a seventh."

"Another career out the window," I joked. His hands were warm, and I was sorry when he let go.

He smiled. "You sure you don't want something to drink? I have ginger ale."

"Uh, sure, that sounds good," I said, but I cringed inwardly. Relegated to the kiddie-beverage category . . .

He jumped up. "I'll even give you a glass, if I have a clean one."

"Rolling out the red carpet, I see."

He returned moments later and handed me a drink in a Doctor Who TARDIS cup.

"Thank you," I said, taking it from him and examining it. "So how much did you put in here? I assume it's bigger on the inside?"

He laughed and put his hand to his forehead. "Oh my God. You just get more and more perfect."

I sipped the drink, hoping to disguise my smile, the fact that his words thrilled me to the core. I loved it that he found me funny, that I amused him. The way we seemed to click astonished me. Maybe it didn't matter that I didn't play an instrument or wasn't very worldly. Maybe it would be enough if I took an interest, if I could demonstrate an appreciation.

He sat back down, put his hands over the keys, hesitated for a moment, then played a few measures of something pretty.

"Hey," I said, my eyebrows furrowing, "what is that?"

"Why, is it familiar?" he asked, glancing at me as he continued to play.

"Yeah! I feel like I know it from somewhere, but I can't think where."

He watched me, silent for so long that I started to get a nervous stomach. "I think you know," he said softly.

"Did you . . ." I took a breath. "Did you play that when I was little?"

He nodded.

"Could I remember something from that long ago?" I asked.

He shrugged, smiling. "I don't know."

I sighed. "I'd give anything to be able to access those memories."

He stood up. "Let me go get something."

He disappeared behind the curtain, then came back a moment later holding a photograph. "It's not the same as a memory, I know, but . . ." He slid in next to me and handed the picture to me.

It was of the two of us, as kids. He must have been five

or six, and he was holding me. His hair was lighter — blond, and straighter than it was now. I was a chubby, dark-haired thing with big brown eyes, dressed in just a diaper. He was puckered up to kiss me, but I was laughing, leaning back, one arm around his neck and the other clutching a light blue stuffed lamb.

My stuffed lamb. I still had it, thanks to my dramatic protest when my mother, on one of her ruthless purges, had suggested it was time to cut it loose. Hard-won victory, that. I wondered if my subconscious remembered the significance of that lamb.

I examined the picture closely, greedy for details. This had been my bedroom. The crib we were standing next to had been my crib, the fabric letters on the wall spelled out my name. I thought again of my scarf — or Luke's scarf, really — whose label just read *Jules*.

"You guys put my name up," I said, turning my eyes to him. "That . . ." I was having trouble with words. Surely I was reading too much into things, and yet . . . "That just seems kind of . . . permanent."

He watched me for a moment, his forehead creasing. "Jules. The thing is . . . we thought it *would* be permanent."

My breath caught. "What do you mean?"

Time seemed to stand still as I waited for his answer. Finally, he raised his eyes to meet mine. "We were hoping to adopt you."

Chapter 10

*Q*uestions ricocheted in my head like Ping-Pong balls. How could this be true? I might have been adopted? Almost actually a member of another family? Almost *Jules Margolis*?

He spoke softly. "You know your mom had problems."

I nodded, thinking about all my mom's meetings lately. I had no idea what her struggle was like. It was a distant, foreign thought, my mother's addiction. It almost had a whisper of myth — I had never seen evidence of it. And she refused to talk about any of it.

He nodded. "So . . . after the first weeks, and then months . . . it started to seem like she wasn't going to get her act together. And we wanted you. We loved you — my parents loved you like their own." He grinned sheepishly.

"Sometimes when I was being a little shit, I accused them of loving you more."

I stood up, unable to think, to process. I went over to the window. A family was strolling down the street, a mom and a dad swinging their toddler by the hands every few steps. An entire parallel life unfolded before my eyes, and the fact that I couldn't remember or feel anything to validate it only made me feel more resentful of my mother.

The bench scraped on the floor as he stood up. A moment later, his voice came from right next to me. "Are you okay?" he asked.

"No." I didn't know what I was, but "okay" was definitely not a descriptor I would have chosen.

"I'm sorry," he said. "Maybe I shouldn't —"

"No," I said, turning to him. "I want to know. I need to know. You're the only person who'll tell me the truth."

He watched me for a second, then reached into his back pocket. "This is the only other picture I have with me," he said apologetically, and pulled a weathered photo out of his wallet. "We have tons more at the house in Milwaukee, though." He smiled. "I've been carrying this around since the day they took you away. It was the whole reason I got my first wallet. At first I wanted a locket. I thought they were kind of cool, with the pictures inside. But my dad suggested a wallet instead."

I couldn't help laughing. I took the picture from him and held it up to the light.

"My dad took it," Luke said softly.

My heart pounded as I took a closer look. Luke and I were outside building a snowman. But we weren't alone. Luke's mother held me in her arms, leaning me over to attach the snowman's carrot nose. She wore sunglasses and a light blue ski jacket, and her smile was enormous, warm. Luke grinned cheesily at the camera, arms gesturing toward our masterpiece. My face was mostly turned away, focused as I was on my task, but peeking out through my fluffy white hat and my many-times wrapped blue scarf, my rosy cheeks and happy grin were unmistakable.

"We're wearing our scarves," I commented.

"My mom knitted them for us for Chanukah."

"For Chanukah?" I asked, turning to him. "You're Jewish?"

He nodded. "Well, mostly. My dad was half-Jewish and wasn't raised with any religion. But my mom's super Jewish. Well, in certain ways. She's weird. She calls herself 'an intense secular.'"

I would be Jewish if they had adopted me? I would have been raised Jewish! With a "super Jewish" mom. Wait till Gab heard this.

"People thought you were ours. You have eyes like my mom's." He shifted his eyes to the floor. "She never got over losing you. None of us did, really."

I stared at a shaft of sunlight lighting a patch of the Oriental rug, working on what he was saying. It was too unreal. All the love I'd always longed for, had always envied about my friends' families . . . Here it was. I'd had it. I'd *had* it.

"You guys really loved me?" I asked. It was a wondrous thought. "Your mom loved me?" Questions bounced to the fore. What was she like? What did I call her? Did she really think of me as her daughter?

"Oh my God." He sank onto the futon and tipped his head back, smiling. "You were the sun and the moon." He turned his gaze to me. His eyes, caught in the late afternoon light, were a bright green, and I thought maybe I felt a tug of the familiar. Somewhere in the recesses of myself, I knew and trusted this person. "She couldn't have more kids after me," he said. "And then we got you. And we fell in love with you — how could we not?"

I shivered at his words. I wanted to hear more. I sat down beside him. "What was I like?" My voice came out a whisper.

He hesitated. "You weren't in great shape at first. You were kind of fearful, and you cried a lot." He shook his head, laughing a little. "I was afraid you'd never like me."

I felt weak, numb. What in God's name had I been through to be a fearful baby?

"But then you just blossomed. You started to smile. And laugh — I could make you laugh! It was the most amazing thing. The way you loved me? And trusted me? I felt like the most important person in the world." He hesitated, then said softly, "I felt like a big brother."

"I must have been heartbroken when they took me away from you," I said quietly. "It's probably a blessing I can't remember it."

"On the day the social worker came for you, I tried to hide you. I mean, how was I supposed to let them take my sister away? So I took you out to the shed behind the garage, and we hid there together. You were too little to understand what was happening. You thought it was a game."

He tried to smile, but he couldn't pull it off. "I brought snacks to keep you happy. Peanut butter cookies — the ones with the peanut butter filling? You loved those."

I still did. "Tookies," I said.

His eyes widened, but then he laughed. "Tookies. Yes." He shook his head, watching me. "It's *really you.*"

Joy surged through me to know how much I meant to him. "So what happened?"

"Hm? Oh." He sighed. "My dad finally found us there."

"Was he mad?"

Luke shook his head, eyes fixed on his lap. "He cried. I'd never seen my dad cry before."

My head swam with too many truths that were too difficult to assimilate.

"You were screaming when they took you away. I can still hear it."

My eyes filled. It was incomprehensible that we had this history, that I'd been so important to him.

"Man. I was one fucked-up kid for a while. And my poor mom . . . she just — fell apart."

"I've been thinking about her," I said softly, discreetly wiping my eyes. "I wish there were something I could do to help — besides just visiting her when she's up for it, I mean. You'd tell me, right, if there was anything I could do?"

"Of course," he said softly, his expression pained. "You know, even when you were little, you had this huge heart. You were always so concerned about everyone. I wiped out on my bike once and came inside crying, and you looked so scared. You gave me your stuffed lamb to hold, which . . ." He smiled. "That was not a thing you parted with easily. And when Mom was finished bandaging my knee, you kissed it."

I hung on his every word. I wanted to know about myself, about those critical first months. And I wanted to know about *them* — the family that loved me and helped me when I was most vulnerable.

But my phone dinged, and my heart dropped. "That's probably Gab," I said sadly, taking my phone out of my purse.

It was. But her message said she was happily partying with Byron and company, and that I should take my sweet time and please plan to be the designated driver.

"Do you have to go?" Luke asked.

I shook my head. "She's having fun. She wants me to drive home later." Suddenly I felt awkward, intrusive. I had

141

shown up unannounced on a Saturday — I should expect him to have no plans?

But then he said, "Good. More time for me."

His smile . . . God, what it did to my belly. I knew it must be the newness of this whole thing, these feelings he gave me. Surely it would wear off at some point.

"We could order takeout," he said. "You hungry?"

I relaxed back into the couch, smiling. "Do you really have to ask?"

We sat on the living room floor in the warm yellow glow of the old lamps, eating Thai food, as Luke filled me in on a past I couldn't remember.

I learned that I had loved food more than just about anything — surprise, surprise. He said no matter what was going on or what I might be upset about, food could always make me happy.

I learned that I called his mother Mima because they tried to pick something close to *Mama* that wasn't *Mama*.

I learned we had a black-and-white cat named Cupcake who used to jump into my crib to curl up and sleep. Luke's mom had worried Cupcake would suffocate me, but no matter what they tried, the cat found a way to sneak back into my crib.

I learned I cut my heel on a piece of glass at Lake Michigan, and it had required stitches. This surprised me — I thought I'd never had stitches. I looked at my foot —"Other foot, Einstein." Luke laughed. And lo and behold, there was a scar on the edge of my heel I never even knew I had.

For the millionth time, I wondered what life would have been like if I'd stayed with the Margolises. Luke would be my brother — my real, forever brother. But: Mima, the only mom I would ever have known, would be dying before I even finished high school. Or maybe she wouldn't be. Some butterfly effect, some possibility that without certain turns of events, others also wouldn't have come to pass? Maybe she wouldn't have cancer. Who the fuck knows for sure?

Luke pushed his plate away and leaned back on his hands, crossing his legs at the ankles. He gave me a pointed look. "You know, don't you . . . now that I've found you? You'll never get rid of me."

I smiled, shy at the way his words thrilled me.

My phone dinged, and I knew it was probably Gab. It was nearly ten, and we were three hours from home. I had messaged my mom, saying, *Still out with Gab.* I'd ignored her return messages, her questions about where I was and when I'd be home. She had a royal lot of nerve, I thought. For starters, it wasn't like she answered me whenever I asked her when she'd be home. And what would she say when I confronted her about my other life? The life I nearly had?

Nothing would ever be the same.

Sadly, Luke and I gathered ourselves up to head out. As he drove me to meet Gab, I alternated between looking out my window at the hazy glow of the moon and gazing at Luke's long legs, his comfortable slung-back posture. Once, during a lull in the conversation, he reached over without looking my way, found my hair, and gave it a soft tug. It was the kind of easy, familiar thing Daniel did with Gab, and I loved that Luke felt comfortable enough to do that with me. But it only made me more worried about the confused and vast spectrum of my thoughts and feelings about him. He seemed to fall into a sibling dynamic so easily, but I struggled to understand the rules, to know if the way I felt was normal. The lost years confounded everything — for me, anyway.

When we arrived at Gab's car, Luke shifted into Park and turned to me. "I want to tell Mom I found you," he said. "I'm going to talk to my dad tomorrow. I know she'll want to see you. Would you be able to come to Milwaukee next weekend?"

My heart leapt. "Oh my God — yes! Of course." Next weekend! That wasn't long to wait even by my impatient standards.

"Jules!"

I turned in my seat. Gab was ambling toward us, hand in hand with Byron.

I waved at her halfheartedly. "That's Gab," I told Luke.

Luke leaned around me to wave, too, which struck me as sweet. "Looks like she had an okay time without you." He turned serious. "You drive safely, okay? Let me know when you get home?"

"Okay."

We hesitated, smiling at each other. Then he reached for me and hugged me tight.

I breathed him in one last time before pulling away. "I'll see you soon," I said bravely.

"Bye, Jules," he said, his eyes holding mine.

"Bye. Duke."

The enormous grin that bloomed on his face filled me up.

As he pulled away, Byron stood by while Gab and I got into the car, then he gave us both a wave and a grin. He sauntered away, whistling, a bounce in his step.

I settled into the driver's seat and scooted it forward — Gab's legs were miles longer than mine — and then pulled the seat back upright. "How does this work?" I asked Gab, pointing at the gearshift.

She reached over and flicked the little gear knob into Drive.

I plugged my phone in and set it to navigate home.

Gab tipped her head back against the seat, her lids drooping.

I shook my head. "Drunk, high, or both?"

"Medium drunk and very high."

"You smoked pot?"

She nodded. "It was, like, extreme weed. Sour Diesel, they called it. I was so high for a while that the walls were moving."

I turned up the volume on my phone so I could hear the navigation instructions, then signaled and pulled out onto the street.

Gab tilted her seat back and put her feet up on the glove compartment, closing her eyes. "So? What happened with Luke?"

"You first," I said. "Tell me about your night. Are college parties everything we've hoped for?"

She turned her head toward me and grinned. "I cashed in my V-card."

My jaw dropped. "You had sex with him?"

Keeping my eyes on the road was a tall order as Gab spilled all the details. I glanced over at her briefly. "Did you use —"

"Of course we did. You think I'm an idiot? I wouldn't even go down on him. I'm guessing he's pretty promiscuous."

"Really?" I winced. "Why did you pick him, if, you know . . ."

A look of annoyance crossed her face, and she leaned her head back again. "I wasn't looking for a life partner, Jules. I was looking for an experience."

Gab and I were about as different as two females of the species could be. "Will you see him again?"

She shrugged. "It was casual."

I wouldn't have one use in all the world for casual sex. The intimacy, the many ways my body seemed so imperfect, all the potential embarrassments . . . I'd never had the kind of feelings for a guy, the kind of trust, that I would need to get that close. And the risks! The countless ways it could change your life: disease, pregnancy . . . to me, having sex seemed about as safe as jumping off a cliff.

I came up behind someone who was driving twenty miles below the speed limit, but I signaled and checked over my shoulder twice and then passed, moving back into the right lane after. Lane changing made me nervous. "Are you going to tell your parents?" I asked Gab.

Gab pulled a pack of gum out of the console. "I'll tell my mom. My dad — no way. He'd flip." She put a piece of gum in her mouth and offered me one. I took it. My mouth still tasted like curry and fish sauce.

"Your mom won't tell your dad?" I asked, chewing the gum. It was cinnamon. My favorite.

She shook her head.

Her confidence in this, her clarity about their dynamics . . . I yearned to understand it, yearned to know what I'd missed, what it would have been like. My relationship with my mother was not much of an education in the workings of marriages and families. I wanted to know what it was to feel comfortable in all the messiness and complexity of a family — not like an alien dropped in as part of some sort of sociological study.

"What will she say when you tell her?" I asked. Gab's mom was pretty damn open-minded, but still . . . a teenage girl tells her mom she went out and screwed a stranger just for shits and giggles? Just for experience?

"I don't know," Gab said. "She'll want to know if we used a condom, of course, and how I'm *feeling* about it all . . ."

"She won't judge you?"

"I don't think so. She's pretty cool in some ways."

"In *some* ways?"

My phone dinged. "It's probably my mom," I said.

Gab picked up my phone and entered my code. "It's Leila," she said, tossing the phone back down.

"Oh, boy," I said. I glanced up over Gab. "We haven't talked to her."

Gab made a face. "You can talk to her all you want. I have nothing to say to her."

"Are you mad at her?"

"Not mad. I'm just not going to subject myself to her judgment. She'd shit kittens if I told her what I did tonight."

"Well," I said, "only because she cares."

"That's not why." She snapped her gum.

An uneasy feeling filled my gut. "You have to tell her," I said.

"Why do I?" She gave me a challenging look.

"Because! It's Leila. If you don't, it's like lying. I mean, there's the assumption that we'd tell each other."

"Jules?" She turned toward me. "I'm eighteen years old. I don't have to tell anyone anything."

I chewed on her words. "I can't believe you'd tell your mother but you wouldn't tell your best friend!"

"*You're* my best friend," she said, surprising me. And then she added, "As much as Leila is."

I wanted it to be true. Really true, and not just that she was irked with Leila. "Well, what am I supposed to do?" I asked her. "Pretend you just sat in the car waiting for me for seven hours?"

"God," Gab said, irritated. "I don't know."

"I don't want to lie."

"Then don't. Tell her whatever you want. I don't care."

"I can't do that, Gab." I looked at her pleadingly. "I can't tell her your — business."

"Fine." She rolled her eyes. "I'll tell her. But it'll just make things worse."

I could see Leila not responding well to what Gab did, but to me nothing seemed worse than Gab keeping something so important from Leila — especially something that *I* knew about. I could only handle so many parts of my life falling apart at once.

"Oh my God, the custard place is open!" Gab pointed. "Pull over. I need a sundae. And a burger."

I signaled to turn. I was the last person who would argue about getting something to eat.

As I pulled into the lot, Gab was already unbuckling. "Let's get our food and then you can tell me about Luke."

By the time we got back to her house, my head was spinning even more than it was when we left. I hadn't considered what it would mean, sharing all this with Dr. Shrink Jr. I hadn't had time to work through what this would mean for my relationship with my mother, but Gab seemed more hung up on that than on Luke.

149

We sat parked in Gab's driveway. "It's a massive betrayal," Gab said slowly. "She lied to you. She stole part of your childhood from you."

"And my Jewishness," I joked, whipping off a quick *home safe!* text to Luke.

She turned to me, her eyes wide. "That is not small, Jules! You were nearly an M.O.T.!"

"M.O.T.?"

"Member of the tribe."

I laughed. "Oh, right. But," I pointed out to her, "I wouldn't have met you. And you're half the fun of almost being a Jew."

She grinned. "My parents will probably insist on making you an honorary Jew." She glanced up at her house, which was dark. Then she shook her head. "Man, what this must have done to Luke's family."

"I know."

"I'm not saying your mom didn't have a right to get you back if she was sober and stable, but . . . shit." She turned to me. "It's amazing the way our choices change history." A troubled expression flashed across her face, half lit in the light of the lamppost by her walkway.

"You okay?" I reached out and touched her knee.

She looked at my hand, then laid hers over it. "Yeah."

"Gab. I have to go home." According to the clock on the car, it was nearly two in the morning. "How are we going to do that? You can't drive."

"Fuck that. Just text your mom and tell her we got home late and you're spending the night."

"I can't."

She was adamant. "Yeah you can. Just stay tonight and talk to my mom in the morning. Then decide what you're going to do."

It probably wasn't a bad idea. "Okay."

"In fact, just stay with me for a few days. There's no school Monday anyway — Presidents' Day. Give yourself some time. You're not going to be any readier to deal with your mom tomorrow. Get some clothes and your computer and just fucking move in. Yes, you can," she said, preempting the argument I was about to launch. "And don't do one of your *I don't want to be a burden* things. My parents would piss themselves with delight if you were going to be a permanent fixture for a while."

She really knew how to get to me. I nodded, trying not to sniffle. "Okay."

Living with the Wassermans . . . I can't say I hadn't thought about it a thousand times, about what it would be like. . . . They were so funny and smart and laid-back. They didn't usually make a big deal about dinner — more than once I'd seen one of them eating cereal while another ate a sandwich, if they didn't order in, which they often did. And good stuff, too. Spinach-stuffed pizzas with two or three different salads. Sushi from the decent place in Barton. Not Hamburger Helper or peanut butter out of the jar.

And they did stuff together. Museums. Trips. Hikes. Gab

151

always was happy to do things with her parents. She *liked* them. And they liked her. And Daniel came home as often as he could. They were what a family should be. They were together by circumstance, but if they had the choice, they'd still pick one another.

Thinking about it made my chest tighten with a feeling I couldn't quite name. Would I have had something like that if the Margolises had adopted me? A real family that liked one another? A unit? An unbreakable, permanent unit?

It overwhelmed me to contemplate. Not least because it meant imagining away my mother, which . . . who does that? It was terrible. But maybe I was terrible. Because I did think about it.

I messaged my mother that I was going to stay with Gab for a few days, and that I'd pick up some things tomorrow. I crossed my fingers that she was asleep so she wouldn't respond; I didn't have the energy to deal with the fallout just now. Fortunately, my phone stayed silent.

In the extra bed in Gab's room, I nudged Faustus, her long-haired tuxedo cat, whose bed this clearly actually was. He relocated to the foot of the bed, then draped himself over my feet, which interfered with my tossing and turning. I lay there, replaying moments from the day.

But also . . . I found myself thinking about Luke in . . . wrong ways. I didn't remember him as a brother enough to disable the mechanism of attraction. Why did he have to be so darling, so sweet, so perfect? It didn't seem *reasonable* that I should not find him attractive.

And so I found myself imagining . . . things. Imagining kissing him. Imagining him realizing his feelings for me were growing too unwieldy to be contained in the previous construct. Imagining his touching me, my touching him. . . . And God help me, I thought about what it would be like to do *all* the things with him.

These kinds of thoughts had to stop. Surely as we reconnected in a more sibling-type way, these odd flashes of misplaced want would rearrange themselves into something correct and appropriate. They had to.

I couldn't fall asleep. I was anxious about meeting his mother. Mima, if that's what I'd still call her. I was afraid I wouldn't remember anything. I was afraid I *would* remember. I was afraid of her dying, just as I was getting to know her, getting to love her, even. But even more than for myself, I was afraid of how hard that would be for Luke, and for Buddy, which apparently is what I'd called Luke's dad — *my* dad — when I was little. When for a certain period of time, I had a dad.

When I finally drifted into sleep, I had dreams — lots of dreams. One piggybacked on top of the one before. Dreams about being little, about cats and strange houses and piano music. I woke, struggling to sort out what was made up and what might have been whispers of memory.

Chapter 11

Gab was right. Leila did not approve of Gab's carefree, carnal adventures. Sitting on the floor in her room the next afternoon, Gab rattled off her actions to Leila as if offering a confession over which she was not the least bit contrite. It occurred to me that Gab rebelled more against Leila than she did her own parents.

When Gab was finished, Leila looked at me as if to make sure she'd heard correctly. "So basically," she said to Gab, "you just hooked up with a stranger."

Gab twisted her mouth and threw her gaze to the ceiling, as if thinking hard, then said, "Yup. That's about the size of it."

"Speaking of the size of it," I quipped, hoping to divert focus and lighten the mood. I petted Faustus, who purred in my lap, seeming to have appropriated me.

Gab flashed a smile at me. "It was just what you'd expect, looking at him. Not that long and kind of thick."

I giggled, then cleared my throat when Leila gave me a look.

"You approve of this?" she asked.

I hesitated. "I don't think it's really my job to approve or disapprove. I'm just, you know, listening."

Leila's lips tightened. Tension filled the air. She turned to Gab and said softly, "Are you ever going to think before you act?"

"Yeah, I knew that was coming." Gab stood up. "Okay, then. That's that. You'll like Jules's story much better." She gave me a pointed *told you so* look and went to her desk. "I have a shit-ton of homework, so can you guys find somewhere else to talk so I can work in peace?" She collapsed loudly into her desk chair and logged in to her computer.

I bit my lip. Leila had just arrived.

"Let's go to my house," Leila said to me.

I glanced at Gab. "Okay, Gab? I'll see you later?"

"Whenever," she said without looking up.

Her words stung. I knew they probably weren't personal, but they brought that feeling I knew and loathed — that sense of being unsure of how welcome I was. "Should I come back tonight?" I asked. A lump formed in my throat, which made me feel stupid.

She glanced at me, then sighed, no doubt realizing she'd hurt my tender feelings. "Of course come back."

Leila gave me a quizzical look.

"I'm staying with Gab for a while," I told her.

"What? Why?" She looked lost. "What else have I missed out on?"

"I'll explain in the car," I said. "If you could swing by my house first, I need to pick up a few things." I gently dislodged Faustus, who immediately turned around and tried to climb back onto my lap. I petted him and stood up. "I'll see you later," I said to Gab.

"Yup."

Leila and I slipped out the front door and into a chilly gloom. The air smelled of damp earth and decaying leaves.

"So what happened?" she asked as she pulled out of the driveway. "And why is everybody mad at me?"

I turned to her. "I'm not mad at you! Why do you think that?"

"You're doing everything with Gab and leaving me out."

"What? I wasn't trying to leave you out." I was horrified to realize I'd hurt her feelings. "It wasn't really a thing *with* Gab," I said. "She just offered to drive me — and you had your cousins' brunch anyway. I've been dying to talk to you!"

Her lips trembled. "Well, it sure hasn't seemed that way!"

"Leila." I reached out and touched her arm. "I'm so

sorry — so much has happened. I'm not mad at you at all! I love you!"

Leila tried to smile. "At least one of you does."

I sighed. "Gab loves you. She just — you know, she feels like you judge her." I hoped I wasn't overstepping. I couldn't deny that Leila was not high on Gab's list lately.

Leila pulled up to a red light, her left turn signal clicking neatly. She turned to me. "Jules. Some of the stuff she does? Come on."

I shrugged. "She's just — living her life. The way she wants to."

"I just don't want to see her get hurt. She does the stupidest things without thinking first, and then she has to face the consequences."

"She did one thing," I argued. "She slept with someone. People do that. She did it of her own free will, and she used protection. Why are you so upset about it?"

"It's not just one thing."

"Well, what else?"

She was silent for a moment. "Nothing." The signal changed, green light washing all over Leila's pale face, and she pulled into the intersection to wait for her chance to turn. "She acts like she's got everything figured out, but she doesn't. She's going to do so many stupid things, Jules — I can see it coming."

"But you're not her mother," I said gently. "You do sort of judge her. Just be her friend."

"She judges me, too," Leila said defensively. "She's always telling me I'm too uptight and psychoanalyzing me, which pisses me off. She acts like she's such an expert because of her parents. I hate that. She thinks she knows everything about me."

"Doesn't she?" I asked, before I thought better of it.

"No."

I wondered what that meant. What did Gab not know? If Gab didn't know, then I guess I didn't know, either. And I wasn't sure how to feel about that.

When she asked me about Luke, I gave her the short version, saving the details for later. My stomach clenched and knotted. We were almost at my house.

"So you're really packing your bags?" Leila said, glancing over as she drove down my street. "That's serious."

It *was* serious. It scared me, and it also made me feel guilty, but somehow it felt important, this literal or symbolic departure on my part. My mom had abandoned me, and some part of me wanted to do the same to her. Was that just spite? Revenge? Or was it me doing some necessary separating?

Leila pulled into the driveway. "You want me to come in? Or wait in the car?"

"Wait, please," I said apologetically. "I'll be out as fast as I can."

I let myself in the front door and called out a hello. I

slipped off my shoes and went in. I found my mom sitting on the floor in her studio, across from her painting. She looked up when came in.

"You got my message?" I asked, pausing in the doorway.

"Why?" she asked. Her expression . . . she looked so hurt and afraid.

I couldn't look at her. I didn't want to feel ambivalent or guilty. I just wanted to fucking be mad for a while. Was I not entitled to that much? "I need to be with my friends for a while. A lot of bombs have been dropped on me lately. I need some space."

I turned and went to my room. I grabbed some makeup and a hairbrush and threw them in my backpack with my books and school stuff. I pulled a tote bag off my closet hook and started shoving some clothes in. I didn't even hear my mom in the hall, so I jumped when she spoke from the doorway.

"You know, all I've ever tried to do is — is just to do right by you." Her voice broke. "I know I haven't been perfect, but do you have to punish me?"

I squeezed past her into the hall.

"I know I'm too wrapped up in my painting. I'm sorry. Is that it? Is it because I can't give you a nice house and nice things like your friends have?"

"Oh my God!" I stared at her. "You think it's about money? About houses? You don't get it at all!" I grabbed my things and ran out the door, worrying that I was pushing my mom into relapse. And I was mad that I was worried. It was on her to stay sober.

But if she didn't, I knew I might never forgive myself.

"I still can't believe you were ever in foster care. Who would have imagined that we had that in common?" We sat on the floor in Leila's bedroom, eating the pillow-soft gnocchi with rich mushroomy meat sauce that her mother had left on a tray outside the door with a discreet knock. Despite my best effort at a cheerful greeting when Leila and I came in, my post-ugly-cry face was unmistakable. Her mom's concerned look just made me want to ugly-cry all over again.

"You were in foster care?" I asked, scraping the last of the sauce from my bowl. "I thought were you in an orphanage."

"It was an orphanage," she conceded. "I just meant that someone else took care of us when we were babies. Not our parents."

I glanced up at her. "And there's really no way to find out who your birth parents were?"

"Nope." She pushed her plate away. "I was left on the doorstep of an orphanage in a dresser drawer, according to the records. I have no idea why, or who my parents were, or if I had siblings or other family . . ." She hooked a lock of hair around her fingers, twisting it.

"Does that bother you?" I asked hesitantly. To me, the very word "orphanage" was a tragedy, conjuring images of cold, hungry, neglected children. I had tiptoed around the subject the entire time I'd known Leila.

"Of course it bothers me," Leila said, her brow furrowing. "Do you have any idea how much I've always envied you and your mom? You look exactly like her! I don't look like anybody. I was dumped on the doorstep of an orphanage, and I have no idea why. Did you know most Ukranian orphans have at least one living parent?"

I was stunned. That didn't fit the definition of an orphan as I knew it.

"I know you and your mom aren't that close and everything but, God, Jules — she got sober for you! It's like, you and her against the world. She fought for you. Do you know how much she must have loved you to do all that?" Leila picked up her glass of ice water and took a sip, then set it back on the tray on the rug. "Not everybody cares that much about their kid."

This was a total 180 in paradigm. I spent my life envying Leila only to find out that *she* envied *me*?

"I know you don't have a lot of money and things at your house aren't perfect," Leila went on, "but your mom moved mountains to win you back and take care of you. If that's not love, I don't know what is."

There was the patter of little feet in the hall. Leila's door opened and Garrett tumbled in, pink-faced and damp-haired and smelling of baby soap. "Night, Leila," he said so softly, it was almost a whisper. He fell into Leila's arms and she hugged him, flipping him over and tickling him. She gave him three kisses and stood him back up. As I observed the love and trust between them, something tugged in me, an ache I could almost name now.

In the hallway, Leila's mom picked him up as he ran out, giving us a gentle smile. "There's cake," she whispered to me, pulling the door closed.

"There's cake," I whispered to Leila.

She laughed. "Want to get some?"

"Yeah. In a minute, though." I shifted and lay on my side on the floor, head propped on my hand. "Leila? Do you — have memories?"

"Of the orphanage?" She lay down across from me, mirroring me (to the extent that a model-thin blue-eyed blonde could mirror me). "Yeah. I dream about it sometimes."

"Really?"

She nodded. "It's the thing I can't control. I mean, I speak English, I dream in English, I live an American life. . . . And then suddenly, there I am. Lying in that hard little bed next to Olga, patting her back while she cries."

"Olga?"

Leila nodded, then looked away. "She was younger than me. She had"— Leila gestured toward her mouth —"that deformity, what's it called?"

"Cleft palate?"

"Yes! It split her whole upper lip and made it hard for her to eat. She just cried and cried."

Suddenly Leila pressed her hand to her face, her shoulders shaking.

"Leila?" I crawled over to her, alarmed. I had rarely seen Leila cry. I was the crybaby of our little group, and God knows I did it enough for the three of us.

"I wish I knew what happened to her," Leila said, sitting up. "I feel so bad, leaving her there. She'd be sixteen now. I doubt she ever got her mouth fixed." She sniffed and gave her head a shake, trying to pull herself together. "I still remember some of those kids, and one of the staff — the one who took care of us most. Vera."

She pronounced it like *Vyeh-ra,* with a hard *r.*

"Do you remember much else?" I asked gently, worrying that I was prying.

Leila took a breath and sighed, leaning back against the bed. "When we went to bring Garrett home, I discovered I remembered a lot more than I realized. It just — came back. But . . ." She trailed off, shaking her head. "It wasn't good. It brought back things I didn't want to remember. I made things so hard for my parents when we there — I was so clingy and whiny."

I scooted closer and put a hand on hers.

"I was afraid to sleep when we were there. I slept with my mom, and my dad slept in the other bed in the hotel room. I just wanted to get back on that plane and get home with Garrett. I was so anxious there. Even now, it messes with my head, hearing Ukrainian or Russian. It echoes. It's

163

like the dreams — I'm just being dropped into the past, out of nowhere, and I can't do anything about it."

I remembered when she went to Ukraine to get her new brother. I never knew it was so hard for her — was hard for her still. "Maybe you should see Gab's mom," I half joked.

"Ha! How do you think I met Gab?"

I stared at her, confused. "Kindergarten!"

Leila shook her head. "When my parents brought me to the States, I didn't talk. After a while, they were worried enough that they took me to a therapist — Gab's mom."

"You're kidding! How old were you?"

"Three and a half or four."

"So Gab's mom taught you to talk?"

Leila shook her head, smiling. "Gab did. I met her when my mom brought me over for therapy in Mindy's home office — she used to work out of the house, and Gab had a nanny. Anyway, Gab just took me by the hand and dragged me off with her, and when Mindy was going to stop her, my mom said no, let them go. My mom had never seen me interact with another kid before."

I stared at her, stunned. "I never knew any of this! How did I not know?"

Leila shrugged. "Gab's probably not supposed to talk about my psychological history. Anyway, my mom would bring me over to play with Gab, and I *had* to talk to get a word in edgewise, otherwise Gab would just steamroll right over me. Everything always had to be the way she wanted it to be." She gave a dry laugh.

"Wait," I said. "So you were there when Daniel was still at home?" I had always thought Leila and I were both after Daniel's time.

She nodded. "He called us Gumby and Pokey."

I tried to smile, but I was stunned. The things I was on the outside of . . . they just seemed to grow in number, and it never stopped stinging. "So," I said finally, "Gab taught you how to talk?"

"Pretty much."

"God. No wonder you two are such a mess. You're practically siblings. It's always felt like that to me . . ." I picked at a loose thread at the hem of my shirt, hesitant to say how left out I sometimes felt. "Like we were all friends, but you two were like something else. Like you had something I just couldn't penetrate."

"Well, don't envy it," Leila said, reaching for a box of tissues on her bedside table. "Your relationship with her is way less screwed up." She wiped her nose and tossed the tissue into the wastebasket. "She was so used to holding my hand and bossing me around and mothering me that she just never stopped."

"It's funny," I said, smiling. "I see you as the maternal one."

"Yeah, but — I just feel oppressed by her, you know? Like she still thinks she's the boss of me."

"I think she feels just as oppressed by you!" I exclaimed.

She raised her eyebrows and let out a huge sigh. "We are seriously messed up." She stood and picked up the tray. "Let's get some cake."

"What kind is it?" I asked, following her downstairs.

"It's a chocolate cake with a mousse filling. Espresso and caramel, I think."

"Oh, sweet Jesus," I said.

We sat at the banquette, kitchen lights dimmed, eating the most perfect cake I could have dreamed up. Chocolate, espresso, and caramel. Rich, bitter, and sweet. As Eli had observed, my favorite combination.

When Leila asked me if I wanted more, I couldn't say no.

Of course I wanted more. When didn't I?

Back at Gab's, I tried to study in Daniel's room, since Gab seemed to be in the zone with her work. At the rate I was going, I was going to end up failing my biology test and turning in my English paper late. I just couldn't concentrate. I thought about the big weekend I had coming up — if all went as planned, I was going to meet Mima. Or I guess I should say *see* her, not meet her. Because five hundred days.

I couldn't resist poking around Daniel's room, looking at his awards and knickknacks and books. I tried to imagine having a brother right across the hall for six years. More, including when he was home from college. Gab was so lucky. So fucking lucky.

By the time I tiptoed into her room, she'd gone to bed. I wondered if she would have preferred for me to sleep in Daniel's room, as opposed to my usual place in the twin bed across from hers. I told myself that I was probably being oversensitive as usual, and I slid into bed in the dark as silently as I could.

"Hey," she said.

"Sorry — did I wake you?" I whispered.

"No. You okay?"

"Yeah." I hesitated, wondering if I should tell her about what Leila had shared about their past. Maybe it would help. "Leila told me that you taught her how to talk."

She laughed softly.

"She really loves you," I said.

"Did she say that?"

I wanted to say yes, but that wouldn't exactly be true. "It's obvious."

Nothing. Finally I heard her sigh and roll over.

Then, just when I figured she was asleep, she said, "I love her, too."

Chapter 12

*A*s anticipated, I failed my biology test on Tuesday. I stooped to the "personal problems" plea for mercy, which I had never done in my life, in hopes of being granted a retake. I was both relieved and ashamed when this worked on Mr. Stewart, who made allowances "due to my exemplary record."

Similarly, Miss Hoffman granted me an extension on my English paper, which I just didn't have the focus to complete. I managed to scrape by in the rest of my classes and get through the week.

I did homework and read books. Spread mustard on rolls. Proofed pages for the yearbook. Caught up with Eli. Stayed with Gab. Worried about Leila. It had been hard for me not to think about her languishing in that orphanage, and what a tiny, sweet thing she must have been. What if she hadn't been adopted? What would have become of her? And Gab and me — what would our lives be like today?

I was also haunted by the little girl with the cleft palate. If I was Luke's lost one, Olga was Leila's. But unlike me and Luke, Leila would probably never find her. And if she did, maybe they'd have nothing in common. Not even language. Maybe Olga would resent Leila for all her unfathomably good luck. Who could blame her? Life was so fucking arbitrary.

Meanwhile, Luke and I talked at any and every opportunity. Daniel's old bedroom had become my private phone haven, where I'd sit in the dark with the door closed and smile at the sweetness of Luke's soft voice, thrill at the sound of his laugh.

After, I'd lie awake, replaying the call. And letting my mind go where it went. It turned out that a mind can go in a lot of directions, some of which required firm redirection. My feelings for Luke were confusing. It felt . . . well, it felt a lot like falling in love. But it couldn't be that. I couldn't let it be. I didn't want to fuck things up. I wanted Luke for the long haul. And he, clearly, wanted a sister.

Gab and Leila and I all slept at Gab's the night before my "family reunion," watching a screwball comedy with her parents and eating junk food. It was like old times. Fun. Easy. It was good. Gab and Leila seemed to roll back together so easily after their disagreements. Despite their disagreements. Sometimes *during* their disagreements. Such was the non-negotiable quality of their relationship. Proton and neutron.

In the morning, the three of us headed for Milwaukee. Despite the gray sky, the mood was warm, and their ceaseless chatter was a distraction and a deep comfort. They sat in the front seat, talking about basketball, laughing and mocking themselves and their bad plays in the last game of the season. And as I sat there in the back, watching their perfect, laughing faces — as familiar to me as my own name — a feeling of boundless love swelled up in me. They were the constants in my life, the sun I faithfully orbited. I wanted it always to be that way.

When they pulled up in front of the designated Starbucks, Leila got out and hugged me, saying, "Call me if you need me. I'll glue my phone to my face."

Gab ran around to join us, wrapping her arms around for a group hug.

Luke came out of the Starbucks and bounded toward us. He wore khakis and a T-shirt with an unbuttoned blue plaid shirt, no jacket. When he reached us, he hugged me tight. He was charming and friendly to Gab and Leila, thanking them for bringing me. After promising them to take good care of me, he gave them a wave and took my overnight bag to his car, parked farther up the street. As we reached it, the rain started.

170

"Mom is beside herself!" he said, holding the door open for me.

Mom. Not *my mom.* Did he still see her as my mom, too? I climbed into the car and buckled up.

He got in and closed the door. "She couldn't sleep last night. She's so excited."

"I'm worried I'll disappoint her by not remembering her." I was hit with the smell of his freshly shampooed hair, which was so intoxicating that I wanted to press my nose to his head. I wondered if I'd think he smelled so good if I grew up with him? Would we find each other annoying and overly familiar sometimes, like regular siblings?

"She knows you were too little to remember. Don't worry. She's just happy to see you again." He smiled, rolling his eyes. "Well. More like ecstatic." He turned on the windshield wipers and pulled into the street. "I hope she's ready for us. She used to be more casual about things, but it takes her longer to get ready now."

I wondered if she had to fuss with a wig, use extra makeup to keep from looking so sick. I tried to push aside the thought. I was so anxious, my knees bobbed up and down. "So what do you think we'll do?"

He slowed for a light. "Eat lunch . . . look at pictures of you . . . watch videos of you. . . . She'll probably have twenty thousand questions." He frowned a little. "We just never know how much energy she'll have. She wants to have dinner at home, too, but she might need to rest. I told her we should just order pizza, or you and I could go out, if she isn't feeling well."

My heart leapt at the idea of going out alone with Luke — followed by a terrible stab of guilt that this was my first thought, rather than hoping Mima would be well enough for the evening. I was having a hard time dividing up the real estate in my heart and mind between wanting to know my foster family and wanting more time alone with Luke.

The rain grew heavier. It was oddly calming, the rhythmic slap of the wipers on the window, Luke's sure handling of the car, his relaxed, leaned-back posture. When I drove, I sat bolt upright, as if good posture would protect me from harm.

We had bursts of conversation punctuated by silence. I thought about things like whether or not I would pretend to remember things I didn't, if out of compassion for his mother and/or my own personal longing, I would feign a sense of connection I didn't feel. I imagined Luke was thinking about his mother. His love for her was plain. The idea of losing her must have been completely unbearable.

Off the main roads, we wended our way through a neighborhood of older homes. Finally Luke slowed and turned into a driveway, taking a breath and glancing at me, eyebrows raised in a *this is it* look.

"Wait," I said as he reached for the car door handle.

He paused and turned back to me. "You okay?"

I had thought of so many questions, but they darted in and out of my mind like bats. "Did you guys have a nickname for me?"

He tilted his head, thinking. "We had a lot of nicknames for you. Dad used to call you his 'little Jujube.'"

I turned it over in my head. *Jujube, Jujube.* I tried to find it in the recesses of my memory, but the word felt as fresh as a spring breeze.

"I remember Mom calling you pet names, like 'sweet cheeks' and 'sugar pie.'"

God. She was like the antithesis of my mom, who never called me anything but Jules. Maybe an occasional "honey," but not usually even that.

I stared at the house. It was large — a Tudor, judging by the decorative dark timber over white and the diamond-patterned leaded-glass windows. Nineteen twenties, I would guess. The kind of house I loved.

"Do your recognize it?" Luke's voice was soft, but I felt the urgency.

"I don't know."

"Maybe you'll recognize it inside. After all, that's where you spent most of your time."

We got out of the car, and he grabbed my bag. I ducked my head against the rain, although it was barely a drizzle now. We headed up the walkway, past the neatly trimmed hedges, to the front entry. A mezuzah on the door frame caught my eye. Gab's family had one, too. The Wassermans' was silver and almost filigree in design. This one was gold with Hebrew letters and jeweled inlay.

A feeling of something like reverence came over me, but there was more to it than that. This was a Jewish home. And it might have been my home — my identity, even. The alternate universe continued to unspool its endless possible trajectories.

Luke pushed open the heavy oak door and called out, "Hello? We're here!"

He ushered me into the foyer, and I glanced around, taking the place in.

It was a beautiful home — elegant, but comfortable. Dark, gleaming woodwork. Oriental rugs over warm wood floors. A crystal chandelier in the foyer, a carved banister leading up the stairs. The kind of house I fantasized about living in. It occurred to me that these longings perhaps were not just random fantasies. Instead, maybe they were echoes of memories — a yearning for something left behind.

Footsteps. A tall, white-haired man walked down the hall toward us, a look of anticipation on his kind face.

"Hey, Dad," Luke said, smiling and turning toward me. "Here she is. This is Jules!"

I smiled at him, suddenly overwhelmed with shyness, and at a loss about how to greet him. If he was once my adoring father, a handshake seemed cold. But he felt like a stranger to me.

He stood in front of me, beaming. He didn't seem to

know what to do with his hands, either. I was aware of Luke standing by, holding his breath.

"Hi," I finally said, reaching out my arms.

He pulled me into a hug, and when he stepped back, his face was a mix of emotions. "I can't believe it . . . seems like just yesterday you were here, such a little thing . . ." He shook his head.

A voice called from another room. "Ted? Are they here?"

"We're coming, honey," he called back.

Luke hung up our coats, and we followed his dad into the house, Luke's hand warm and reassuring on my back.

We stepped into a huge kitchen, and in a windowed breakfast nook, there she sat. *Mima.* Her bony hand fluttered to her mouth, almost smothering the small noise she made when she saw me.

Luke guided me to her.

The emotion on her face made me weak. And in that moment, everything changed. In that moment, I knew that all these unreal things that had unfolded were incomprehensibly real.

It was clear how much I meant to this woman. Her hands trembled and her eyes spilled over as she reached out to me.

I leaned down and hugged her.

She was so slight, she was barely there. She shook as I held her.

Luke's dad reached out and touched her arm. "Take it easy, Sarah," he said quietly.

After a moment, she pulled back, taking my face in both her hands.

"Look at you," she whispered. "I'd know you anywhere." She smiled even as tears streamed down her cheeks. "Those big brown eyes. Those cupid's bow lips. You're just beautiful. You were always beautiful."

I smiled at her, wondering if she'd ever seem familiar to me. I hoped more than anything that she would. "Thank you," I said. "Thank you for . . . taking care of me."

Luke's dad pressed a tissue into her hand, and she dabbed her eyes. Then she glanced up at Luke, smiling. Thanking him with her eyes. She took a breath and gestured at the table. "Sit! I can't wait to hear all about you."

"Sure. Um." I glanced at Luke. "Could I just use the bathroom first?"

He directed me to the powder room in the hall, and once inside I closed the door and leaned against it.

This was hard. Harder than I expected.

I used the toilet and washed my hands, examining the details of the powder room. I probably wasn't even toilet-trained when I left, so it made sense that this room didn't spark any memories. I wondered what would, if anything.

I gazed into the mirror, trying to see myself as she did. The color of my eyes, the shape of my mouth. What else did she remember about me? She knew me when my own mother didn't. She heard my first words. Saw my first steps.

Changed untold hundreds of diapers. Fed me. Made me safe. Loved me.

I took a breath. She had said she wanted to hear all about me, but what could I tell her? They were clearly sophisticated, educated people — what could I even talk to them about? I was petrified of disappointing them with my bland mediocrity.

When I went back to the kitchen, the table was set and Luke and his dad were ferrying dishes from the counter to the breakfast nook.

"Something smells good," I said, moving toward them. A savory, buttery smell mingled with the aroma of coffee. "Can I help?"

"No, no, just come sit next to me," Mima said, patting the seat next to her. "There's nothing to do. I just made a quiche and some muffins and a fruit salad. I hope that's okay. Luke said you still eat everything."

I felt my cheeks color as I sat beside her. "Accurate," I admitted.

She smiled at me, which made her whole face look younger, more alive. She wasn't wearing a wig. Her hair was very fine, though. Thin, and on the short side. A mix of brown and light gray. "I loved that about you," she said, patting my knee. "Luke was so picky when he was little. But not you. You were such a good eater."

"That's an understatement," Luke said, pulling plastic

wrap off a ceramic bowl of mixed fruit. He glanced up and gave me a wink.

"When we first got you," Mima said, taking my hand in hers, "you were on formula, but you had trouble keeping it down. You were just tiny. But when we started you on solids, oh, boy . . ." She smiled, shaking her head. "Everything turned around. You *loved* to eat — you liked everything."

"Except peas," Luke's dad said, cutting the quiche into slices.

They all laughed.

"We have footage of that." Luke smiled at me as he sat down. "You have to see it. You were scraping the peas off your tongue!"

"And such a terrible face she made!" Mima laughed.

I was fascinated — it was hard to get my arms around the fact that they were talking about *me*.

Luke's dad handed me a plate with a slice of quiche on it and passed me the bowl of fruit. The coffee maker beeped, and he got up. "Coffee, Jules?"

"Uh, sure. Thank you." It wasn't going to help my nerves, but I wanted to have coffee with everyone.

When he brought over a cup for me, I asked him shyly, "What should I call you?"

He paused, then looked at his wife.

"You used to call him Buddy," she told me.

I nodded and glanced at him. "Would that be okay? If I call you Buddy?"

He swallowed, his Adam's apple sliding up and then down. "Buddy's great," he said softly.

As we ate, everyone regaled me with stories about myself. More coffee was made, juice was poured, the quiche — crab, goat cheese, and scallion — was demolished, although I was too nervous to have seconds, and I noticed that Mima didn't eat a bite. Twice Luke prompted her quietly to eat, but she waved him off. At some point during the meal, I don't know when, someone put a container of Ensure in front of her.

When we finished eating, Mima asked if I'd like to see my baby videos, which of course I very desperately wanted to do.

But first, I helped clean up, despite protests. I felt a need to be useful, to demonstrate that I'd turned out well. As I rinsed dishes, Mima pushed herself up to her feet. Luke's dad — *Buddy* — rushed over.

"What do you need, Sarah? For Pete's sake, just ask!"

She swatted at him. "I can get up. I want to show Jules something." She gestured toward the cabinets. "Let me do it," she said, moving slowly past him.

Her gait was stilted, careful. I recalled the picture I'd seen of her, from before she was sick. She had been so beautiful. She still was, in a fast-fading sort of way. How long did she have? What were her odds? Imagining she might be dead in a few months gnawed a hole inside me.

She held on to the counter with one hand and opened an upper cabinet. Buddy stood behind her, on alert. I could tell that it was hard for him to stand by and watch her struggle. But she turned around, triumphant, and held something out to me.

"Do you remember this?" she said, smiling. "It was your favorite sippy cup!"

I wiped my hands on a towel and took it from her.

"Buzz Lightyear," I said, staring at it.

Buddy chuckled. "Only back then you pronounced it *Buth White-year.*"

"*White-mear,*" Luke corrected.

"Buth White-mear," I repeated.

It was quiet for a moment as everyone watched me.

"Do you remember it?" Mima finally asked.

"Mom," Luke said softly. "She'll tell us if she remembers something."

She nodded, glancing at me apologetically. "It's just — it was the only cup you would drink out of."

I turned it over in my hands. The more I looked at it, the more unsure I was if it was familiar or if it was just my imagination, just wishful thinking.

Also, I couldn't help thinking of my mother, who would have tossed something like this out long ago. Raised in this family, I would probably have had keepsakes galore.

I would have liked that a lot.

I handed the cup back to Mima with a smile I hoped didn't look too sad. "Thank you for keeping it," I said. "It means a lot to me."

"Of course," she said. "Our memories of you are so wonderful, Jules. You'll see."

And so we migrated into the adjacent family room, which had a wall of windows that displayed the continuing rain outside. It looked like something from a painting, the periwinkle and slate of the sky through all the tall trees in the backyard. It made me think of my mother, and I wondered whether she was painting. And fucking up the sky.

A gleaming grand piano held court in the family room. A large leather sectional faced the fireplace, a flat-screen TV mounted above. Displayed on a gorgeous weathered sideboard were framed photos of Luke, throughout childhood. He was adorable. My hand went to my heart when I spotted myself in one of them. I sat in the bathtub, pouring water out of a cup, and Luke knelt on the floor near the tub, grinning at the camera. My first thought was, *They displayed a picture of me!* Followed quickly by: *He's seen me naked* — a thought that was actually sort of jarring, for some reason. Had I seen him naked, too?

I sank into the leather couch next to Mima, and Buddy propped throw pillows behind her until she was comfortable. Luke flipped through discs, setting up for viewing the home movies.

I took a shaky breath at the thought of seeing myself at that age for the first time — it might be like falling into a wormhole to that alternate universe. In a way, that's just what it was: a universe where I was a member of this family, where, if my mother hadn't emerged victorious over addiction, this would be my home, my mom, my dad, my brother. I'd go to high school here. I might think of myself as Jewish. I never would have met Gab or Leila. And I would never have known anyone who looked just like me, the way my mom did.

Would I be fatter? Skinnier? More confident? Better-educated? Or would I feel like a rejected throwaway living off the fat of charity? Leila fit so well into her family. . . . Maybe I would have, too? But Leila and her brother were both adopted; in my case, I would have been the only unrelated one. Maybe that would have been hard. Or maybe it wouldn't have. Maybe the kind of love these people would have given me would have mitigated a mountain of potential psychological or emotional issues.

Suddenly Luke was settling in next to me on the couch, close enough that his arm touched mine. I was glad for his warmth. Did he intuit what this might be like for me? I felt barely tethered, and his closeness was an anchor. I was intermittently aware of Mima narrating . . . "This was the day we got you — we'd only had a day's notice! Look at that expression! You're so gorgeous, but you have the most skeptical look on your face! Don't you think? Well, who could blame you. Poor thing . . ."

My ears pricked up when I heard her say, "Oh, this is the first time Luke held you!" I heard her intake of breath, saw her hand go to her mouth, saw Buddy reach for her other hand.

Luke, who was as adorable at five as he was now, sat in a rocking chair, grinning at me as Mima helped arrange me in his skinny, awkward arms. I, dressed in one-piece pink pajamas, was clearly irritated by the fussing. *She doesn't like it, Mama,* little Luke said. He looked crestfallen.

I chanced a peek over at Luke now and caught his eye. "Do you remember that?" I whispered.

He nodded slightly, his eyes on the screen.

Mama, she's gonna cry! What's wrong with her?

My present-day eyes filled as the baby on the screen started to wail, and not just out of compassion for her. It was Luke's distress that was breaking my heart.

She doesn't like me. Take her back, Mama.

Mima's arms picking me back up, patting my back, soothing me. And Luke, sitting there in the rocking chair next to us, arms crossed, staring down.

She's tired. Mima's voice assuring him from the recording. *She's going to have to get used to us. Don't worry, sweetie. She's going to love you. Just give it time.*

In the video, Luke glanced up doubtfully and rubbed one eye with his fist.

I glanced over at him. Like mine, his eyes were damp now, too.

"I'm sorry," I whispered. "I feel so bad!"

He nodded, laughing softly. "Yeah, you pretty much broke my heart."

I wanted to comfort him, to hold him. To be alone with

him. It was confusing, all of it. He was my brother, but I knew fuck-all about what it was supposed to feel like to have a brother. I did, however, know something about how it felt to be attracted to a guy.

This was not good.

I stared straight ahead at the screen. Several clips in, baby Jules was laughing. Playing. Grinning at Luke. Learning to pick up Cheerios (in the video, they all applauded when I managed to finally get one in my mouth). I looked happy. The transformation over these months on the screen was unmistakable.

These people had saved my life.

"I think we'll have to continue this later," Buddy said softly to us, standing and nodding toward Mima, whose eyes were drooping. "I'm sorry, Jules."

"Of course — that's okay!" I felt bad, suddenly, like an interloper. Had I overstayed my welcome?

He leaned over to her, taking her hand. "Come on, Sparky. Let's get you some rest."

She protested. "No, no. We haven't finished the videos. We haven't even looked at the photo albums."

"We're not going to get through everything in one sitting," Luke said, holding up the remote and pressing Pause. "We'll watch more later. Besides, Jules'll come back — right, Jules?"

"Of course," I said, standing and turning to Mima. "There's no rush. I'm not going anywhere."

184

As soon as the words were out of my mouth, I could have kicked myself. *I* might not be going anywhere, but *my* timeline wasn't the problem.

But Mima reached out her arms and hugged me. "Oh, my sweetie," she whispered. "I never stopped missing you."

When she released me, Buddy slipped his hands under her legs and behind her back.

"No, I can walk," she protested. But he ignored her, picking her up. I tried not to cringe — she was such a bag of bones. She turned toward us. "I'll just rest awhile, and then we'll have dinner later, okay? So don't go! You hear me, Luke? Don't go."

He nodded. "We won't go anywhere."

She blew us a kiss as Buddy carried her out.

I dropped my face into my hands, pressed the heels of my hands into my eyes.

I heard Luke step over. "Hey," he said softly. And then his arms were around me.

I leaned into him. He felt so good, and, God, he *smelled* so good. I didn't want him to let go. It was all I could do not to hold on too tight, not to cling too long. I didn't want it to be weird. I just . . . wanted.

This was all so fucked. I sniffled, trying to pull myself together.

"Jeez," he said. "You *still* cry when I hold you."

I laughed, stepping back and wiping my eyes.

He smiled at me, those fleck-y green eyes so warm and

close. His mouth . . . it looked so soft. What would it feel like to kiss that mouth? I pushed the thought away, trying to get my head on straight. He was a brother to me. A brother was for life. This was everything I'd ever wanted. Family. Connection. Mattering to someone. To have a crush on him would be idiotic. It would ruin everything.

He raised his eyebrows at me. "Want to see your old room?"

My old room. I wanted to see everything, but the pressure of recall was wearing me down. I took a breath and nodded.

On our way upstairs, he picked up my bag from the foyer. At the top of the stairs, he pointed left to a closed door at the end of the hall and said, "Mom and Dad's bedroom is that way. Ours are this way." He guided me down the hallway to the right. "This is my room," he said, pausing so I could peer in. Unlike his apartment, it was tidy — which made sense, since he mostly didn't live here anymore.

Music-related posters plastered his walls. Awards and medals lined the shelves over his desk, but I didn't have a chance to examine anything because he propelled me farther down the hallway to the room that was, at one time, mine.

I hesitated in the doorway. The walls were a soft peach, and there was a simple white four-post bed. A floral quilt. A small desk off to the side.

"It's different now," Luke said, stepping in behind me. "Mom uses it as a guest room. But she kept it the same for years, thinking maybe we'd get you back."

My hand went to my chest, which felt suddenly full with trying to take in what he was telling me. "How long?"

He pulled his mouth to one side, thinking. "I must have been thirteen or fourteen when she finally changed it — when my aunt from Arizona was coming for a visit. So, what, six or seven years?"

Jesus. That was a long time to wait. To hope. For me.

I stepped into the room and went to the window, looking out.

"You okay?" Luke asked, moving toward me.

An ache swelled in my chest as I realized that during those years, people I didn't even know about were thinking of me, longing for me, hoping for me. I must have missed them terribly for a while — they were the only family I knew. My mom had robbed me of something precious. Even if she did get sober and "win" me back, did she have to erase my past? Cut me off from people I'd grown to love, people who loved me? Maybe I could have stayed in touch with them, like extended family. Was my mom so selfish and insecure that she wouldn't even consider it?

"Come here." Luke gestured with his head. "I want to show you something else."

I followed him to the end of the hallway, where there was a tiny white door midway up the wall, with a little white knob.

I hesitated a moment. Something about it . . . "What is it?" I asked, pulling on the knob.

"Laundry chute. Goes all the way to the laundry room in the basement. You could barely reach this when you were here. I had to pick you up for you to drop stuff into it. Which you loved to do. Clothes, toys — anything. And then we'd go downstairs to get them." He laughed. "You never got tired of that."

The little door creaked open as I pulled. I stared at the tiny door, examined the chipped paint around the frame, the square metal interior. Was it familiar? Was this a memory? I turned to Luke. "Can we go to the basement?"

Luke nodded and turned to go, but then stopped. "Wait, we have to put something down it." He felt his pockets. Neither of us had anything. So he slipped out of his flannel and handed it to me. "Go ahead," he urged, smiling.

I didn't want to put it in the chute. I wanted to bury my face it in and smell it. I wanted to keep it.

Not helpful. Not normal.

I obediently pulled open the creaky door and slipped it in.

He grabbed my hand, and we flew down the stairs. We circled around on the first floor to a door near the kitchen that led to the basement. "Careful," Luke warned, flipping on a light switch at the top of the stairs. "The stairs aren't level."

He was right — the steps were wonky, the treads shallow, like they were made for tiny feet. At the bottom, Luke tugged a pull chain, and a single bulb illuminated the unfinished space. Boxes were piled along one wall, as well as stacks of folding chairs, card tables, and an extra refrigerator. It smelled old and musty, like Eli's basement — a smell I kind of liked. Luke led me to the back, ducking under some pipes midway, and we stepped into the laundry room. A white basket sat on top of the washer, his shirt topping the pile of laundry in it.

He stepped over by the dryer and patted it. "Sit here."

I pushed myself up onto the dryer, confused.

He scooted the basket over and jumped up onto the washing machine next to me. He turned me around to face the laundry chute. "Remember anything?"

I closed my eyes. I smelled fabric softener and a whiff of bleach. I searched and struggled and waited and thought. What was I supposed to be remembering?

After a moment, I turned to him and shook my head, sorrier than I could possibly express.

"It's okay." He smiled gently, but I could tell he was disappointed. "So, I'd sit up here with you, and Mom would send treats down the chute. You thought it was magic. Your face would light up each time a Hershey's Kiss came tumbling down — you'd turn to me, all amazed and excited."

I didn't know if it was just the suggestion, but I could almost see a video in my head, suspended in the middle of nowhere, no context, no tethers to place or time. Like something I saw in a movie. Was I remembering scraping those wrappers off the chocolate with my eager little fingers, the delicious, melty chocolate in my mouth? Or was

I imagining it? Was I confusing it with memories of other chocolates from later years? Our old neighbor, Mrs. Borski, had a dish of candy in her living room. Was that what I was remembering?

"Do you remember at all?" he asked. His expression was so full of hope.

I hesitated. I couldn't bear to disappoint him.

"It just . . ." He shook his head. "It seems unfair if you don't remember. To you, I mean. You had so much love . . . I wish you had the memory of how much we loved you."

My chest flooded with warmth. "I don't have to remember it to know it," I told him. "I feel it."

And I did feel it, the love this family had for me. I gazed into eyes the color I loved more than any other, and I thought, *If only that's all I was feeling.*

Chapter 13

*W*hen the sun started to peek out from the vast swaths of gray, Luke took me outside. We wandered around in the wet grass in our unzipped coats, looking for clues, bits that might spark something buried in the far depths of my mind. I felt like I almost had a memory of the birdbath, where apparently I used to slap at the water with my hands, but it could easily have been anything — a different time, a scene from a movie, the power of imagination fortified by longing. I didn't at all remember the rose garden. Or a swing set that was no longer there. Or the crib in the garage, which had been Luke's before it was mine.

Back inside, he showed me pictures of my old bedroom. Pictures from holidays. Pictures filled with things I didn't remember.

It was exhausting, the tax on my mind, on my memory. The expectations, the silent pressure to recognize something, anything. It was too much for one day. What I wanted was a long nap, but we had a dinner and evening to get through. By 5:00 the sun sat on the verge of the horizon. Mima was still resting, and I hadn't seen any sign of Buddy, either. Maybe he stayed with her when she rested. He seemed totally devoted to her. A more opposite upbringing I could not have had.

I made Luke play piano for me. I sat next to him on the bench. Occasionally his upper arm would skim past my breasts as he reached for the lower keys, shaming me with confused feelings of pleasure and yearning. I should have leaned back, more out of his way. But I didn't want to. I wanted that contact. Everything he did felt so good.

I forced myself to focus on his playing. I was mesmerized by his command, by the movements of his hands, the invisible intricate matrix of nerves and impulses that resulted in such beautiful sounds. Already my thoughts were turning toward the countdown, the bits of time we had together before I would return to Maplebrook and he would return to Appleton, three hours away from me. I tried to enjoy being near him in the moment rather than obsessing about being apart, but it was there now, hovering around the edges and coming into focus. But we still had a night ahead. I would gladly stay awake all night to have every possible moment with him. I hoped he'd also want to stay up late. Just us.

After a while, Buddy came down and found Luke and

me in the breakfast nook with the photos I'd brought — two slender volumes whose contents petered out almost completely by the time I was eleven or twelve.

"Can I see?" Buddy said.

I nodded, and Luke and I scooted over so Buddy could sit on my other side. I was a sad excuse for a narrator. Most of the pictures were of just me, and there wasn't a lot of story to them. I guess that's one of the casualties of growing up in a family of two: one person is the subject, the other the photographer. There was only one picture of me with my mom. She was holding me in front of a Christmas tree in an apartment I couldn't remember. I must have been almost two. She had a stiff smile on her face, and I just stared blankly.

"I always wondered what she looked like," Buddy said quietly. He shook his head. "Boy, you look just like her, don't you?"

A rhetorical question if ever I heard one.

Dinner was pizza, ordered in. Mima didn't eat anything. She sat next to me on the sofa, bundled under two blankets, while we watched more videos. I finally saw the footage of me learning to walk. I was thirteen months old. Mima and Luke sat on the floor of my bedroom, Buddy videotaping as they widened the gap between them foot by foot and propelled me back and forth. Finally I had managed about eight lurching steps on my own. That feat was met with many hugs and applause from Mima and Luke. To my embarrassment, baby Jules responded to the praise by grinning at Mima, turning her hands palms up, and asking, "Tookies?" Cookies. They all laughed in the video, as they did now.

There was even brief footage of Luke and me running around at a cousin's bat mitzvah. Apparently Gab's wasn't my first. I wore a beautiful green velvet dress and white tights. Boys in yarmulkes, a klezmer band . . . I looked comfortable, happy. It was surreal.

We looked at photo albums. A picture that especially tugged at me was one of me asleep in Luke's arms. Luke gazed at the camera, his shy smile revealing his pleasure and pride.

Mima didn't say much as I paged through the photos I brought, nestled beside her. I didn't know if it was because she was disappointed by the life I'd ended up with, or because she was too exhausted to react. I had the feeling the day had taken a lot out of her. But I also wondered if she'd had higher hopes for my fate when they lost me. Was she disappointed in how I'd turned out? The thought hurt unbearably.

She made it to 9:00. She kissed me good night and said that knowing I'd be there when she woke up, just like the old days, was the best gift she could ever receive. She laid a hand on my cheek and told me, "I love you, Jules. I never stopped."

When she hugged me, I thought maybe something about her did feel familiar. Maybe I did remember her. She was the most loving, reassuring presence. And at that moment, I really, truly, wholeheartedly wished my mother hadn't taken me away from these people.

Luke asked if I wanted to watch a movie. He held up a DVD. *Cinema Paradiso* — one of his favorites, he said.

"Will it make me cry?"

"Oh, for sure." He grinned.

I heaved a sigh.

"But I think you'll really like it."

As if I could say no.

We went into the kitchen to get something to drink. Luke offered me a beer and I said okay, glad to somehow have made the leap to adult beverages. He gave me a bottle of Two-Hearted Ale, which bore no resemblance to any of the cheap, pissy beers I'd ever tasted. It was darker — rich and a little bitter. Naturally, I liked it.

I took another sip and smacked my lips. "Chewy!"

Luke laughed. "Exactly. It's one of my favorites. Don't tell my parents I gave you a beer. They think you're still a baby."

I spotted a popcorn popper, so I made us some buttery popcorn with Parmesan. We shared a bowl of it while we watched one of the most beautiful movies I'd ever seen, pausing it to get more beer at one point. I don't know why I didn't see it coming, the way the movie ended, but Luke was right. I was undone. I wondered if he knew how it would hit me, that whole idea of never being forgotten, even when you had no idea someone still thought about you, still cared about you. I cried like a slobbering jackass.

Luke reached for a box of tissues on an end table and handed it to me. "See?" he said. "You love it!"

I laughed as I wiped my eyes and nose.

He smiled gently. "I always wished you could know that I was still thinking about you. That I never forgot you."

I wanted to hug him, but I never quite felt like I could reach out and do it. I wished he'd do it more so I wouldn't have to work it out. I said, "Thanks for never forgetting me."

"Thanks for coming back."

When he didn't make any movement to hug me, I gave up and asked, "Can I have a hug?"

"Of course." He held out his arms and I leaned in, spilling cheesy popcorn into his lap.

We both laughed and pulled back. Luke started picking the popcorn off his pants, glancing up at me and smiling. "It's just like old times. You and a big mess of food."

I laughed as he stood and brushed the crumbs off himself. "Anyway," I said, "I did love it. The movie."

"I'm glad." He picked up the remote and flipped off the TV. "We should probably head up," he said.

I felt a stab of regret. I wasn't ready to end our evening.

I followed him into the kitchen with our empty beer bottles. I rinsed them and set them quietly in the recycling bin as he dumped the last of the popcorn into the garbage, then flicked off the kitchen light.

In the guest room upstairs — my old bedroom — I checked my phone for the first time the whole day. Lots of frantic question marks from Gab and Leila. And a string of messages from my mother, some angry, some apologetic, and some desperate.

It was weirdly gratifying. She was having feelings about me. Suddenly I mattered.

Luke appeared in the doorway in pajama bottoms and a T-shirt. "It's unreal that you're here." He came over and sat next to me on the bed. "Is it really you? Are you really here?"

"It's really me. I'm really here." He smelled like soap and toothpaste.

"Are you tired? Or do you feel like talking more?"

"I feel like I'll never be finished talking to you."

He smiled — those pretty teeth, so close. "Should we go to my room?" He shrugged. "That's where the music is."

"Sure," I said slowly. "Maybe I'll change first?"

"Okay. You know where to find me." He stood and disappeared down the hall.

My pajamas, ugh. Gray fleece bottoms and a faded baseball shirt with a peeling number eighteen on the front. They were comfortable — a fact that offered little comfort now. Still, what was I supposed to wear for this? Lingerie? Clearly not.

I quietly closed the door to change. I hesitated after I pulled off my shirt. To bra or not to bra? That was the question. Obviously I slept without a bra on, but my chest in the fairly snug, faded shirt . . . Yeah, no. The bra stayed on.

I stopped in the bathroom to wash my face and brush

my teeth, then continued on to Luke's room. When I tapped on his door, which was open, he didn't respond. He was lying on his bed with headphones on, hands behind his head.

Christ. His stomach . . . His shirt had ridden up, and in the dim light of a table lamp, I could just make out the faint whisper of hair trailing down from his belly button. He was wearing boxers — the elastic peeked above the top of his pajama bottoms. I stared at the spot, transfixed, my heart rate suddenly skyrocketing.

He glanced up and smiled when he noticed me there and pulled off his headphones. He propped his pillow up against the headboard and patted the spot in front of it, scooting out of the way. "Sit."

On the bed? With you?

I edged my way inside and swung the door partially closed behind me, which I hoped was okay. It seemed wrong wide open, but wrong closed tight, too.

I sat cross-legged on the bed, leaning back against his pillow. He sat halfway down the bed, leaning his back against the wall.

"So did you always live in this house?" I asked, grasping for something to say.

"Almost always," he said. "It was my grandparents' house. My parents bought it when I was three, when my grandparents decided to downsize. They bought two condos — one here and one in Florida, for the winters."

"Are they alive still?" I unfolded one leg, positioning

198

my foot in front of his feet. If he decided to straighten his legs, we'd have a traffic situation.

He nodded. "Both of them. That's my father's side. My mother's parents have both passed."

I didn't want to conflate thoughts of death with his mother. "Did I ever meet them?" I asked.

"Oh, yeah! They were here a lot when we were little. And we sometimes stayed with them for the weekend or for an overnight."

More people who had taken care of me.

"You know, it's meant everything to my mom, seeing you again." He nudged my foot with his.

I stared at my feet, my self-styled toenails painted a rich shade of purple called, interestingly enough, *Sole Mate*. "It's meant everything to me, too," I said. Our eyes met. "I can't thank you enough for making this happen. For both of us. I mean, for both her and me."

"Well. It was for me, too," he said softly, nudging my foot again. He grinned, suddenly all mischief. "Are you still ticklish?"

"I'll never tell," I said, yanking my foot away and crossing my arms.

"Ha! Look at your defensive posture. Asked and answered." He scooted off the bed. "Let me put on some music. What do you feel like?"

"Whatever you like."

He messed with his phone over at his dresser. "Let's go

with the mellow acoustic list." When the music started, he went over and closed the door all the way. He caught my eye. "Don't want to wake them up," he explained.

"Right."

He hesitated. "I can open it, if you'd feel more —"

"No, don't be silly. It's fine — keep it closed."

As if. As if he'd try something, as if he'd make a romantic advance.

But God help me, my stomach fluttered at the thought.

We talked about everything. Our parents, our childhoods, our friends, school . . . we gradually worked our way to the subject of girlfriends and boyfriends. He asked if I'd had many boyfriends, and I admitted I hadn't. He, on the other hand, had had a lot of girlfriends, three of whom had lasted longer than a year, one of whom had lasted over two years. Four-plus years of monogamy = a lot of sex, I couldn't help thinking. He must be so very good at it. Why was I even thinking about this?

I asked about his last girlfriend, Makayla, who apparently he had been with until last fall. "Why'd you break up?"

He sighed. "Long story."

"Let me guess: she wanted you to commit and you weren't ready."

He gave a short laugh. "No, it wasn't like that at all. She broke up with me."

Was she crazy? Who'd break up with Luke? "That had to hurt. After two years."

"Yeah. Well. It's not like I didn't see it coming. I think my mom was more upset than I was. She had us married off in her mind."

Something flared in me at his words. Was it jealousy? "She liked her?"

He nodded. "She did. She does. But Makayla . . . she's ambitious. And she should be — she's a very accomplished violinist."

Of course.

"She wants to spend a couple of years in Europe after we graduate, to have adventures. And I don't feel I can do that right now. So . . . we just don't want the same things. And, being the logical girl she is, she didn't think we should stay together."

I picked at the pilling on my pajama pants. "Did you want to stay together?"

He chewed on his lip. "Yes and no. I mean, I didn't want to break up. But she's right — it probably wouldn't have worked out. And if you can envision that it's going to end at some point, sooner's better than later, right?"

"Probably. But I'm sorry you went through that." I rotated so I was sitting next to him, leaning against the wall instead of the headboard. And leaning a little on him. He turned to look at me. I'm sure he didn't know what I was doing. I didn't know what I was doing, either. I was sleep-deprived — it was after two — and I'd had a couple of beers.

"You know," he said, giving me a serious look. "I used to change your diapers."

I was so jarred that I struggled to form words. My *diapers*? The sudden clarity of all the ways he really saw me as a kid sister hit me hard. I covered my face. "Did you really?" I asked through my hands.

He laughed softly. "Well, I mean, I helped. Mostly Mom cleaned you up, and I got to fasten the diaper. Oh, and if it was a poopy one, I was out of there."

I pressed my lips together and closed my eyes. Deep breaths. The idea of him not only seeing my nethers, but seeing them smeared with poop . . . if there were a hole I could slip into and disappear forever, I would have leapt without a moment's hesitation. "Good news," I said, unable to meet his gaze. "I'm completely house-trained now."

He laughed. "Listen." He gestured with his eyes toward the speaker. A song was starting. "Great Lake Swimmers. This one's called 'The Man with No Skin.' They recorded it in a silo."

Grateful for the shift in focus, I leaned back and listened to the music. So mellow and melancholy. So dreamy . . .

I must have dozed off, because suddenly Luke was nudging my shoulder and whispering my name.

"Huh?" I blinked. "Oh — sorry."

"That's okay. Great Lake Swimmers'll do that."

I turned my face up to his. I was hazy, not quite in my

right mind . . . I couldn't take my eyes off his mouth. I wanted to kiss him. He was so close, so fucking close.

"I don't want to say good night," I said softly.

"I'll see you in a few hours," he reminded me. "Breakfast. More family time."

And then you'll take me home. I frowned at the thought — I couldn't help it. Everything that meant: dealing with my mom. School. Camping at Gab's. No Luke.

"Hey. What's wrong?"

I closed my eyes. "Just . . . gonna miss you."

He bumped my shoulder with his. "We'll see each other," he said. "Come on, cheer up. I can't sleep if you're down the hallway all sad."

"Okay," I said, pulling myself off the bed. The ache I was getting from not being able to get close enough with him was unbearable.

He turned down the music and opened the door, and we crept down the dark hallway quietly. There was no light under the door in his parents' room. I hoped that meant they were resting peacefully.

When I went into my room, Luke paused in the doorway, his face lit amber from the little lamp by my bed. "Okay, I'll see you in the morning." He held up a hand in a wave.

Not the good night I wanted. I gave him an exaggerated wave back.

"Don't mock me," he said, laughing. "Wake me up if

you're up before me. Unless it's, like, four a.m." He gave me a pointed look. "You used to holler from your crib before the sun was even up."

"Probably wondering where the hell my breakfast was."

He laughed loudly, then quickly covered his mouth and ducked his head. He leaned into the hall to glance toward his parents' room. He turned back to me, eyes wide. "You're trouble," he whispered.

I shrugged. "Never claimed I wasn't."

"That's true, you didn't." He raised his eyebrows. "Okay. G'night."

I opened my mouth, then closed it tight.

"What?"

I shook my head, horrified at myself. I had almost told him I loved him! I was off the rails. Too much fatigue, too much beer, too much *something*.

"What?" He tilted his head and took a step closer.

"It's nothing."

He looked confused, almost hurt.

I laid a hand over my eyes, weighing my options: confess to my over-the-top thoughts or leave him feeling hurt. "I was going to tell you . . ."

"What?" he prompted when I petered out. "What is it?"

"I was going to say I love you," I blurted. I didn't dare look at him. "I mean, I think I remember loving you. Or maybe I just know somewhere inside that I did love you?" I winced, sure I'd finally gone too far, and peeked out through my fingers. "Psycho, right?"

He stared at me, which could have meant anything and therefore filled me with terror. I lifted my other hand to better hide my face.

"Come here, you goon." He pulled me into a hug. "I love you, too."

I sighed with relief and hugged him back. His arms were the warmest, best place I'd ever been.

He pulled back long before I was ready, but he did plant a kiss on the top of my head. It was a sweet gesture, very brotherly. I was glad he did it. It seemed correct, and good, and promising.

And yet . . . When he was gone, I climbed into bed and lay there, wide awake, for most of what remained of the night, trying — and failing — to control the unchaste direction of my thoughts.

In the morning, Luke was in the bathroom when I went to see if he was up, so no one got to wake anyone up. I could hear Buddy and Mima downstairs in the kitchen, clanking and clattering. The aromas of bacon and coffee wafted up.

We had a simple breakfast, watched some more videos — a few of which featured Luke's grandparents, which was especially surreal: I'd had *grandparents*! Doting, white-haired grandparents! We talked some, but the energy was low, maybe stemming from the fact that Mima clearly was exhausted and weak. I felt guilty—I was sure I was the reason she was so spent.

I had hoped to spend the afternoon alone with Luke, maybe go to the movies or out to dinner, but he told me he was in the weeds with homework. Well. So was I, but I would have blown it off to spend time with him. Which told me that the scale of feelings was probably tipped.

Around noon, I gathered my things and hugged Mima and Buddy good-bye, and Luke and I headed out. He was quiet, and I wondered why. Did he wish we had more time together, too? Did he feel weird about last night? Was he worried about Mima? What was I thinking—of course he was worried about Mima! Guilt nudged at me. The point of this visit had been for me to meet Mima, and all I could think about was Luke.

The sun shone brightly, sending the temperature soaring up near fifty. I rolled down the window for a moment, just to breathe the air. It woke me up, whipping my face and flinging my hair in all directions. It smelled like change, like new things. Spring was coming—fresh and watery and full of hope.

In that moment, I realized, with some surprise, that I didn't want to go to Gab's house.

I wanted to go home.

I was still angry with my mom, but home, however imperfect, was home. And I felt a pull to return to it. Despite my resentment. Despite my anger. I had upset my mother, and even though I thought she deserved it, even though it gave me satisfaction in the moment, I couldn't live that way. For better or for worse, she was my mother. And of all the possible lessons I might take away from having found the Margolises, one stood out. Life is short.

"You sure?" Luke asked when I told him to drop me off at home. He glanced over. "You'll be okay?"

I nodded. His concern for me was something I felt in my chest, in my core, a gratitude that almost seared. He steered with his left hand, his right fingers tapping out a rhythm on his leg. I wanted to reach over and lay my hand on his, but I was pretty sure that wasn't right.

"So this is where you live," he said, pulling into the driveway. "It's different from what I pictured."

I snorted. "I'm sure it is. What did you picture?"

He shifted the car into Park. "I don't know. Something beautiful, I guess." He looked flustered. "I mean, not that it isn't nice."

I smiled. "No worries."

"Hey," he said, shifting toward me, "do you think next month you could come for another visit?"

Next month? "Of course," I said. I hesitated. "I could come sooner, if that would be better." It wasn't just that I didn't know Mima's exact prognosis. It was that next month was a thousand years away. I didn't want to not see them for a month. Especially Luke.

He gave me a warm smile. "I really appreciate that. But between classes and rehearsals, I don't have much free time over the next few weeks. And Mom probably needs a little while to recover from this visit." He tilted his head at me. "Hey, don't look so sad!" he said. "This weekend meant everything to her. And we'll do it again. Okay?"

"No, you're right." I nodded and reached for the door before I cried like an asshat.

He got out and opened the trunk.

"Thanks again for what you did for my mom," he said, holding the bag out to me. The afternoon sun glinted gold on his hair and lit up his green eyes. "What about *your* mom?" He winced, like he knew it was a tough question.

I lifted a shoulder. "I don't know."

He nodded. Then he took a deep breath and stepped forward to hug me again.

I squeezed him hard. "I'll miss you."

"I'll miss you, too." He let go and smiled as he backed away from me.

I stood on the walkway as he pulled out and drove off, and then watched him disappear into the distance.

My heart went with him.

Chapter 14

I stood at my front door.

I'd lived in this house since I was five — thirteen years now. A crooked crack ran through the cement front step. Teal paint peeled off the door. The dingy opaque rectangular window in the door let in light, but you couldn't really see in. Or out.

I pushed the door open and stepped inside. "Hello?" My mom's clogs weren't in their usual spot by the door. Her coat was gone, too. I took out my phone and messaged, *I'm home.*

I dropped my stuff, went into the kitchen, and habitually opened the refrigerator. There were a lot of Chinese take-out containers in there and also, to my surprise, a red velvet layer cake. When was the last time she baked one of those? More years than I could remember.

I pulled the loose plastic wrap off the cake and dabbed at the frosting with my finger to confirm what I already knew: it was from a can. The cake was from a mix, too, obviously. My mom was no pastry chef, but at one time this cake had totally rocked my world. The little girl who knew nothing about scratch baking or fine food went apeshit for boxed/canned red velvet cake. Until I discovered there was a world outside of my tiny bubble. Leila's mom's handiwork. Restaurants with the Wassermans. Laroche's. It struck me that every good thing that happens in life, every discovery of the next best thing, stands to breed discontent for what came before.

I got a fork out of the drawer and took a bite of cake. It tasted fake to me. Too sweet, almost caustic. Cheap.

I wasn't the same girl.

Still, I ate it. It no longer appealed to me, but somehow I wanted it anyway. It was the connection I was after, I supposed — the link to an earlier time. Too many tethers to my past were broken already. I couldn't bear to give up another.

When I'd eaten all the bites I could stomach, I put it away and went to my room, where I immediately stopped short. Propped against the headboard was a pillow covered in buttons. Curious, I went over and picked it up. The buttons — they were from my tin. Mom had repurposed an old throw pillow from the living room as a display for them. Dozens of them, all shapes and sizes, were sewn onto the pillow front.

She'd done an amazing job — they were more artfully chosen and arranged than I ever could have managed. Her eye for color and composition was not limited to the canvas. I traced my fingers over the buttons. I couldn't believe it — how long had that taken her?

But beyond the time and effort that went into this, what made my eyes fill was the message inherent in it: she was acknowledging something that was important to me.

I messaged her again. *Such thoughtful things waiting for me here. The pillow is amazing — I love it.* I added, *Ready to talk when you are.*

I caught up on my e-mail, which included one from Eli, subject line: "Best recent obituaries." This was a favorite pastime of his, finding unusual or humorous obituaries, and I always played along because it was one of the few things he shared with me. So I read them and texted him, *SPLENDID. Loved the line about Little Debbie Snacks stock prices falling sharply following Ida's death.*

He wrote back *AN ORDER FOR SIXTEEN MOCHA FRAPPES! TWEENS! LOUD STRAIGHT TWEENS! SHOOT ME NOW.*

I wrote, *"Shoot me now" is not a thing you want to hear from your friend who is obsessed with obituaries fyi.*

Silence. He was probably frantic with blender action.

That left schoolwork. With a resigned sigh, I gathered up my materials and dove in.

* * *

A couple hours later, just as I finished my overdue English paper, my phone dinged. I picked it up, thinking it would finally be my mom, but it was Luke.

Home safe. Everything okay?

It warmed me to hear from him, and to know he was worried about me. I wrote, *Yes. Mom isn't here, so no big scene or anything. Also, she baked a cake and sewed my antique buttons onto a decorative pillow??*

Him: *Aw, that's nice! Guilt? An attempt to disarm?*

Me: *Ha, no idea.*

Him: *Let me know what happens. Going to make coffee and get started on work. Possible all-nighter ahead.*

I smiled. *Me too.*

He wrote, *Had a great weekend with you.*

It felt like the sun breaking through the clouds. I wrote, *Same. I had an incredible weekend.*

He sent me a smiley face and wished me happy studying.

So I tried to study. I imagined us shoulder to shoulder, even if virtually, pushing through the work together. I started with biology — my makeup test was a mere twelve hours away. But my powers of concentration were nearly nonexistent. All I wanted to think about was the weekend, the Margolises . . . Luke.

By 9:00 I was yawning. I decided to follow Luke's lead and make a pot of coffee. When I opened the cabinet, I discovered a small bag of fresh-ground French roast from Laroche's next to the giant plastic vat of Folgers. I knew my mom was upset, but I couldn't imagine her spending so much time and thought on me, on things that I'd like. I opened the bag and inhaled, closing my eyes. Heaven.

Where was she? Why didn't she answer? Could she have gone to the movies? Was she driving? All this time? I pushed aside thoughts of her going out and wrecking herself. But the longer I didn't hear from her, the more I worried. I'd ignored all her pleas, left her to her own devices. I hoped she was okay.

I poured a mug of coffee and returned to biology. ATP, ADP, AMP . . . I couldn't keep the acronyms straight. I lay down for a minute, exhausted. After a while, I texted my mom again: *You okay? Answer, pls.*

I thought of all the hours I'd left my mom alone with her thoughts, her worries — all the suffering I'd caused her. I didn't know if I would ever be able to forgive her for the things she'd done. So I didn't entirely understand how I could also feel worried for her, and guilty, and moved that she'd made an effort in my absence, despite my refusal to cooperate or communicate. She had hurt me, but I was hurting her, too.

I picked up my phone again and messaged: *I missed you.*

I fell asleep and woke up around five. My mom had left a message in the wee hours: *Sorry, phone died. Stayed with a friend — didn't expect you to come home. I'll be home tonight after work. Will you?*

A friend? What friend? My mom rarely went out, let alone stayed out the whole night. I sent a quick *yes*. I had only two and a half hours to get my affairs in order for school and maybe squeeze in a shower. I'd really screwed myself with that untimely nap, but my exhaustion was bigger than I was.

I did pause, though, to answer a message from Luke. He'd gone to bed around two and hoped my studying was going well. I confessed I'd passed out and was up early.

I spent the day trying to be the student I used to be. I passed my biology test with a shameful C+. Caught up with Gab at lunch and Leila by text when we could sneak them in. After school I zipped straight home and hit the books again — no Laroche's, no phone calls, no messaging with Luke. When my mom texted that she'd be home by six, I took a break from studying and surveyed the pantry for dinner options.

Well, there was ramen — always ramen. I found a chicken breast in the freezer, and there was cheddar and cream cheese in the fridge. In the pantry there was also a can of hot roasted green chilies, and so was conceived the newest in a growing line of ramen perversions: jalapeño popper ramen with chicken. I found some scallions in the crisper drawer that had about a minute of life left in them, so I chopped the most verdant strands to top our dinner.

I was grating the cheddar when I heard the front door open. I turned and peeked out.

She was kicking off her shoes, a pile of mail in her arms. I could almost pretend this was any other day — any day before I learned the truth about her, about my past. But the guarded look she gave me made clear that pretending was not possible on either side.

"Hi," I said.

"Hi." She hesitated, then stepped into the kitchen and set the mail on the table. "What smells so good?"

I described dinner, and she smiled as she got herself a glass of water. "I never would have come up with that. Thanks for cooking."

"Thanks for all the stuff you got me."

She glanced up quickly over her glass. She swallowed and said, "You liked?"

"I did. The pillow . . ." I shook my head. "I never would have thought of that."

She smiled. "There were some amazing things in there — some of those look really old!"

I nodded.

"You really like that stuff, don't you?" she said, tilting her head.

"Yeah." My eyes bored into hers. "I do." I was grateful that she was seeing me, really seeing me. But why did this have to be new? Why did it take so many years?

We ate mostly in silence, apart from discussing the food, which my mom enjoyed. It was creamy and cheesy and spicy. I wished Luke could try it.

As I watched my mom clean up, I reflected on how comfortable I felt, despite the storm cloud hanging over us, the wreckage that was us. She was utterly familiar to me. Could it really have been like that with anyone else? Could I really have seen Mima as my mother the way I did this woman standing before me, looking like me, executing all her idiosyncratic maneuvers? Dumping the whole cutting board into the trash and shaking it off, or picking up a dirty paper towel from the garbage to wipe out a bowl (no garbage disposal in our kitchen, and why use a clean paper towel for that?). She was shortcutty and frugal. She could live with messy but not with dirty. She wouldn't be bothered by days of mail on the counter, but a smear of coffee would be a nonstarter.

I loved her and I hated her. I was proud of her and disappointed in her. She was indifferent about things that mattered to me and consumed with things that didn't matter to me. She was irritating, yet elusive. Too close and too far. She was the nearest thing to my own self that existed — genetically, experientially, geographically, viscerally. She was a part of me.

"Want a cup of tea?" she asked, putting the last of the silverware into the drainer.

"Sure." I watched her, my head propped up on one hand on the table. "Peppermint, please."

She put the kettle on and fished out a Red Zinger and a peppermint from the boxes in the cabinet.

When she sat down at the table, I opened with, "I spent the weekend with my foster family."

"Ha." She dunked her tea bag in her favorite mug. "Is that what you're calling the Wassermans now?"

"No, Mom." I waited until she met my eyes. "My real foster family. In Milwaukee."

I guess I hadn't fully considered how that announcement would strike her, but I watched the blood drain from her face, watched her lips go pale. She let go of her mug and sat back a little, clasping her hands together.

"Their name is Margolis," I said. "And they took really good care of me when you were . . ." I trailed off, unable to find words that didn't seem pointedly harsh.

She stood up suddenly, her chair scraping the linoleum. She dropped her cup of tea in the sink. It shattered as it hit the old porcelain. No more NO SOUP.

I followed her into her studio.

"Do you know where I was last night?" she asked, going to her desk.

I leaned in the doorway. "No. Obviously."

"I went to a meeting." She shuffled through a stack of postcards — inspiration for the canvas. Places with brilliant waters and impossible skies. Beautiful places other, luckier people had seen, reduced to glossy paper rectangles for the less fortunate. "I hate meetings, I hate AA, I hate talking."

"Then why have you been going to them?" If she said it was because of me, I was going to lose my shit. It wasn't my fault she was an addict. And it wasn't my fault she lied to me about my past and it came back to haunt her.

She stared at the postcards in her hands. "This whole situation has brought up some really tough memories."

That made sense, I supposed. These were memories of the very things that knocked her off the wagon in the first place. But whatever they were, I was out of patience over not knowing. "Mom, what happened when I was little?" I pressed. "And why did you lie to me all these years?"

She set the postcards down. "You mean about the foster care? By the time you were old enough to understand, I didn't think you remembered it anyway. It just seemed pointless."

"Convenient for you." I crossed my arms, still leaning in the doorway. "You could just erase your mistakes, right? Like they never even happened. Like the Margolises never happened."

She paused, wringing her hands. When she finally spoke, she surprised me. "You're right. I let myself off the hook. I told myself things that would make it easier for me." She glanced at me. "But I meant to tell you. So many times I would gear myself up for it, and . . ." She shook her head. "I could never bring myself to do it. It's so hard to face what I did."

She was finally owning her shit, and I didn't want to kick her when she was down. I crossed the room. "Mom. What *happened* to you? Tell me. Help me understand. You've been alone with it for so long. But it didn't just happen to you." I gripped one of her hands in mine. "It happened to *us*."

When she squeezed my hand and began to cry, it felt like something heavy breaking free in my chest.

And then, finally, she started talking.

It wasn't long before I understood my mother's inability to talk about the things that had happened in her past. Our past.

How do you tell your child you left her in a car seat for an indeterminate number of hours outside a bar when she was four months old, before the police were alerted and she was turned over to Social Services?

How do you tell your child you lied about not knowing who her father was? (He was indeed the waifish boy in the delivery room at my birth. His name was Ethan Whitman.)

It was his death that sparked Mom's relapse. She'd gotten sober when she found out she was pregnant. And then, months later, it all fell apart.

It was unknown whether his death was a suicide or an accidental overdose. My mom believes the latter. She said he was trying too hard and loved us too much for it to be anything but an accident.

I didn't argue. I was pretty sure that's not how addiction or depression or suicide works, but I saw no reason, after all she had been through, to take that belief away from her.

I was greedy to know more about this fragile, tortured

boy who fathered me, but my mother was quickly nearing her limit. The final detail she shared with me was that Ethan and his father never got along, and the older and more independent Ethan got, the harder on him his father was. "He kicked Ethan out of the house when he found out I was pregnant," Mom said, bitterness thick in her voice. "I hated that man. If it weren't for him, Ethan might have stood a chance."

Mom couldn't bring herself to talk about my dad any more after that. We were both exhausted. I hugged her good night and wandered in a daze to my room. Thoughts swirled in my head. What if my dad had lived? What would it have been like for me to be raised by a mom and a dad, even if they were both recovering addicts, both impossibly young?

But I would never know. And it was so devastatingly, infuriatingly unfair.

But also unfair? The fact that my mother had blocked me from knowledge of my father my whole life. Everything I had ever longed for, she had single-handedly blocked.

I lay in bed that night, unable to sleep, tormented over the father I would never remember. If he had lived, if they had recovered, I might have had everything I'd ever wanted — a mom, a dad, maybe even siblings. Or maybe my life would have been chaos. After all, how stable would two eighteen-year-old addicts really have been? Maybe they would've broken up and fought over custody of me, or maybe I'd have been raised by junkies.

One thing was certain, though: in any of these scenarios, there would be no Luke, no Margolises. And it was confusing to factor them out of my mind and heart now. They had already loved me. I couldn't imagine them away.

Luke. Oh, what I wouldn't give to talk to him right now, to be held by him. It would be so sweet, so comforting. I imagined how he might tenderly stroke my back as we hugged, how he might whisper that he loved me.

I knew I should shut down this train of thought, but I was too gutted to be strong. And so I let myself picture the kinds of things I'd been wanting to picture since I met Luke. And it made me feel wrong, ashamed. But admonishing myself not to feel that way was useless.

I nearly jumped out of my skin when my phone rang. I checked the screen, stupidly hoping it might be Luke. But it was Eli. I frowned; it was almost one.

"Hello?"

At first I wasn't sure if he was laughing or crying. But when he choked out the word "Jay," I knew.

"I'm coming, Eli. Hang on."

I pulled on some clothes, grabbed the car keys, and tiptoed out.

His house was dark except for the yellow glow emanating from the basement window wells. I let myself into the front door and crept down the stairs. I found him curled up on his bed, crying like a little boy — a sight that tore my heart in half. I petted his head, glancing toward the cage.

I couldn't see anything from where I was, so I tiptoed over.

I shuddered. Jay lay on his side, his limbs curled stiffly, his mouth open. Daisy, awake, sat on the mezzanine level, staring out at me.

I crept back over to the bed to lay down next to Eli, rubbing his back as he wept. I reminded him that Jay had a wonderful life — as good a life as a rat could ever have. And that Eli would always have wonderful memories of him.

"What do I do?" he asked. "I can't even look at him. What am I supposed to do?"

I drew in a slow breath. Was I going to have to remove Jay's body from the cage? Because I wasn't sure I was the person for the job. And assuming I could make myself get it out, then what was I supposed to do with it?

"Have you ever . . . lost a rat before?" I asked.

He shook his head and wiped his nose on his arm. "Jay was my first rattie."

"Well . . . should we bury him?"

As soon as I said this, I remembered that it was still winter — was the ground still frozen?

Eli started to cry again. "I don't know."

I sat up and started googling on my phone "24-hour animal clinics." When I found one nearby, I tiptoed over to the stairs and called.

After being told I could bring Jay in to be cremated and assured that he would be treated with the utmost respect, I gently shared the information with Eli, who nodded, but remained curled up on the bed. I sighed resignedly.

I poked around the basement until I found an empty shoe box. I found some rags in the laundry room, which I used to remove Jay's stiff body from the cage, coaching myself through each horrifying second of it. How would all this affect Daisy? Those two loved each other. They stayed so close — as close as they could be. The idea of Daisy left alone for the rest of his days, lonely and bewildered, tore at my already-torn heart.

And that's when it hit me: that's what was coming for Buddy. To be left behind, bewildered and alone, missing his one love. And it was more than I could bear to think about.

I wrapped Jay in some extra rags and tucked him in the shoe box. "Um, go with God, little guy," I whispered, feeling some ceremony was in order but having no prayers or blessings at the ready.

"Can you bring me Daisy?" Eli called to me.

"Sure, of course . . ." I set the box on the table and reached in gingerly. "You sure he won't bite me?"

He made a muffled sound I hoped I could interpret as an affirmative.

Daisy turned and sniffed my hand as I reached for him, making me jerk back. "How do I pick him up?"

"Just pick him up around his middle and then cradle him in your hands."

I slowly reached a hand around Daisy, who didn't seem

to mind. When I lifted him out, I supported him with my other hand. "Good boy," I said softly, taking him over to Eli, who sat up and took him from me.

"Did you . . . ?"

I nodded. "I tucked him in with some nice soft rags and said a little prayer for him." I sat down next to him. "He's at peace, Eli. And it's better this way, that he passed suddenly, without a lot of suffering. He had a good, long life. You said so yourself."

"Daisy's going to miss him so much," he said, looking at me imploringly, his eyes swollen and red. "How can I make him understand he's gone?"

"He knows." I petted Daisy's head, another rush of tears filling my eyes. "Animals know things. He'll miss him at first, but he'll be okay. You'll see."

Even though I wasn't sure I believed this, I knew I had to say it. Eli needed to hear it — whether or not *he* believed it, too.

I stayed by Eli's side until he was calm. Somewhere around five, he finally fell asleep and I took Jay to be cremated.

The receptionist at the clinic remembered Jay. It was the same clinic Eli had brought Jay to when he was having breathing problems. She sent her condolences to Eli, then got up and gave me a hug, telling me I was a good friend. It made me tear up, because damn. People can be so fucking decent.

Oddly, they charged by the pound for cremation. Jay was cheap. I paid in cash.

As I drove back to my house, a yellow-peach haze glowed at the horizon. I was glad for the new day — it felt correct. In some small but important way, I had temporarily risen above my own muck to be there for Eli, who didn't even think to thank me or hug me or anything. And he didn't need to — I didn't care. It didn't escape me, despite all my angst about family, about finding family and having family and missing out on family, that this was a very real thing I had: friends I would drop everything for. Friends I'd take bullets for. Friends I'd handle dead rats for.

There is more than one kind of family.

Chapter 15

*M*y mom and I forged the kind of existence that only the conflation of familiarity and physical proximity make possible: the kind where you just can't deal with your shit at every moment so you have an unwritten agreement to set it aside in order to proceed with the doings of life. Anyway, I needed my energy for my faltering academic career, my friends, and my hopes for Luke — and the Margolis family. I'd be seeing them again next weekend. Luke had said the time would pass quickly, and maybe for him it did, but for me, the combination of anxiety about Mima's condition and longing to be with Luke resulted in days that crawled like years.

I thought through endless trajectories of the alternate universe. The one where I was a Jewish kid with a loving family and a brilliant, doting older brother. Maybe we would have been peas in a pod. Maybe he would have been protective with me about boys. Maybe — Jesus. Maybe I'd also play piano? The idea that I might have been knowledgeable about music, maybe even able to play an instrument, brought yet another stab of longing and regret.

But running through these other versions of reality also meant thinking about the impact on *this* reality — not knowing my own mother. Not having Gab or Leila or Eli. Not knowing a china pattern from a Chinet plate.

Would I have felt in the other reality as I do in this one? Like someone who didn't quite belong, someone who always wished for something different? Maybe I would have obsessed about my "real mother" and the life I'd missed? That sounded about right, if I was honest. Maybe I was just a chronic malcontent. Nothing was ever enough.

And what about my mother's fate? If she hadn't gotten me back, would she ever have sobered up? In an alternate reality, she could be homeless, or even dead. Or she could have sobered up and, unencumbered by a child and the demands of single-parenting, she might be a celebrated, famous painter. The alternate realities were an endless mindfuck.

Winter was giving up the ghost. It was March now, and it felt every molecule of it. The last of the snow melted, revealing limp grass in sepia tones that would rally to verdant redemption in the coming weeks. Of course, in Chicago there were no guarantees; an icy or even snowy relapse remained a possibility far into spring. Still, the grass was dotted with purple clusters of crocuses, and the daffodils wouldn't be too far behind. As far as I was concerned, we'd made it.

One rainy afternoon after school, I huddled under an umbrella and headed for Laroche's. I wanted to check on Eli. He had taken bereavement leave from work after Jay died, but Madame V. was short on sympathy when she learned who — or what — the dearly departed was. His job, he felt, was hanging by a thread. Sometimes I worried he was, too.

On my way there, I stopped in at Tina's to say hello and discuss my summer schedule. She greeted me by wrapping me in a fur stole, one of her recent estate sale scores. She asked if I wanted to join her on a scouting venture sometime, which I answered unhesitatingly in the affirmative. Her happiness about my coming aboard warmed me.

I pulled open the door to the café with all my might and got in somewhat gracefully for once, despite also having an umbrella to contend with. "Hey," I said to Eli as I approached the counter. "How are you doing?"

He shrugged as he unloaded a box of napkins.

"How's Daisy?" I asked.

He looked up and his eyes reminded me of my father's in the photos — waifish, lost. "I think he's depressed. He sits and stares a lot, and every time I see him sleeping alone, it kills me. I hate leaving him. I wish I could bring him to work with me."

"Oh, Eli." I searched for words of comfort, but sanguine platitudes were not exactly my specialty lately.

The door dinged and a pair of forty-something women in yoga pants came in, jarring the quiet with loud laughter. I went to find a seat at the window.

I tried to think of something I could do to cheer Eli up. There was no replacement for a lost loved one — I knew that better than ever. But I suddenly realized there was maybe something I could do — something only Eli would appreciate and only I would know. I pulled out a pen and grabbed a napkin.

Jay Gatsby
Departed this world at age almost-four, aka at least
100 rattie years, Jay was a black-hooded fancy Dumbo rat
who lived his whole life in Maplebrook, Illinois. He loved
snacking and cuddling and staying in or near his cage. He
was sweet and full of love and objectively better than most
humans.

Jay is survived by his one-and-only life partner, Daisy,
and his beloved person, Eli, who made Jay's life happy and,
well, gay.

In lieu of flowers, please sprinkle Cheerios around your
local garbage dumpster.

As I finished, my phone dinged. It was an e-mail. From Luke.

Jules, sorry to do this, but this weekend isn't going to be good for a visit after all. Mom's having trouble breathing — she has a lot of fluid around her lungs that they have to keep draining. We're bringing in hospice care so this can be handled at home. Looks like the end might be sooner than we thought.

Sorry for the change in plans. Will keep in touch. L.

I sat back, my hand pressed to my mouth. My God — was she about to die? Like, any week now? Any day? Would I never see her again?

I picked up my phone, wanting so badly to call him, to hear his voice, to connect with him, to tell him how much I cared. But he had e-mailed me — not called, not texted. Did he want space from me? Was I just an intrusion at this point? Sometimes I felt like I was on the inside, richly, warmly on the inside. Like I belonged. And then there were moments when it all fell away, and I felt like I was intruding. And it was unbearable.

But I couldn't just ignore something like that. I texted him:

My heart is breaking. Please send Mima all my love — a whole lifetime of it. I wish I could be there for you. If you need me . . . I'm here.

I glanced up as Eli sat down across from me. I told him

about Luke's e-mail. "I was supposed to go see them this weekend," I told him. "But now . . ." My eyes welled up.

"Jeez," Eli said, looking kind of shaken. "Shit, that sucks."

I pushed the napkin toward him. He glanced at it in confusion, picking it up. As I sniffled, I watched his face change. He chewed lightly at his lip ring, then glanced up at me. "You wrote an obituary? For Jay?"

I nodded.

"Fuck," he whispered, turning his face away.

"Oh! Eli." I reached across the table.

To my shock, he reached out for my hand and squeezed it. "That's . . ." He glanced at the napkin again, and I swear his eyes went a bit misty. "That's maybe the nicest thing anyone has ever done for me."

I hoped that was an exaggeration. "Eli? Do you remember your mother?"

He blinked, clearly caught off-guard, and sat back. "Yeah."

"What do you remember about her?"

He shrugged. "A lot of things."

"Good memories?" I asked hopefully.

He glanced out the window, fingering the line of little rings along his ear, and for a moment I thought he wasn't going to answer. But then he said softly, "All of them."

I went into the bathroom, sat down on the toilet, and cried.

* * *

My mom and I ordered pizza that night and ate on the sofa in front of the TV.

She flipped the channel to *House Hunters,* where a young couple was looking for a starter home close to the wife's parents in Savannah. "I guess this is as good a time as any to tell you," my mom said, licking sauce off her thumb. "We're house hunting, too. Well, apartment hunting."

"What?" I stared at her, confused. "He's selling the house?"

She nodded, setting her plate down and brushing off her hands. "He's tired of waiting on the market. He just wants out."

I blinked, stunned. "When do we have to leave?"

"May first. He's buying out the rest of our lease, though, which goes until September first. With our security deposit, that will be almost six thousand dollars."

"Wow."

"Yeah, we'll need it. Rent in this area has gone up a lot over the years."

"Well, we could probably get by with less space in the future," I said. "Since I mostly won't be at home from this point forward."

Mom blinked, as if she'd forgotten or maybe hadn't fully processed the upcoming changes in our lives. "Have you heard back from everywhere you applied?"

All three places? At about fifty bucks a pop, I wasn't applying to a dozen schools like most people I knew. I nodded. "Accepted at all three: Beloit, Augustana, U of I."

She smiled. "That's my girl."

I tried to smile back, but conflicting feelings rose up in me at her words. Warmth at her pride and proprietary expression. But also, discomfort at how new and foreign they felt. I wished we had arrived at a point like this long before now.

"Hey," she said, "aren't you seeing the family again this weekend? I could drive you, if you want. I was thinking . . . I could show you the houses where your father and I grew up, and the high school, and maybe the diner we liked to go to, and . . ." She shrugged. "If you're interested."

My mixed feelings continued to do battle inside me, but something swelled in my chest at the realization that she was trying to right some wrongs. "I would've loved to," I told her. "But I'm not going to Milwaukee this weekend."

"Why not? Did something happen?"

"I think she's . . ." I wound my fingers together. "I think she's dying."

She looked stricken. "Jesus. That poor family."

I nodded, and we were quiet for a moment.

"We should still do it — go to your old neighborhood," I said, surprising us both. "I'd really like to."

She smiled tentatively. "You would?"

I nodded. "I want to see where you and . . . Ethan grew up." I stumbled over what to call him. The yearning to say "Dad" was an unbearable ache deep inside me.

"I haven't been there in years." She took a breath. "I wonder if I'll even recognize it."

"It was yellow when we lived in it." My mom shifted into Park and peered out the window at a small two-story house, slate gray with white trim, 1950, plus or minus, I'd guess. I tried to imagine it twenty years earlier.

"It's cute," I said. "Has it changed much?"

"Someone fixed it up." She squinted and lowered the visor to block the sun.

It was the kind of piercingly clear and bright March morning that makes promises you aren't convinced it can deliver — a morning temperature in the upper thirties giving way to a sixty-degree afternoon seems unlikely, but if Chicago-area weather ever had a rule book, it threw it out eons ago.

"How long did you live here?" I asked. In the front yard, near the street, stood an ancient-looking willow tree with a gnarly trunk. Its naked branches hung like strands of wheat-colored hair in the morning light.

"We moved in when Mom was pregnant with Dawn. I was five, just about to start school."

Dawn. A four-letter word. I knew my mom had lost a sister, but it was not a subject she'd ever wanted to talk about. Until this morning, anyway. On the drive up, she told me about growing up in Milwaukee and about how her dad ran off after her sister died. Another grandparent who might still be out there, might still be alive. She wasn't sure. But given her feelings about him, I wasn't going to push. If the things she said about him were true, then I didn't want to know him anyway.

"That was my bedroom." She pointed toward the left side of the house, upstairs. "I used to sneak out my window and shimmy down that tree on the side."

"To see Ethan?"

Her mouth curved into a wistful smile. "Yeah."

"Did you guys really love each other?"

She looked surprised by the question. "Oh, yeah," she said emphatically. She reached out and touched a lock of my long hair, identical to hers. "Oh my God, yes. *So* much."

I hadn't realized it mattered to me, but the fierce rush of warmth that ran through me suggested it did. My eyes stung.

"I should have told you that. I'm sorry. Yes. We loved each other a lot." Her face creased with emotion. "Fuck," she whispered, sitting back in her seat. She took a moment to compose herself, then glanced at me. "Ready to go see his house?"

I nodded.

She started chewing on her thumbnail. "We won't be able to park this close. I don't know if his parents still live there, and I'm not prepared to run into them."

I nodded again, to show her I was okay with this. I was more than okay, to be honest; I could only imagine how hard it was for her to be here, to remember whatever it was she was remembering. She'd spent my whole life trying to forget all of this, and now she was sharing it with me. That was huge.

She glanced at me. "Does he know you're here?"

I didn't have to ask whom she meant. I turned and looked out my window. "Well, I messaged him. Told him we'd be up this way."

When he didn't respond with the question I felt my message raised, I sent another explaining the trip. In return, there was only radio silence.

I had hoped he'd ask me to stop by while I was in town — hoped Mima would be okay enough that it was possible. Barring that, I'd hoped he'd at least want to know about all these developments in my life. A few weeks ago, we were so close — or at least it felt that way. Now it was starting to feel like a dream.

I pulled out my phone and typed another message before I could talk myself out of it.

Just wanted to let you know that Mom and I arrived in Milwaukee.

I struggled with what to say next. *Hope everyone's well* was a clear nope. *I love you* would be idiotic. I finally settled on *Sending love to you all.*

When my mom slowed the car, I glanced up. My nerves were jangling, but not nearly as bad as hers. She drove with one hand on her stomach, the other trembling on the wheel.

"That one," she said, pointing up the street to the right.

I stared out my window, taking in the house, the

property. It looked like, well, a grandmother's house. It was a Cape Cod style, and there were window boxes filled with spruce branches and pine cones. Maybe their scenery changed with the seasons.

A tidy, white-fenced yard was filled with sturdy shade trees and magnolias. A wide, arched arbor led to the backyard, its wood barren now, apart from a weave of twigs, but I imagined it was covered over with vines and blossoms in the summer. This was not the setting I imagined for that pierced, punk-looking teenager. Could it be that all this 1950s white-bread sentiment was what he was rebelling against?

"Oh, God." My mom took a shaky breath. "The porch swing is still there." She pointed. "That's where we had our first kiss."

I squinted, trying to see it better. Most of the red paint had peeled off, revealing weathered, pale wood underneath. I tried to imagine my mom at my age, kissing the wild boy in the picture.

"My heart is pounding," she said, laying her hand on her chest.

I turned and laid a comforting hand on her arm. And that's when my phone dinged. It was Luke.

Jules, can you come? Mom wants to see you, and she wants you to bring your mom. If you could be here within an hour, that would be best. It will need to be a short visit.

"Oh my God," I murmured.

"What is it?"

I turned the phone toward her.

She read it and sat back. "Oh, Jesus. I don't know, Jules. I'll take you, but . . . I don't think I . . ."

"You have to. She's *dying*. She wants to see you."

She shook her head.

"Mom." I waited until she met my gaze. "Don't you owe her that much?"

Chapter 16

*L*uke opened the door with his usual friendliness and warmth, but he looked like he hadn't slept in days. I wished I could pull him aside somewhere private and just hold him. Instead, we had a brief hug, and then he shook my mom's trembling hand.

She was a mess. Watching her drive over, I almost wished she smoked or something. She could have used a cigarette. *I* could have used a cigarette, just watching her nerves play out through her shaky hands, her shallow breaths, her blinking, darting eyes.

"It's great to meet you," Luke said to my mom, ushering us in the front door. "My mom's so glad you could come."

She stammered out a response as we followed Luke up the stairs.

When we approached the master bedroom, Luke held up a finger to us in a *wait one sec* gesture and peeked into the room. After a few soft exchanges, he opened the door for us.

Flowers filled the room — they were everywhere, all kinds, almost too cheery, too bright. Mima watched us from the bed, her face completely washed of color. Her concave chest rose in staccato short breaths. A machine fed her oxygen through tubes into her nose.

Buddy turned from fixing her covers and gave us a tired smile. He hugged me, then quietly introduced himself to my mom.

I looked toward Mima, who lifted a hand to gesture me over. I approached her carefully, afraid I'd cry, afraid I'd do something wrong. She was so gaunt. I reminded myself that she was still Mima, the woman who had loved and taken care of me. I tried to slip my arms around her to hug her, carefully avoiding the tubes.

"Jules." She smiled at me through cracked lips. "You're a . . . sight for sore eyes." Her speech was punctuated by short breaths, and it sent a chill through me. She glanced behind me. "And this is . . . your mother?"

I turned to make way for my mother to approach, but she didn't step forward. She stood there, lips trembling, then pressed both hands to her face and started to silently cry.

I was mortified, even as it pierced my heart. I stepped over to her and put an arm around her shaking shoulders, coaching her in a whisper. "It's okay. Shhh." And finally, "Mom, pull yourself together — please."

She dropped her hands and shuffled forward, still sniffling and trying to contain herself.

Mima patted the bed beside her, and my mom perched on the edge. Between my mom's hiccup-y breaths and Mima's intermittent and sudden shallow ones, I felt like I was suffocating.

Mima glanced up at us with a smile. "Give us . . . a minute?"

I nodded, my eyes connecting briefly with my mom's, which were full of terror.

Luke and I stepped into the hall, swinging the door almost closed. "Come on," he whispered, leading me down the hallway to his room.

He sat on his bed, which was unmade, and dropped his face into his hands. I sat down next to him, struggling to know how to comfort him, what the parameters were. I rested a tentative hand on his back. He startled me by turning to me and hugging me, his forehead pressed into my shoulder.

I held him, stroking his back softly. I whispered meaningless phrases of comfort, helpless to do anything that could make a real difference. He clung to me, and I was elated with the feeling of his needing me, of wanting to get closer, but also hated myself for taking any pleasure when what compelled him to cleave to me in this moment was a deep well of pain.

"I'm not ready for this," he whispered. "I don't want her to die."

"I know."

"I know I'm all grown up, but . . . she's my mom. You know?"

"I know."

"She won't be at my wedding. My kids won't have their grandmother."

My eyes filled at all the terrible things he was beginning to realize.

"She should have been a grandmother," he said. "She'd be the best grandmother a kid could ever have."

"Yes."

"And my dad . . . he'll be all alone." At this, his voice tore into ragged sobs. I held him tighter as he shook under my arms.

After a moment, he pulled back and wiped his face. The light streaming through the window lit his eyes a bright green.

"How long can you stay?" he asked. He sounded like a little boy, and I realized in some ways, that's what he was. A little boy who was about to lose his mother.

"I don't know," I said, wiping away my own tears. "I

imagine my mom is going to want to head back pretty quick."

He wrapped his hands tightly around mine. "If I drive you home tomorrow, would you stay the night?"

I blinked. "Really? You — you want me to stay?" My heart soared.

He glanced down. "I don't want to be alone. Besides . . ." He looked up at me. "She was your mother, too. You should be here with her. With us."

I looked at that beautiful face, so open and raw. "Of course I'll stay." I pulled him into a hug without even hesitating.

I jumped at a rap at the door. I quickly pulled away from Luke as Buddy pushed the door partway open. "Mom's just about spent," he said. "Probably should wrap it up."

I nodded and stood up. When I stepped into the hall, Buddy offered me a weak smile. "How's our girl?" he asked.

I was unable to answer. Instead I teared up and nodded. He patted my back as we walked down the hall, Luke following behind.

My mom emerged from Mima's room carrying a paper bag. She looked a little shell-shocked, but she wasn't crying anymore.

"What's that?" I asked softly, eyeing the bag.

"Pictures and home movies." She took my arm before I could follow Buddy and Luke into Mima's room. "Can we go? Please."

I winced. "Luke asked me to stay with him. He'll drive

me home tomorrow." Watching her process that, I felt terrible. "Will you be okay?"

She nodded, but I wasn't convinced.

"Are you sure? I could tell Luke I can't —"

"No, it's fine. If I'm struggling, I'll go to a meeting. Or maybe see my friend." She glanced toward the bedroom door. "Tell Luke and his dad thank you."

"Will you message me when you get home? Right away?"

She nodded and started to move away, but then she turned back for a hug.

"You did good," I whispered.

She squeezed me a little tighter. When she headed down the stairs, I was not at all sure she was going to be okay, and I almost called after her to wait, that I'd go with her. But I'd told Luke I'd stay with him, and this was probably the last time I'd ever see Mima.

My mom would have to take care of herself.

I tiptoed in and sat next to Mima, whose eyes were drooping. She saw me and moved her lips, but nothing came out.

"It's okay," I said, squeezing her hand. It was bony, cool to the touch. "You don't have to say anything."

But there were things I wanted to say — things I needed to say. There was no way I could do this without crying. I didn't even bother to hold it back. "The way you took care of me . . . The love you gave me — it's why I'm okay. It's part of who I am. I'll carry it with me the rest of my life. I love you, Mima." The words felt awkward but important.

She swallowed with effort. Her lips were so dry and cracked it was hard to look at them. She nodded, mostly with her eyes, somehow. "I love you, Jules." Her eyes fluttered closed.

Buddy patted me on the shoulder kindly, cuing me that I should let her sleep. When I glanced up at him, his chin quivered slightly — a sight so terrible I wished I hadn't seen it. As he adjusted her sheets, I slipped out.

"Do you have any fours?"

Luke and I had been playing card games for over an hour — part distraction, part reliving lost childhood, I supposed.

Luke squinted at me, leaning back against his bed. "You're cheating."

I snorted. "How would I cheat? What, do you think I have mirrors set up or something?"

He threw his cards down. "I forfeit. I don't play with witches."

I actually laughed — which felt amazing but also completely inappropriate. But when I risked a glance at Luke, he was smiling.

I picked his cards up off the rug and put the deck back together. "Okay, but you owe me seven cents."

"Man, you're brutal." He stood up. "I'm not sure I would have survived an entire life with you as my sister." He went over and picked through a mug of change on his desk. He turned and handed me a nickel and two pennies. "Don't spend it all in one place."

I grinned and slipped the coins into my front pocket.

He glanced toward the door. "I'm gonna go check. I'll be right back."

I nodded, the smile falling from my face. When he left, I stood up and shook out my leg—my foot was asleep. As I set the cards on his dresser, I spotted a photo—a small one in a silver frame. I picked it up. It was Luke and a girl. Not just any girl, but a beautiful redhead—possibly the one who kissed him after his recital. She was in a red dress, and both her arms were around Luke, who was in a suit. She smiled into the camera like she owned the world. His eyes were on her.

"Makayla."

I jumped, glancing up. "Oh my God, I'm sorry," I said, setting the photo down where I found it. "I wasn't snooping—"

"It's fine; it's just a picture." He walked over and shoved his fingers into his jeans pockets.

I swept my hair out of my face, flustered. "How is she?"

He had his eyes fixed on mine, and it made me forget what universe I lived in. "She's sleeping. The nurse is here. Dad handed me some money and told me to go get us some dinner." He smiled. "You're hungry, right?"

"I assume that's a rhetorical question," I said, a slight blush warming my cheeks.

"That's my girl." His smile melted me.

My phone dinged. I grabbed it from my purse on the floor. "My mom, probably."

It was. She was home, grabbing a bite, and heading to a meeting.

I glanced up at Luke. "She's okay, apparently." I quickly typed, *Good — thanks for letting me know.* <3

He tilted his head. "You were worried that she might . . ."

I hesitated, feeling caught out. I didn't want to imply my mother was unstable, that this was a thing I needed to worry about.

He stepped closer. "Jules. You know you can't be responsible . . ."

"I know." I wanted to touch him, to let him know I appreciated his concern, but everything I wanted to do seemed like maybe too much.

"Okay." He nodded. "So? Dinner. Does Mexican sound good?"

"I love Mexican. If it sounds good to you, it sounds good to me." I picked up my purse and slung it over my shoulder. *"Su casa es mi casa."*

He laughed softly and shook his head. I loved that. I loved that I could make him laugh.

In the car on the way to the restaurant, I took in one of my favorite sights: Luke behind the wheel, relaxed. His beautiful hands, his lean thighs, his command of the vehicle. The doubt surfaced in my mind that Gab ever looked at Daniel this way, but the comparison suffered. They were actually related. And they had always known each other. Was it so weird that things felt not exactly like that with Luke?

"Hey, how are you at driving?" he asked, glancing at me.

"Well, I haven't driven through any storefronts or mowed down any pedestrians yet."

He grinned. "Good enough for me. Will you drive home? I could really go for a margarita. Or three."

"Oh! Sure, no problem." But I was immediately nervous that I'd drive like a dolt and embarrass myself.

Luke pulled into the parking lot of a strip mall and found a space in front of a place called Juanita's Cantina. Though bland on the outside, the interior was warm and awash with colors. Mariachi music played, which I detested, but I'd listen to fingernails on a chalkboard accompanied by dental drills if I could do it in Luke's company.

We were seated in a booth near the back, a candle flickering on the table. I settled in and opened my menu. "What's good here?"

"I have a thing for the veggie enchiladas." He leaned forward and pointed to them on my menu. "They have spinach and they're in a cream sauce."

"Yum." I sat back as a busboy set a basket of chips and salsa in front of us.

"But they also have this insanely spicy shrimp thing. It's

in this red sauce with smoked chilies, and it is seriously hot."

I closed the menu. "There can't be anything on this menu that sounds as good as those two things. Get both and share?"

He closed his menu. "Girl after my own heart."

Well, yes. I was, in fact. Any way I could get it.

After he'd ordered a jumbo margarita (with salt, on the rocks), guacamole, and the entrées, we talked about everything but Mima and, man, did it feel good. It wasn't as if we could forget about it, but to be able to distract each other, safe in the knowledge that neither of us was truly forgetting . . . we had cried enough that day, and we'd no doubt cry tomorrow. This was a precious time-out from life.

So we talked about college. About childhood. About Gab and Leila. Music. Religion. Where we'd like to travel. If it were a date, it would be the best date I'd ever had — and probably the best I ever would have. It was meaningful; it had depth. We clicked. It was such a rare thing for me, this kind of connection. He was so right for me in so many ways. And yet so tragically wrong.

Luke was the best example of a boy, of a man, I'd ever encountered. He was sweet and thoughtful and respectful and gentle. God, he was so fucking *appealing*. Why did he have to be so much what I had always wanted and never found? Why did he have to be so perfect?

When we finished eating, Luke ordered a burrito to bring home to his dad and finished the last of his jumbo margarita.

His *second* jumbo margarita. They weren't kidding about "jumbo": they looked like small fishbowls on stems.

While we waited on the burrito, he tipped his head to the side, regarding me. I would have given anything to know what he was thinking. Did he find me attractive? Or was he marveling at how grown up his little sister was? Or simply having second thoughts about entrusting me behind the wheel?

After he paid the check, he helped me on with my coat, giving me a little hug from behind after my arms slid into the sleeves. I shivered, despite the added warmth.

Outside, a cool mist swirled and glittered like diamond dust under the sodium lights in the parking lot. We walked to the car, arm in arm, Luke making me laugh by singing a silly song about a mouse named Gerald and gingerbread men and a bike with a basket. He opened the driver's-side door with a flourish, and I climbed in. A moment later, he tumbled into the passenger seat and laid his head on my shoulder. "Thank you," he said.

"You don't have to thank me for anything," I said softly, quietly inhaling his fragrant hair. I couldn't resist.

"This is the best I've felt in days," he mumbled. "I wish it could stay like this."

Happiness swelled in me. "I know. It's okay. Hey. We'll go back, we'll hang out, maybe have a beer, have some laughs. Tomorrow is for tomorrow. Tonight is still tonight."

"Can I say something terrible?"

"Sure."

"I wish we'd never lost you."

My breath caught at those words. "That's not terrible."

"But it's like wishing your mother never got you back. It *is* wishing that."

"Yes, but . . ." I knew his wish *wasn't* terrible, even if it had a dark side. After all, how many times had I wished the same thing? "It's a wish born of love. I understand." I let myself pet his head, just a little, but when he didn't seem to mind, I kept going.

"We should go," he finally said.

"Right," I said, trying to keep the regret out of my voice. "Your dad's burrito is getting cold."

He sat up, his hair all flopping in the wrong direction.

"Seat belt," I reminded him.

"Right." He buckled up, and then, tiredly but cheerfully, he directed me home.

We pulled into the driveway and then traipsed up to the house arm and arm, both a little off-kilter for various reasons. Inside, he grabbed a couple of beers from the fridge. We tiptoed upstairs, and I went to Luke's room while he brought his dad the burrito.

He was back in no time. "Dad's asleep next to her with the TV on," he whispered. "Hey, do you need something to sleep in?"

Well, yes, there was that. A shirt probably would be easy

enough, but I was worried about the "bottoms" category. "What do you have that's loose and comfy?"

He opened a dresser drawer and started tossing things at me. "My Derrick Rose shirt is huge. . . . These pajama bottoms are pretty big. But ugly." He tossed me a pair of green-and-black plaid pants. I held them up. They did seem pretty big.

I disappeared to "my room" and changed. Chicago Bulls shirt and ugly plaid pants for the win.

I tapped lightly on Luke's open door. He'd put on music while I was gone. He was propped up against his headboard, drinking his beer, nodding to the beat.

Luke glanced up at me and smiled. "There you are."

"I look like a sporty Christmas tree," I said.

He laughed.

I picked up the other beer off the floor and sucked back almost half of it, eyes closed against the burn, then sat on the bed next to him. "You should probably drink some water," I said, worried he might end up with a hangover.

He tilted his head and watched me. "I'm so glad you found us," he said. "I never want to lose you again."

"I never want to lose you, either," I said weakly, thrown off-balance by the seriousness of his statement.

"Listen." He nodded in the direction of the speakers. "Listen to the lyrics."

I leaned back against the headboard next to him and tuned in to the dreamy acoustic sounds.

"Great Lake Swimmers," he said softly. "This is 'Song for the Angels.' It reminds me of you."

The music, almost ethereal, filled the room, buoying me, rocking me. I could see why the lyrics reminded him of me — especially the chorus, which was about feeling someone there, even when you don't see them or hear them. The idea that he had always been thinking of me made my chest feel full and warm. I finished my beer as I listened, then set the bottle on the floor.

I glanced at Luke. His eyes were closed. He must have been so overwhelmed, so exhausted. I watched his face, his relaxed mouth, the soft-looking lips whose draw confused me so badly. I thought about that good sweet heart of his, breaking inside him. It seemed that he lost every girl, every woman, he ever gave his heart to. And as much as I understood that meant the most important thing was my permanence, my stability, I struggled with the longing to be closer to him, the longing for more.

When he reached out a hand, without even opening his eyes, it was as if he had read my mind.

I took his hand, shifting sideways so I could watch him more closely. As the music washed over us, I began running my thumb softly over his knuckles.

I knew I was treading directly on top of a line, but the want . . . the want was so much. I leaned forward, my lips hovering inches from his. On some level, I knew it was the equivalent of a one-way ticket, if I crossed this line. But that moment, I couldn't bring myself to care. There was nothing I wanted more, no perspective or logic that outweighed my need to be close to him. I wanted to kiss him so badly, I was incapable of clear thought.

Before I could talk myself out of it, I closed my eyes and brushed his lips with mine, so, so lightly. And he made a sound, this breathy, tiny sound, and oh, God, it ping-ponged all over in me, lighting me up. Emboldened by his not pulling away, by the thrilling echo of his little sound, I touched his lips with mine again, and then . . . it was happening. We were kissing, and it was the softest, most tender thing I'd ever felt.

I met his pace, gentle and slow, almost delirious that this was real, that it was so, so good. Never had a kiss felt like this — not even remotely. When his tongue swept my lip, something exploded in me. I opened my mouth to his and pulled at his neck, his back, not wanting our lips to let go, not for a second, not for anything.

And then he abruptly broke away. "Oh, God." He pressed his hand to his eyes. "Oh my God. I'm so sorry!"

I blinked at the sudden withdrawal, my lips still hungry for his. "It's okay." I touched his shoulder lightly.

He jerked away, then scrambled off the bed and crossed the room. "Jesus," he muttered.

My stomach dropped. I scooted off the bed and went to him, wanting to hug him so much that I wound my fingers together to stop myself. "Luke, it's okay."

"It's not okay." Louder now. He scraped his fingers through his hair. "It's fucked up."

My chest tightened, and I clutched my arms to myself.

"You're supposed to be my little sister!" he cried. "All I wanted was to be your brother again. Not to be — to do *that* . . ." He made a disgusted face. "God, what would my parents think if they knew about this?" His hand went to his forehead. His fingers shook.

I wanted to remind him that we weren't related and that it's okay, but I finally understood: it wasn't about our DNA. It was about how he saw me, about who I was to him. It was about how he felt about me. And how he didn't feel.

I was sick over my actions, over my complete stupidity and recklessness. Part of me wanted to run and never look back, pretend I'd never met him. . . . But the thought of losing him entirely was more painful even than my shame. How could I have fucked things up so badly?

I had to salvage what I could. I had to somehow assure him we were okay. "It's not your fault," I told him. "*I* kissed *you*. You didn't do anything."

He remained turned away from me as he spoke. "I didn't stop it fast enough. I was caught off-guard and I wasn't thinking and —" Suddenly, he turned, his expression changing as my words sank in. "Why did you . . . ?" He lifted a hand, palm up. "Was that just an impulse? You don't, like, have feelings for me, do you?"

His expression was a knife in my heart. He looked horrified at the idea. If I said yes, if I admitted that not only had I kissed him with full knowledge of what I was doing, but that I was actually *in love* with him . . .

Then it would be over.

I couldn't lose him.

So I lied. "I don't know what I was thinking," I said, wringing my hands together. "Today was so overwhelming, and I was really tired, and I think the beer went to my head. . . . I'm sorry, Luke. I don't know why I did it."

He watched me for a minute, the doubt on his face plain. He turned away again, his eyes fixed on the floor. "It's late. You'd better get to bed. I'll drive you home in the morning."

The knife in my heart twisted. He wasn't going to soften or come around. Nothing I said would change the way he saw this. There was nothing for me to do.

I got up, opened the door quietly, and walked down the hall to his baby sister's bedroom.

Chapter 17

*T*he night was hell. I cried through most of it. I kept hoping Luke would knock on my door because he couldn't sleep either. That he'd say he was sorry for overreacting. The truth was, I wished for foolish things, too. I wished he'd come back and take me in his arms and say he'd been fighting these feelings, too, that he'd also been dreaming of that kiss. But of course I knew that wasn't going to happen. I hated myself for being so stupid.

As the minutes and then hours ticked past, I wished for smaller things. I wished he'd come and say that he understood, that it was just a weird blip, like I'd said, and that those things happen and we'd be okay. . . . But that didn't happen, either.

I felt sick with regret over what I'd done. Had I ruined things permanently? What if Luke couldn't ever look at me again without feeling disgusted?

What had I done?

As the first light of dawn filled the room, I thought about tiptoeing out of the house, finding a café or something, and calling Gab or my mom or someone to come get me. But the thought of not seeing Luke, of not fixing things, was as agonizing as the thought of seeing him was terrifying.

I lay on the bed for who knows how long, contemplating the terrible new reality. Finally, my bladder forced me into action. I got dressed and tiptoed to the bathroom, wondering if Luke was sleeping — his door was closed — and wondering how Mima was this morning.

I stared at myself in the bathroom mirror. I had never looked so ugly. My face was puffy, splotchy — my eyes were swollen halfway shut.

I hated myself. After a lifetime of being afraid to step a toe out of line, I had fucked up wildly, epically, egregiously. And the stakes had never been higher.

My stomach took a dive as I realized not just that I had crossed a line I shouldn't have crossed, but I did it when Luke was most vulnerable — with grief, with alcohol, with exhaustion. The idea that I took advantage of him sent a wave of nausea through me so fierce that I turned and knelt at the toilet. I threw up twice, leaving my throat burning as badly as my eyes.

When it passed, I stood up and rinsed my face. And then I remembered, fuck — I was stranded without a toothbrush. I rubbed toothpaste on my teeth with my finger and rinsed over and over, then went to my room and sat on the bed, waiting for something to happen.

After a few minutes, I was yawning so hard my eyes were tearing, so I tipped over and lay on my side. I was dreaming a series of random, frenzied scenes when I realized someone was saying my name. I opened my eyes to find Luke standing over me. He was dressed, and his hair was dripping wet. I sprang up to sitting.

"Hey. You ready to go?" His voice was low, almost gravelly, and he looked as wrecked as I felt. But what sent a chill through me was the fact that he wouldn't meet my eyes.

I lowered my feet to the floor. My sinuses stung with the need to cry; it was unbearable, the absence of his warmth and humor.

"What about Mima?" I asked softly. "Should . . . should I say good-bye?"

He hesitated. "She's asleep. Dad is, too. They might not be up for a while. I'll tell them you said good-bye."

So I picked up my things and followed him downstairs. I felt like I was being put out like yesterday's garbage. Worse, given Mima's condition and the way Luke seemed to feel toward me now, I realized I would likely never see her again, never say good-bye. Would he tell her what I'd done? My stomach seized at the idea that he'd tell his parents, make them think badly of me. I wanted to beg him not to, but I had no right to ask anything of him.

"Do you need to eat something?" he asked, slipping his shoes on by the front door.

My stomach was growling, but I still felt sick. Maybe something to settle it would help, but I couldn't eat now — not while he was like this. Even just his choice of words — did I *need* to eat rather than *want* — made clear his desire to get me out of there.

I shook my head, trying to hold in my tears. He handed me my jacket.

We stepped out into the cool, sunny morning. A fine mist covered the windows of his car, and he pulled a rag out of the trunk and wiped them down. The air smelled of cold, wet spring.

I got in and fastened my seat belt, shaking. I had never been so anxious, so miserable and fearful and distraught. I had to make something good happen during this car ride, had to carve out some hope of healing, of coming out okay.

But before I could even take a breath to speak, he reached out and turned on the stereo. And then he turned it up louder than usual. The message was clear.

The tears spilled over — I couldn't stop them. I was afraid he hated me. I wanted him to tell me we'd be okay, that it wasn't over. That I hadn't lost him, hadn't lost the best thing that had ever happened to me by being a silly, stupid, greedy fool.

Nothing was ever fucking enough for me. I always, always wanted what I didn't have.

The ride stretched interminably. I cast occasional glances at Luke, at the way the morning sun lit planes of his face through the window, lit the stubble on his chin. I loved him. I loved him in wrong ways, yes, but didn't I also love him in right ways? I loved who he was, how kind and funny and warm and good. Could I in time let go of the romantic feelings in favor of something more correct, more sustainable? If it meant not losing him? I *had* to. I wanted that chance.

Finally we reached Maplebrook. When he pulled into my driveway, he turned down the stereo and addressed the dashboard. "Look. I think it's best if we take some time."

This was another excruciating blow. I knew it was well within his rights to ask for this, but the thought of being cut off from him was unbearable. "Luke. Please. Can we just — can we just forget about what happened?"

But even as I said it, I knew I'd never forget about the most exquisite, amazing kiss of my lifetime.

"I'm sorry, Jules, I just . . . I can't deal with this right now." He looked out the window. "I really need to get back."

I started to cry. "I know things seem fucked up right now, but I still — I care about you all so much and . . . I don't think I could take losing you."

He blinked at his lap. "I just need some space right now."

What did that mean? I fought panic. "Can just tell me

how long you think . . ." I couldn't bring myself to finish that sentence.

The crushing, desperate humiliation of begging. Actually begging.

When he didn't answer right away, I knew I didn't want to wait to hear what he might say. My hand hit the door handle, and I stumbled out of the car. I closed the door behind me and made my way up the walk, praying he'd call after me. But no — he was already backing out of the driveway.

I closed the front door behind me and slid to the floor.

"Jules?" I heard my mom's footsteps in the hall. "I'm glad you're home so early! I have something to show you." She appeared from the hallway and her face fell. "What happened?" she asked, squatting down next to me. "Did she — is she gone?"

Oh, God. Of course that's what Mom would assume! I shook my head. "It's Luke. I fucked everything up."

Words tumbled out, tangled up in sobs. At some point my mom pulled me to the couch. And I told her everything.

Because among all the other things that had happened that weekend, I had learned that my mom had been in love once. And had fucked up many times. She was the one I wanted to tell. She wasn't perfect like Leila. She didn't have a safety net like Gab. She wasn't lost in an imaginary world like Eli. She was mostly, well, like me.

So I told her about my feelings for Luke and my idiotic actions and the aftermath.

And she didn't try to fix things, didn't tell me I was twisted or gross or stupid. She just listened. And the truth is, in those moments, I wouldn't have traded her for Gab's mom or Leila's mom or anyone's mom. By some miracle, my own mom was all I needed.

"The worst part is that I didn't get to say good-bye to Mima." I wiped my eyes with a tissue. "If I had known yesterday was the last time I'd see her . . ."

"You got a lot," my mom said gently, laying a hand on my arm. "You got more than a lot of us ever get."

My breath caught as I realized what she was referring to. Ethan. My father. Of course — she never got to say good-bye. "I'm sorry, Mom."

"No, don't be! That's not why I'm saying that. My point is you might never have met her again, but you had this time with her, and you got to reconnect and express your love and gratitude to her, and she got to tell you that she loved you. Did she tell you she loves you?" She smiled softly. "She told me."

That started me crying all over again.

"She said you were a gift to her once — 'like an angel.' And then you were a gift again, now. And you are — you're such a gift." And then her eyes welled up, too, and I leaned into her arms.

When I had cried myself out, she stood up. "Come on. I want to show you something." She pulled me by the arm into her studio. Propped up on her easel was a finished painting, track lights all pointed at it. "I did this painting nineteen years ago. For Ethan."

I took in the art in front of me, or tried. But to do so, I had to realize something:

I didn't know shit about my mom.

It was like finding out that the house you had lived in your whole life had secret passageways, and they led to amazing rooms that were filled with astonishing treasures. And all this time, those rooms were right there, but you never knew. "Where was this?" I asked.

"Wrapped up in the back of my closet. I finally took it out yesterday, after . . ." She stared at the painting, her face a mix of emotions. "Everything in this painting is something he loved or was fascinated by or obsessed with."

I stared at the painting. Contained within a few square feet of canvas was a veritable map to my father.

The painting itself was unlike anything I'd ever seen before. It seemed like several disparate scenes blended into one, like a number of paintings superimposed into one space that somehow just *worked*. The first thing that drew my eye was a psychedelically colored dragon near a green river that sparkled with silver (upon closer inspection I saw that the sparkles were actually stars). The dragon held a top hat in both hands, and a mermaid leaned out from the hat, her wavy blue hair trailing down the embankment and into the river. A dazzlingly white baby bassinet was cascading down the river of stars. There was a path paved with playing cards that led to a picnic table, where a tea party was set up. A rainbow arced from the sky into a teacup, where a little blond girl sat, gesturing as if talking to someone across the table, but there was no one there. The sky was the most beautiful one my mom had ever done — somehow a hazy swirl of lilacs and gold and wisps of bright coral. It almost seemed to be lit from behind. There was so much to take in. It was staggering how talented she'd been even then, at my age. And there was no question that it was a work of love, of complete devotion.

"The thing about your dad," she said, "is that he wanted magic to be real. The most important things about him are all in this painting."

"Mom. This is amazing."

She turned and hugged me so tightly and suddenly that it jarred me. I couldn't remember the last time she'd embraced me like that. Clearly something that she'd bottled up for years had been set free, and it meant everything to her to share it with me.

"You were there, you know," she told me, pulling back. "I was pregnant with you when I painted this."

"You were?" I gazed at the painting, imagining being inside the artist as she painted this. "Is that the significance of the bassinet?"

She nodded, smiling. "That's how I told him." She held her hands tightly at her chest. "I really wanted to believe we could have it all. Have a baby, be sober, and still have all the magic, all the art, have everything. And I wanted him to believe it, too." She stared at the painting, biting her lips together. "It sounds so naive, I know."

It sounded . . . lovely. And not at all like my mom. "How did he take it?" I asked softly. "That you were pregnant."

She turned to me, emotion creasing her brow. "Oh, he was so excited, Jules." She touched my hair. "So excited. And I was so . . . *hopeful.* I thought we were on the path to a perfect life. It felt like you were a *gift,* like you were the key to everything."

A gift. My throat tightened. My whole life, I'd felt like a curse.

I thought of her being my age and pregnant, and losing the person she loved most in the world — unexpectedly and in a horrible way. Being left alone with a baby and nothing else. Giving in to addiction, then losing even her child. Losing everything, literally everything.

She had suffered in ways I could barely even fathom.

Maybe Leila was right about my mother, about how huge it was, *is,* that she fought for me.

Maybe the narrative I was stuck in about my mother and myself was only one version of reality.

Chapter 18

I heard nothing from Luke that week, which I should have expected, but it decimated me anyway, every day, every hour. I'd try to focus all day on what it would mean to be his sister, and what I could do to show him that I could be that, show him that we'd be fine if he just gave it a chance. Then I'd lie in bed at night remembering the feel of his mouth, his mind-bendingly slow, soft kissing.

My days were composed of millions of agonizing, Lukeless moments, and there was nothing to do but push through them.

And what about Mima? Was I to assume that because I hadn't heard otherwise, Mima was still with us? Would Luke even contact me to let me know if she'd passed?

And the other agonizing thought: Had Luke told his parents about what had happened? If not, then how had he explained my abrupt departure? And if he had . . . did I disgust them, too? Was the whole family glad to be rid of me?

For the first time in what felt like maybe ever, I kind of clung to my mom. She was there for me in ways she never had been, and I depended on her in ways I never had.

Together, we started looking for an apartment, but the places we saw were ugly boxes: square and carpeted and plain. I thought of Luke's darling, idiosyncratic attic space. Would I ever get to visit him there again? It seemed unlikely, since he would be graduating soon. . . .

Over spring break I cat-sat Faustus while Gab sent me photos of herself at her top two East Coast contenders — Middlebury and Amherst.

Leila sent me pictures from their family vacation in Costa Rica. One in particular hit me in the heart, although I know she didn't realize it. It was a picture of her and Garrett in front of a waterfall. Garrett was on her back, clinging tightly to her, a big grin on his face.

How that little boy loved his sister.

How lucky they were.

Eli was a comfort, in his way. At least he understood playing the hand you were dealt, even if it wasn't the hand you would have chosen. He held his terrible job and worked his way toward the end of his great American novel. Late one night, he sent me a picture of Jay's napkin obituary, which he'd framed and put up on his wall next to his mother's. After, he texted me, *You also are objectively better than most humans.*

It made my eyes fill with tears. It was unlike Eli to say things like that. It was timely, as these days I mostly felt like a worthless, horrible person.

I went through the days in a numb fog, just trying to endure all the moments.

And then Gab came back from her trip to the East energized, organized, and galvanized. "Pack a bag," she said by way of greeting when I answered her call. "I have a plan."

"What is it?" I said. I was reading *The Heart Is a Lonely Hunter,* and I didn't want to put it down.

"You'll see."

An hour later she showed up and packed a bag for me herself, since I still had my nose in my book, randomly picking clothes and toiletries and dropping them in. She dragged me out to the car.

"Are we getting Leila?" I asked as she backed out.

"Yup."

"Just tell me what we're doing."

"Nope."

We lassoed Leila, who had just gotten back from the airport and was tanned and glowing. She climbed into the backseat, and Gab headed down Kingston and then turned on Summit, slowing in front of our grade school. She parked and jumped out of the car. "Come on!"

Leila and I followed her past the magnolias in front of the school, not yet in bloom, past the mulberry trees, which had yet to stain the sidewalks with their inky berries, and behind the school to the playground, which, at 4:30 on a Saturday, was deserted. The old play structure had been replaced with a new one — plastic, neon orange and blue.

"Good," Gab said, heading off to the right. "It's still here."

"The roundabout?" I asked.

"Get on," Gab said, grabbing one of the bars on the rudimentary carousel and waiting.

"Why are we doing this?" I asked, climbing on after Leila.

Gab didn't answer — she just held on to the bar and pushed.

"I'm probably going to puke," I told her as she ran alongside, spinning us faster and faster. She finally let go, then stood back and waited for the right time to jump on. She launched herself after a couple of rotations, lurching to her knees, then pulling herself up and standing in the center, facing us. "Who remembers something that happened on this roundabout?"

"I showed you guys the note I got from Jake Herman in second grade," Leila said, holding on to a bar with both hands as the world spun around us. The wind blew her hair into her face. "Where he told me I was pretty and if I wanted to be his girlfriend, I should wear a blue shirt the next day so he'd know the answer was yes."

I smiled. I remembered that. Mostly I remember being jealous, wishing I were as pretty as Leila so boys would be smitten with me and give me notes.

"Excellent," Gab said, turning her gaze to me. "Jules? Whatcha got?"

I sat down, wrapping both arms around a bar. "Fourth grade. I remember eating Wild Cherry Life Savers that Gab stole from Mrs. Silberman's desk."

"Yes." Gab grinned, lowering herself to a seated position as the ride began to slow. "And I remember Jules crying because Mrs. Hall yelled at her for touching the glitter after she told everyone not to. We fantasized about egging her car and booby-trapping her front porch."

"With a bucket of pig's blood," Leila added, "like in *Carrie*."

Gab pulled a little bag out of her hoodie pocket.

"What's that?" Leila's voice was sharp.

Gab stuffed something into a little ivory-colored pipe.

"Where did you get that?" Leila demanded. "What, are you, like, hooking up with drug dealers now?"

"Ha. Been there, done that," Gab said, pulling out a lighter.

I couldn't help smiling at that. "Did you get that from Byron when we were there?"

"No, I just got it. It's not like trying to find the lost ark of the fucking covenant. It's not hard to get."

"I'm not smoking that," Leila said as Gab held the flame to the bowl and sucked on it until it glowed. Gab passed me the bowl, holding her smoke.

I hesitated because of Leila's disapproval. And other things.

"Is pot really addictive?" I asked Gab, staring at the pipe. "Or is that just a scare tactic?"

"In my semi-professional opinion," she said, breathing out the smoke at last, "you are in very little danger of becoming a pot addict."

"But . . ."

"You're not your parents, Jules," she said softly. "And there is no gene for pot addiction that I'm aware of." Gab took another hit, then tipped her head back and stared at the sky, which was darkening. She exhaled through pursed lips. "We three have experienced many rites of passage together. Getting high is another rite of passage. I think we should do it together. Besides . . ." She grinned. "It's the perfect warm-up to our next stop."

She held out the pipe to me, a question. I thought back to the day we went to Lawrence, how much pot Gab had smoked, and she was okay. I didn't think one or two puffs would be the end of me. I took the pipe.

She peered over at it. "Is it still lit? Take a hit, let me see."

Keeping my eyes far from Leila, I took a puff.

"Here," Gab said, flicking the lighter and holding it over the bowl. "Try again."

This time the weed crackled and lit up red. My throat burned. I tried to hold it, but I made it about a half second before I started coughing.

"That's okay," Gab said softly. "You'll get it."

I looked at Leila, who was watching us, arms crossed, leaning on the vertical bar behind her.

Gab turned to Leila. "Your rite of passage can be saying no drugs."

"Shut up, Gab."

The sharp edge to her tone caught at me. It made me sad. It worried me.

I glanced at the sky, which was now a dark gray. "I don't think it's so wrong to try pot, Leila," I said. "It's not worse than alcohol, I don't think."

"You drink, and that's completely against the law," Gab pointed out. "So even if you spend the rest of your life coloring inside the lines, you're already an outlaw." She turned to me. "Here, try again."

I took another hit — a little less this time, so I was able to hold it. After a long moment, I let it out and lay flat on my back. Gab lay down next to me.

After a while, I said, "My head feels like there's helium in it."

"Cool," Gab said. "Not everyone gets high the first time."

I heard Leila shift. "I guess it's true, I'm already an outlaw."

Gab sat up and helped Leila take a hit. She did better than I did, holding it longer before coughing.

There wasn't enough room between bars for Leila to lie down next to us, so she lay the opposite way, tucking her head between ours, her feet facing the other direction. No one talked for a while. There was a rumble of thunder in the distance, and Gab started to laugh.

"What's so funny?" I asked.

"A thunderstorm is coming, and we're out in the middle of an open area on a large metal structure."

Leila snorted, and that started me up. Soon I was laughing so hard, I had to sit up. I crawled off the edge of the roundabout and pulled on the bar to spin it. I caught each bar as it came by, pushing them, rotating it faster. I went to jump back on and hit my head on one of the bars as I lost my footing and fell down, which made me laugh more. I crawled over to them and resumed my position, watching the sky spin above us.

"This is so cool," Leila said.

Thunk. A huge drop of water hit my eye. A moment later, another hit my hand. "You guys? It's raining."

As it started coming down harder, none of us moved. We just lay there getting wet, still spinning slowly.

A loud crack of thunder nearby jerked us out of our stupor.

"Come on," Gab said, rolling over and climbing off. "Let's go to the play structure."

We ran after her over the freshly laid mulch, which stank of manure and wet bark. As we got soaked with rain, the sky lit up. "Did you see that?" I called to them. "That lightning looked like a human skeleton! Did you see?"

Gab climbed up the wooden rungs and ducked under the roof of the encased portion of the structure, near the tube slide. We all squeezed in there, the rain needling off the plastic overhead.

"Anyone want another hit?" Gab yelled.

"I don't think I need one," I said.

Leila reached out her hand, and Gab held the lighter for her.

"Where are we going next?" I asked. It was getting darker, and the cracks of thunder seemed to get closer each time. "This better be about food."

"Where was our favorite place to eat when we were younger?" Gab asked.

"Mario's?" I asked. The sudden thought of hot, cheesy pizza made me ravenous.

"No, before that."

"Taco Bell," Leila said.

"Ding, ding, ding!" Gab said. "Next, we slay the munchies the way we did when we were ten."

"Technically, we didn't have the munchies when we were ten," Leila said. "But, oh my God — I could go for some tacos. Or that new nacho burrito thing! With lots of sauce. And extra sour cream."

So when the rain died down, Gab took our baked, hungry asses to Taco Bell, where we ate an embarrassing amount of fake Mexican food with about a thousand packets of sauces. The stubble-bearded slacker behind the counter side-eyed us the whole time. He could probably smell the weed.

"Our favorite movie in junior high: go!" Gab scooped some shredded cheese and diced tomatoes from a taco wrapper with her fingers and slurped them up.

"*Pitch Perfect*?" I asked.

Gab pointed at me with one hand and pointed to her nose with the other. "Next stop, Lou's Quikmart for . . ." She looked at us expectantly.

Leila's hand darted up, as if she were in a classroom. "SweeTarts!"

"And Peanut M&M's," I added.

"You guys are good at this," Gab said, wiping her mouth and tossing her napkin down on her tray. "Let's hit it."

Half an hour later, Leila and I were cozied up in Gab's basement, candy poured into bowls, movie cued up. Gab's parents were out for the evening, which was convenient to the next part of her plan. She came down the stairs, holding out a green liquor bottle for us to inspect.

"Absinthe?" Leila said. "What's that?"

I looked at the label, which featured a dreamy rendition

of the "green fairy." "It was really popular with artists and writers in the late eighteen hundreds and early nineteen hundreds. Supposedly it brought, like, visions. Van Gogh and Oscar Wilde were big absinthe drinkers. I don't know who else — Eli probably knows." I took the bottle and examined it more closely. "I thought it was illegal."

"Don't know, don't care," Gab said, squeezing in between Leila and me.

I opened the bottle and sniffed. "It smells intense. Like medicine. But licorice-y. Holy shit, Gab, this is a hundred and twenty-three proof!"

Leila reached for the bottle. "Ooh, I like the smell."

"I think you're supposed to add water or sugar or something," I said. "I could ask Eli."

"Then we'd have to invite him over, wouldn't we?" Gab said, pulling out her phone and opening a browser window. "No offense to Eli, but tonight is about us three."

"Yeah, what is this, Gab?" I asked. "Is this, like, renewing our vows or something?"

She smiled. "Something like that." She got up and sat on the coffee table so she could face us. "Here's the thing. This fall, we're all going our separate ways. We've never not been together. You guys have been one of the biggest parts of my entire life."

A sinking feeling hit me. This day, this evening . . . it felt so good. I didn't want to think about the future.

"Visiting that last round of schools," Gab said. "It made

it real. You know? We're really going to be apart. We might only see each other a few times a year. It just — it hit me. Oh, Jules. Don't cry — we're going to be okay."

I wiped my eyes. "It's really going to happen, isn't it." It's funny how you can know things without really understanding them.

"I know people don't always stay friends forever," Gab went on, "but losing you guys would be like losing a part of myself. I would not be okay, ever. So I'm hereby pledging thee my troth, both of you." She reached for our hands. "Even if I sometimes do stupid shit that freaks you out or makes you mad." This was addressed to Leila. "And even if I'm not always perfect about keeping in touch and reminding you guys that I love you. I do. Both of you. And I always will. Okay?"

She leaned forward for a group hug.

"I'll always love you guys, too," I said.

"Me, too," Leila said.

"Now," Gab said into our hair, "let's have some absinthe."

We tried to do it according to instructions we found online, but we didn't have the right utensils or sugar cubes. So we just added some sugar and water, and it was pretty good. Gab liked it least, probably because she hated licorice. Leila and I liked the taste, though, and the high-proof thing was no joke. We were seriously buzzed after one glass.

"How much more do you think we'd have to drink to see the green fairy?" Gab asked, staring at the TV screen. "Do you think that's really a thing?" We were watching the movie on mute, which wasn't a problem because we knew the dialogue by heart.

"It's probably a myth," Leila said.

We fell into a companionable, buzzed silence. I examined an etched pink bowl from a side table, wondering if it was Depression glass. I was pretty sure it was — 1930s, then.

After a little while, Leila turned to me. "Hey. Any word on . . . ?" She let the sentence dangle, unfinished.

I shook my head.

"Have you heard from Luke at all?" Gab asked.

I shook my head again.

Leila sighed.

I glanced at her, puzzled. "What?"

"I don't know," Leila said, cringing a little. "It's just . . . it's pretty messed up, what happened."

I realized, with a sinking feeling, what she was referring to.

"Hey," Gab said to Leila. "Don't do that."

Leila glanced at me. "I'm sorry. I mean, I know you're not technically related, but . . ." Leila shrugged. "I mean, that's how he saw you."

Why hadn't Leila said any of this when I'd first told them what had happened? Were the pot and alcohol making her more honest? What else did she secretly think about me?

"Lei! Don't judge her." Gab put a protective arm around me.

Leila said, "I'm not judging! I just can't help thinking of it from Luke's point of view."

As her words stung me, Leila and Gab exchanged a tense glance. I felt bad that my stupid actions were causing friction between them, as if all the grief I'd caused myself wasn't enough. I said, "Hey, could we maybe not talk about it? I just want to forget it ever happened."

Gab jumped up. "I'm getting more absinthe." She disappeared up the stairs.

Leila turned to me. "I'm sorry for the way that sounded. I'm really not judging you."

Well, yes. She was. But I could never stay mad at either of them for very long. "Have you decided about college?" I asked her, changing the subject.

She leaned her head back on the sofa. "I think Michigan. It's the biggest. I want a big pond. I want to disappear."

"Beautiful girls can't disappear, Leila. It's one of the laws of the universe."

"Well, then, I guess you can't disappear, either." She smiled at me.

When Gab came back with replenished drinks, she pushed in between us and sat down. She unmuted the TV, so we watched for a while, sipping our drinks.

"Can I tell you guys something?" Gab said. "About Byron?"

"Of course," I said, turning to face her. I tucked my legs up and leaned against the arm of the sofa.

She stared at her lap. "The thing is . . . well, it wasn't that great."

My eyes met Leila's, but she quickly looked away.

"Maybe he just wasn't very good at it," I said.

"He wasn't," Gab said. "It was kind of rushed and, I don't know. I mean, I didn't even . . ." She rolled her eyes. "You know. It was kind of a letdown." She glanced down. "I was embarrassed to tell you."

"Maybe you just weren't into him," Leila said. "I'm not being a priss, I swear, but when you do it with someone you're really into, and they're really into you, it's different."

I knew that was true — for me, anyway. My kiss with Luke, compared to every other kiss I'd ever had, was proof enough of that. But I didn't want to talk about it. I was trying to forget my broken heart, not trample on it.

I glanced up, tuned in to a sudden silence. Gab was staring at Leila.

"You speak from experience?" Gab asked.

"Well, yeah."

Gab raised her eyebrows. "You and Brett?"

Leila gestured and made a *duh* face. "I mean, we went out for eight months."

I sat frozen, my eyes going back and forth between them. This felt unprecedented. To Gab, too, apparently. But the awkwardness — and my own curiosity — soon got the best of me. "How many times did you do it?" I asked, leaning forward to see around Gab.

Leila shrugged. "I don't know. A lot."

"Where?"

"His house, mostly. In the car a few times."

Gab lurched off the sofa and stomped upstairs.

Leila sighed, her shoulders slumping. "Great."

I felt caught. I didn't want to make anything worse, but . . . I was kind of stunned that Leila had never told me she'd had sex — and shocked that she'd withheld it from Gab. For what, a year? How could Leila think Gab wouldn't be upset? Maybe it was the booze, because finally the question spilled out: "Why didn't you tell us?"

She glanced at me. "Probably because I was never drunk before."

I couldn't help smiling, which made her crack, and then we were both giggling. And then, clutching our dangerous drinks, we scooted closer and Leila told me about her sex-capades with Brett, which were much more colorful than I would have imagined.

"Are you going to tell Gab this stuff?" I thought about her upstairs — how hurt she must be.

Leila shrugged, looking uncomfortable.

There was a time when I would have been happy that one of them shared something with me and not the other.

But that time was gone. I needed Gab and Leila to be okay. I needed this stability.

A wave of guilt washed over me as I thought of Luke, who had also needed some stability. I could have given it to him. Instead, I blew it all up.

I had never regretted anything more.

When at last we tiptoed upstairs, Gab's door was closed, her lights off. I thought about checking on her, but the closed door and darkness seemed like a clear message. So Leila and I slipped into Daniel's room to go to sleep, sharing the full-size bed.

I was almost asleep when my phone dinged. I glanced at it, then shot up to sitting when I saw it was Luke.

Hands shaking, I opened the message.

Just wanted to let you know that we lost Mom early yesterday morning. It was peaceful. Dad and I were with her.

My hand went to my mouth. *No.* I knew this was coming, of course. And yet. I wasn't prepared.

Mima. A mother of mine, at one time. Someone who had loved me was gone from this earth. I would never see her again.

I typed back: *Oh, Luke. I can't find the words. I'm so, so sorry. Can I do anything?*

He wrote back: *I'm okay. Makayla's here.*

My chest tightened.

Of course he'd want her there. She was practically a member of the family. Mima had loved her. She was an adult and beautiful and capable. Not a clueless, insecure high-school girl with zero judgment or moral compass.

My phone buzzed again: *Mom will be buried tomorrow in a private service. I just wanted you to know.*

A private service? As in, I wasn't welcome? Was that what he was saying? I wanted to be there — for him, yes, but also for Buddy, and to pay my respects to Mima. Was Makayla going? As loath as I was to see her and Luke together, perhaps that meant that the definition of "private" could include me? Makayla had only been Luke's girlfriend; I had been Mima's *child*. Luke himself had said, *She was your mother, too.* I gathered my courage and messaged: *Would it be all right if I came?*

An eternity passed, then finally: *I think it would be best if you didn't. I'll pass your condolences to Dad, if you want.*

His words were an anvil to my chest. That he didn't want me there, didn't want me included — it was more than I could bear. But what was I going to do, argue? About his mother's funeral? I had no choice in this matter.

I wrote: *Okay. You'll be in my thoughts, and if there's anything at all I can do, please let me know?*

It was almost incomprehensible that one stupid move on my part had caused all this destruction, that one lapse in judgment had rendered me a persona non grata. Before I did what I did, *I* was the one he wanted with him. *I* was the one he might have sought out for comfort.

I hated myself for countless reasons — not least of which was the realization that I was as upset about losing Luke as I was about Mima's death.

My crying woke Leila, who sat up and hugged me when I told her. But when she went back to sleep, I lay on my side, awake. Miserable.

I had no idea I was capable of sinking so low.

Chapter 19

*I*n the morning, I told Gab that Mima had died and Luke didn't want me to come. And I just wanted to be alone. She drove both Leila and me home. None of us spoke.

So much for Gab's renewal of vows.

I found my mom in the kitchen, making coffee. She glanced up. "What's wrong?"

"She died."

"Oh," she whispered, turning and leaning back against the counter. "I'm sorry. Did — did Luke call you?"

I sank into my chair at the table. "He messaged me. He doesn't want me to come to the funeral. He says it's private." I lowered my head onto my arms.

She sighed heavily. "Jules." A moment later, I felt her hand on my back. "I'm sorry. That sucks."

I appreciated that she didn't try to talk me out of feeling bad or make excuses or criticize Luke or anything. I didn't want pep talks or platitudes. I just wanted to be heard, just wanted the acknowledgment that yes, it sucked.

"We'll send a card," my mom said. "I know you're worried about him."

I rested my head on the table, eyes closed, listening to the sounds of her making coffee. Mug from the cabinet. Pouring. The click of the fake creamer lid. The clatter of her spoon against the mug. What mug was she using now that she'd broken NO SOUP?

I lifted my head. It was a black mug with white bold lettering: DEATH BEFORE DECAF. I hadn't seen it before. Where had it come from?

"Mom?" I asked, sitting up. "Who did you spend the night with? That night."

She stiffened visibly, her back to me. "He's a friend."

He. Wow.

"Where'd you meet him?" I picked at the old tape on the table. "At a meeting?"

She laughed and turned to me. "No. He was . . ."

When she hesitated, I watched her curiously. "Oh my God — you're blushing!"

She sighed and sat down next to me with her coffee. I could smell the amaretto creamer, almond-y and sweet. "Remember that time you walked into my studio? When I had a model?"

My eyes bulged. *"The yam? You're dating the yam?"*

She tilted her head. "The yam?"

"He was uncircumcised!"

"Jules!" She put a hand over her mouth and turned away from me. I couldn't believe how embarrassed she was.

"So what does he do?" I asked. "Apart from dangle his bits in public."

"Oh my God, stop it!" She whacked me in the arm with the back of her hand. "He's an art history teacher at the college. We became friends. He's asked me out a couple of times, but I don't want to date him."

"Why not? Do you not find him attractive?" I tried to remember his face, but it was useless; all I could think was *yam*. But it felt weird, asking her that question. I never thought of my mom that way.

"No, I do," she said, putting her hair behind her ears. "He's definitely attractive. But young. Younger than me, I mean."

"How much younger?"

She bit her thumbnail, fidgeting. "A handful of years. A generous handful." She sipped her coffee.

"So he's, like, thirty?"

"Not quite."

"Oh my God." My hands went to my face. "He's in his *twenties*?"

She cringed, nodded.

Luke was in his twenties. Jesus.

"Does he know how old you are?" I asked.

She looked offended. "Jeez, Jules, it's not like I'm eighty. Yes, he knows how old I am. And thirty-six is not actually that old. Anyway, we're not really dating."

"But you spent the night with him. How did that work?"

She gestured with one hand. "We watched TV. We got a pizza. We laughed. He showed me pictures of his daughter."

"He has a kid?"

She nodded. "He's divorced. His daughter is eight."

"Wow. Okay, so then what?"

"And then suddenly it was two in the morning, and I was about to keel over. He offered me his bed like a gentleman, but I slept on the sofa. In the morning he made pancakes and joked that it was the best sexless date he'd ever had."

My eyebrows went up.

"And that's when I knew we could be friends. Because he let it be funny. Because we could laugh about it." She sipped her coffee. "He's a really nice guy. His name is Casey." She looked at me curiously. "Didn't you think he was cute?"

I shrugged an apology. "Not gonna lie. All I remember is his dick."

She rolled her eyes and grabbed her phone. "Here." She turned the phone to me.

Whoa. Yeah, he was cute. He had short blond hair and a blond beard. Cornflower-blue eyes. Amazing smile. He was wearing a T-shirt and he had muscles. "Um, Mom?"

"I know, right?" She put a hand to her eyes. "So not what I need right now."

I squinted at her. "Why? I mean, you've been alone my whole life. You're young. You're attractive. You're interesting. You've finally met someone who's really into art and really into you. . . . What's the problem?"

She blew a breath out, thinking. "It just feels risky. I feel like I've been trying my whole life to get my shit together. And I still don't have my shit together. And I have no one to fall back on but myself." She raised her eyebrows at me as she lifted her mug for a sip. "Sometimes it's better to play it safe."

I wanted to tell her to follow her heart. But the thing was, maybe she was right. I wished I'd played it safe with Luke. She could end up fucking wrecked, like me. And at least my wreckage didn't cost me my sobriety. I suppose one rough break for her could be deadly.

She stood up to top off her coffee. "I'm seeing a few apartments this afternoon," she said, "if you want to come."

"Are they all boxes?"

"Probably." She stirred creamer into her coffee and glanced at me. "There's something I could consider, but I don't think it probably works."

"What is it?"

She sat back down. "There's a three-to-eleven shift at the library. It pays more than my shift. Not a ton, but it would be two, maybe three hundred dollars a month more."

"Three-to-eleven shift would suck."

"Not for me."

Then it hit me. *Duh.* "Your painting," I said. "My God, you'd have all the daylight."

"Yup."

"You have to do it."

She shook her head. "Jules, think about it. I'd barely see you in the morning, I'd be gone before you got home from school, and I'd get home after you went to bed. We'd never see each other. And these are your last months at home!"

"We'd see each other on weekends. And we'll see each other more over the summer; you've seen my schedule at Tina's. And I can get myself dinner — I usually cook anyway."

She chewed her lip, watching me. "You really wouldn't mind? You're not just saying that? You'd be alone all the time."

"I really wouldn't mind. It would change your whole life, being able to paint. It doesn't make sense to sacrifice your dream just to eat Hamburger fucking Helper with me at night."

She turned her eyes to her lap. "I feel like I'd just be putting another nail in the bad-mother coffin. I should be here for you."

"Mom." I leaned toward her, forcing her to look at me. "I don't need you to be *here*. I just need you to *be* here. Just, to love me."

Her shoulders went slack. "Of course I love you. I've always loved you."

"Well . . ." I shrugged, feeling a sting in my eyes. "Maybe love me louder."

She smiled. "I can do that." She took a breath. "I've always felt sort of . . . like a fraud, I guess. Like I don't deserve you. Impostor syndrome. And I've been waiting your whole life for you to figure it out and call me on it." She blinked rapidly. "I thought . . . I thought that when you found your foster family, that would be it. You'd see a family more like Gab's or Leila's and you'd—" Her voice broke. "You'd think you got a bum deal, and you'd never forgive me for it."

"Oh, Mom." I hugged her, but even as I did, I thought of how close I'd come to this very thing—to blaming her for depriving me of a better life. I still struggled with thoughts about that other universe, but I was working to make peace with this version of reality. "If I'd grown up with the Margolises, I would have spent my whole life wondering about my real mother."

A choked sound came out of her. She hugged me tighter.

"Look," I said, pulling back to look at her. "Nobody's perfect. Nobody's life is perfect. But . . . we're okay." I tried to smile. "And, you know, you kind of have your whole life ahead of you yourself. You're in your thirties! You should start living the life you want, doing what you want to do. I'm all grown-up. And I turned out okay, right?"

She looked at me with an expression that gave me goose bumps. Love. It was what love looks like. "You turned out amazing."

I smiled. "Now, what are you going to do about that late shift?"

Excitement washed over her face. "It would be incredible to be able to paint every day. I mean, if we found an apartment with a room that had good daylight —"

"We can! We can find a place. You can take the three-to-eleven shift and earn more. And if you can paint more, you'll sell your work — I know you will. You're so talented. And we'll have that extra six thousand dollars from this lease. We should just expand the stupid budget and find the perfect place!"

"But what about college? I still worry."

"Mom, we've done the math, and my college counselor at school has done the math. Between grants, scholarships, and work study, I should be fine. I'll save my earnings this summer for books and stuff. It'll be okay. Really." I almost joked that when times were hard, I at least was the ramen queen. But I couldn't joke about ramen.

I didn't want to think about ramen.

She reached for her phone. "You're positive about this? Because I'm going to try to get that shift. If you're sure."

"I am totally sure."

She smiled as she poked in a number. She walked off toward her studio, and a few seconds later I heard her talking to her boss. It was a short call. She came back still smiling.

"It's mine. I can start a week from Monday." She clasped

her hands together. "I'm excited for us to see apartments today."

Today.

Today, in the wee hours, I found out that Mima died. And that Luke still wanted nothing to do with me. I hadn't even begun to process all that.

"Would you mind if I didn't go today?" I asked, feeling bad for dampening her good mood.

But Mom surprised me yet again. "Oh my gosh, of course you don't want to go. You've had such a rough day. Do you just want to crash? I'll take pictures and show you later, okay?"

"Crashing sounds good," I admitted.

But before I did that, I went over for one more hug.

Chapter 20

*W*hen I finally did join my mom in the apartment search, it did little to lift my spirits. The endless depressing string of dark and boxy cookie-cutter apartments was beyond demoralizing. But then a small miracle came from an unlikely source: Eli.

I was at Laroche's one afternoon, drowning my apartment sorrows in a chocolate croissant, when Eli asked if we'd seen the rental on Linden.

And so it was that we found an impossibly charming vintage coach house on a pretty street right in Eli's neighborhood, surrounded by gorgeous old homes and beautiful gardens and mature trees. The enormous bank of north windows convinced my mom that we could splurge a little — the coach house cost a little more than the brown box, but it was worth it.

The rental was above a three-car garage that originally was a carriage house — an idea that excited me and sparked my imagination. It had two tiny bedrooms with slanted ceilings and low sidewalls. A good-sized living room with built-in bookcases. A bathroom with vintage fixtures and a claw-foot tub. Radiators. A small but functional kitchen that shared space with the living room. And — best of all — a screened porch! And the windows — the windows! The light was glorious. I hoped my mother's days of wrecking skies were over.

We wrote a check for the security deposit and started packing. Things filled the days, and the days passed.

But, even with the passage of time, I could not get over what had happened with Luke. I missed him dreadfully and thought of him constantly. I fantasized about reaching out to him — I had composed dozens of messages I'd never send. Knowing he really didn't want to hear from me — and worse, imagining Makayla there looking over his shoulder — was enough to keep me from pulling the trigger. I dreamed of him often. In some of the dreams, he called and everything was warm and wonderful and okay. But he didn't call. And nothing was okay.

Sometimes the dreams were awful — he said terrible things or I did terrible things. In one, I walked in on him having sex with Makayla. It was confusing and graphic and passionate. I woke up crying, in an agony of jealousy I wasn't sure was all dream or part real.

In another dream, it was me having sex with him. And it was tragically good sex. There was amazing kissing. There were sounds; there were feelings. There was that particular brand of often-elusive dream ecstasy. I woke up out of breath, still coasting on the relief of an ache I had tried (and failed) to repress.

I didn't know how to reach out to him. I didn't know how I'd survive it if he rejected me, if he never talked to me again. The way he cared about me . . . he would have loved me always, I was sure. If I hadn't fucked it up.

Another wrecking ball to my heart came when Eli found and sent Mima's obituary to me. Even though it was stupid to imagine I might be included in the "survived by" list, it stung a little that I wasn't. Mima was my mother almost and sort of. I felt so excluded from all of them. (Petty though it was, I was glad Makayla *wasn't* mentioned. It would have been too much.) But did they even consider listing me? Would I ever know if Luke had told them what I did, what had happened between us? If he'd told both of them, and that was the final image Mima ever had of me . . . The thought made me want to crawl into a hole.

I sometimes almost wished I'd never found him. The adage "better to have loved and lost than never to have loved at all"? Not convinced. Not even a little. But part of me still clung to the hope that I *hadn't* lost him, that we were just "taking some time," though how *much* time I didn't know. The limbo was almost worse than knowing for sure we were over. At least then, I could stop hoping, stop waiting for the shoe to fall. At least then, I could try to move on.

That weekend, Daniel came home to celebrate his thirtieth birthday. I took a break from packing to join them.

Leila didn't come. She had a family thing, she said. I hoped that was the truth.

As the Wassermans put up streamers, made Daniel's favorite deviled eggs, and got an early start on the champagne, I couldn't help watching Gab with a keen eye. She was so excited he was coming home. When he pulled up outside with a cheerful beep of his rental car horn, she rushed out the door. I stood watching at the dining-room window, a jumble of emotions crashing through me. He hugged her, grinning, lifting her off the ground, even though she was at least two inches taller than him. When he put her down, they fell into chatter immediately as he pulled his duffel bag out of the car. They walked back up to the house, his arm slung around her shoulders.

It made my heart ache. But it was beautiful.

I watched them throughout the party, feeling shy and very much on the outside. I studied them for cues, constructing a paradigm for how I might be, or might have been, with Luke. "This is my sister, Jules," he might introduce me to people. "My brother, Luke, is a brilliant pianist," I might say to friends in college. Maybe he'd even visit me. Maybe he'd hug me and pick me up and who knows — maybe other people would envy *me*.

Those were the thoughts I tried to focus on. Not his mouth. Not how slow and dizzying his kisses were. Not how good he smelled. Not those.

That night, envy still swirling in me over Gab and Daniel, I decided to take a chance and reach out to Luke. If he ignored me, it would just be more of the same. If he told me he really didn't want to see me again, then I could move on. If he was receptive, then that would be good (*really* good), but it seemed like anything that might happen was no worse than the situation I was already in.

It was almost eleven when I finally, after endlessly struggling for words, fired off a message: *Hey, Luke. I hope it's okay that I'm reaching out — I know you suggested we take some time, which I respect, but I've been thinking about you and hoping you're doing okay.*

I lay in bed, holding the phone to my chest, praying for it to ding. Minutes passed, each one a deeper stab into my heart. I'd been foolish to think that his ignoring me wouldn't be any worse than the status quo. I was already feeling devastated by the passage of four little minutes.

But then my phone sounded, sending adrenaline surging through me. *Let it be Luke,* I prayed.

And it was. But I set my phone down quickly, because

what if it was bad? What if he asked me to not contact him again? My hands shook while I finally raised the screen to read his words.

Your timing is impeccable. I was just thinking about you.

Did I dare to hope it was for positive reasons? Before I could think of responding, another message came: *How are you doing?*

It was such a simple question, but it seemed cause for hope. If he were going to banish me forever, he wouldn't ask how I was doing. Right?

I'm okay, I wrote. *Sad about Mima, though. Worried about you. And so desperately sorry for what happened.*

I watched my screen, heart thumping, until his reply came: *I'm sorry, too. I'm sorry I didn't stop it right away, and I'm sorry for being so hard on you. Those were not my best moments.*

Tears welled in my eyes at his kindness. This was going somewhere. I wrote: *Nothing was your fault, Luke. I don't blame you for being jarred or upset. It was a dumb thing I did, and I wish I could turn back time and undo it. What I really want is the chance to be the sister you've missed.*

He wrote: *Do you really feel that way? I'm not clear on what exactly your feelings are. I'm sorry — this is awkward.*

It was more than awkward; it was precarious, dangerous. If I told him the truth, he might not want to see me again. And I couldn't bear that. I could get over the feelings I had for him. In time, surely I could. But to salvage our relationship, I had to convince him now.

I had drafted countless messages that I never sent, and now I resurrected the best lines, the sentiments I felt had the best chance of actually making things better. I wrote:

Luke. What happened was a mistake. I think it was the confusion of so much intense emotion — so many years apart, all that lost closeness. I think the longing to be close to you again caused me to take that mixed-up wrong turn. But we can move past that — I know we can. You're the only brother I have. And I am the only sister you have. Without you, who will screen my boyfriends for approval? Who will help me through rough spots in college? Who will tease me about my appetite? And without me, who will teach you how to cook? And stop you from letting your future wife choose a dumb china pattern? ☺

He wrote, *Those are good points.* ☺

Hope rose in my chest.

He added, *I would love it if we could get things right again. I've missed you.*

His words warmed me to the marrow. *I missed you, too.*

We messaged a little while longer. It felt like we were nearly us again — it felt good. And I knew for sure Luke felt the same way when he suggested getting together.

We made a plan for me to visit the first weekend in May.

* * *

The days passed in a flurry of activity—school, packing, and daydreaming about the kind of close, enduring relationship Luke and I would build.

In the meantime, Gab and Leila chose their college. Yes, singular. In the end they both decided on University of Michigan. They joked about it, all "what are the odds," but there was nothing surprising about it to me. The attachment between them ran deep, both ways. I don't think Leila was any more capable of living without Gab than Gab was of living without Leila. They were a proton and a neutron, bonded together by nuclear force.

For me, though, it was the end of an era, and nothing was certain. But certainty was often an illusion, I was beginning to understand. We had no choice but to live without it.

But there were upsides to uncertainty, too. The massive financial aid package from Beloit was the best kind of surprise. We weighed it against U of I, which was still a little cheaper all told, but my mother wanted me to have my dream as much as I wanted her to have hers. We decided to let a visit to Beloit make the decision. It was barely a two-hour drive—even closer than U of I, to my mother's delight. She took a day off work, and we hit the road.

And I fell in love.

The campus boasted expansive green lawns, winding walkways, Victorian Gothic architecture . . . it was the actual dream. It was the oldest continuously operated college in Wisconsin, founded when Wisconsin was still a territory.

The oldest. And, as tiny as it was, it had two museums! One was a museum of anthropology, which I had begun to consider as a possible major. They even offered a minor in museum studies — and study-abroad opportunities in places so far from home they seemed impossible.

It was while we were in the anthropological museum, looking at Japanese ceremonial prayer sticks, that my mother turned me to her and told me that I must, *must,* study abroad — that she'd work two jobs to pay for it if she had to. "I've never been more than a few hundred miles from home," she told me, her tone urgent. "I want you to see more. I want you to have it all."

And immediately, I thought of the painting she'd done for my father. She'd wanted him to have it all, too. She had more generosity and goodness in her heart than I'd ever known — and if it weren't for the rough year we'd had, I might never have figured that out. It was my anger at her and the damage to our relationship that had shown me we had the thing I'd always envied in my friends' relationships with their families: permanence. Dependability. We would always be mother and daughter. She loved me; she was there for me — I knew that now. As we stood hugging in front of the Ainu exhibits, I was beginning to understand that in an increasing number of ways, she was the mother I'd always wanted.

We stopped for lunch at a café on campus and enjoyed coffee, panini, and live guitar music (courtesy of an adorable guy whom I rather fervently hoped was not a graduating senior). After, we wandered around the campus. The building called Middle College — a Wisconsin historical landmark — was built in 1847. It seemed impossible that I would soon have the right to appropriate some of that history for myself, as a Beloit student.

And it felt so good, the anticipation, the happiness, that I gave myself a pardon for my problem of wanting more. More, in this case, seemed like a fine thing.

Chapter 21

*M*oving day arrived with rain, which my mother claimed was auspicious. Around the neighborhood, daffodils receded as tulips advanced. At the new apartment, we'd be trading a magnolia for a couple of dogwoods and lilacs (and more windows to enjoy them from, not to mention the screened porch). Mom's "friend" Casey rented a truck and corralled a couple of his friends to help us on moving day. My mother's anti-hoarding sensibilities made for an easy move — I didn't even take Gab and Leila up on their offer to cancel their scheduled activities to help us. Five of us and a truck was more than enough.

As my mom and I looked around our dusty, emptied-out house for the last time, I said it felt like we should have some meaningful parting words. "Good riddance?" she'd quipped. She was in a good mood. The combination of her new work hours, the new place, and, I suspected, Casey were doing wonders for her. And maybe the incipient closeness between us didn't hurt, either.

By noon we were moved in, and by bedtime we were mostly unpacked. Things would be looking nice in no time. My bedroom already looked great, especially after I plugged in the lamp I'd found. It was a score from Tina's, more treasure than thrift — a Tiffany-style desk lamp with dragonflies and flowers in a mosaic of colors. I loved its warm glow. It went perfectly with the small Oriental-style rug we'd nabbed at IKEA, along with some dark espresso-stained bookshelves that Casey and his friends assembled for me. Despite their modern source, if you looked at them just right, they almost had a vintage feel — my whole room was taking on the sensibility of another era. I filled the shelves with books — old editions of important novels, books about classic architecture, travel books I'd collected from places I dreamed of visiting.

Casey hung my mom's painting for me — the one she'd made for my dad when she was pregnant with me. He affixed a picture light to the top to illuminate it. It looked spectacular.

After making my bed and placing my button pillow at the headboard, I was ready to call it a day. All I wanted was a hot soak in that deep Victorian tub before bed. But on my way to draw the bath, Gab called.

"Hey, are you moved in?"

"Yes," I said. "I'm exhausted. About to climb into the tub. I might never come out."

"Oh, okay. Never mind, then." She sounded disappointed.

"What? What is it?"

"I was just — I thought maybe I'd stop by to talk for a few minutes. But if it's not a good time . . ."

I thought longingly of my bed, but if Gab needed me, then there was no question. I told her to give me half an hour for a bath and then come on by.

Soaking in hot water up to my chin was divine. I had dumped in some lavender Epsom salt my mom had already unpacked and put away under the gingham skirt attached to the pedestal sink, and I probably would've stayed submerged until I was a total prune if Gab weren't about to show up. Reluctantly, I pulled the plug from the drain and was just drying off when I heard my mom let Gab in. I wrapped my towel around myself, then padded into my bedroom.

"This place is awesome," Gab said, coming into my room. "It's so you. Do you love it?"

She hugged me, and I hugged her back with one arm so I could hold on to my towel.

"I do. I finally love my house, and it happens right as I'm moving out." I smiled. "I'm hoping I can re-create some of this vibe in my dorm room, though."

Gab's eye was caught by the painting on the wall. "Oh my God, this is amazing. This is the one you told me about?"

"Yeah. I had no idea my mom could paint like that." I crossed to my dresser and pulled open a drawer to get underwear and pajamas. "I'm going to change. Be right back."

She gave me a funny look as I slipped out to the bathroom to change. When I came back in, I asked her, "So what's going on?" I dug through a box, looking for my hair stuff.

She sat down on my bed, watching me. "How come you won't change in front of me?"

I blinked, caught off-guard. "Um, because I'm modest?" I could feel my face getting hot.

"Do you change in front of Leila?"

"No. I don't undress in front of anyone. I have a whole ridiculous method of changing in the locker room, too. I know it's stupid, but . . . why? Why is it a thing?" I sat in my desk chair, crossing my arms. Now I was self-conscious.

"You started getting all private about it when we were, like, fourteen," Gab pressed.

"Well, yeah. I mean, isn't that a normal age to start to feel shy about your body?"

"That, or . . ."

"Or what?"

She pursed her lips and looked at the floor. "Leila really never told you what happened?"

"What are you talking about?"

She squirmed. "There was just—this thing happened.

Once. With Leila." She wouldn't look at me. "For a while I sort of had . . . feelings for her."

"Feelings?" I said carefully. I came over and sat next to her on the bed. "Like, *feelings* feelings?" My brain scrambled to catch up. Gab was attracted to girls? And to Leila in particular?

"Kind of." She avoided my eyes. "I . . . I did something I shouldn't have. And things have never really been the same since then." Her eyes met mine, but they quickly flitted away. "And after that, you got funny about taking off your clothes in front of me. So I thought maybe she told you, and maybe you thought . . ."

"Gab." I laid a hand on her back. "I had no idea. The way I am has nothing to do with you. And Leila never said a word to me about — whatever happened between you."

She turned away, her lips trembling. "It was so stupid."

"What happened? Do you want to tell me?"

She stared at her lap. "It was the summer after eighth grade. Remember how her family and mine sometimes went to Door County together?"

I did remember, mostly because it made me so jealous. Jealous that I didn't have a family that could fit in, jealous that we couldn't afford even small vacations, jealous over the time they spent together without me.

"We had spent the day on the lake, swimming and everything, and she was sunburned, and she was wearing this little white nightgown." She covered her face. "And I'd been having all these ridiculous, like, thoughts about her . . ."

I nodded, but she wasn't looking at me.

"She was lying on my bed, and we were talking, and I just . . . I couldn't stop looking at — oh, God, this is too embarrassing." She continued to avoid my eyes. "Anyway, I . . . I tried to kiss her."

My mind spun. How could I not have known about this? How have we all been going along like this for years, after that? It hurt to realize that they shared even more things I was kept on the outside of, but it was a familiar ache and an increasingly dull one.

"Well, you can imagine how she reacted. She jerked away and looked at me like I was sick." She sat up and wiped her eyes. "God, it was such a fucking stupid thing to do."

I was struck with the similarities between what we'd done — Gab with Leila, and me with Luke. I realized that must have been behind Leila's reaction to what happened between Luke and me — her remark: *Think of it from Luke's point of view.* It was all so much to digest. "Were you . . . in love with her?"

She shrugged. "I guess I was, a little. It felt like that."

I hesitated. "Are you in love with her now?"

She shook her head. "No. But I just can't get past it. Because I don't think *she* can get past it. That's why she never told me she was having sex with Brett. She doesn't want to talk to me about anything having to do with sex."

310

"Did you never talk about it? About what happened?"

She gestured helplessly. "At first, she was all, 'How could you not tell me you like girls? How could you not tell me you had feelings . . . ?' But I was so mortified by her response that I didn't know how to talk about it. And really, they were feelings that meant something I hadn't really found the language for yet, and it wasn't all just about Leila. You know?"

"So," I said slowly, "are you . . ."

She shook her head. "I'm not a lesbian. But I guess I might be a little . . . bi. I don't know — none of those terms feels right. Blech. I hate words." She turned to look at me. "Does it bother you? If I'm bi or whatever?"

"Of course it doesn't bother me. Don't be silly." I hugged her. "I love you, Gab. I don't care who you're attracted to. I can't believe you even worried about that!"

And it was true, of course — it didn't matter one whit to me whom Gab was into. But my mind still reeled as I tried to reframe everything I thought I knew about my best friends. All in a moment, nothing was as it seemed.

"Does your mom know?" I asked her.

"About what happened?" She shook her head. "I didn't tell anyone. Except Daniel."

I paused at this, my thoughts derailed at the idea of having a brother you were so close to, you told him things you told no one else. Not even your best friends. Not even your wonderful, supportive, open-minded shrink parents. Could it ever be that way for Luke and me?

Gab gave me a wry smile. "I told my mom a while ago that I was pretty sure I wasn't straight. You want to know what she said?"

I nodded, smiling in anticipation.

"She said, 'Oh goody.'"

I shook my head, laughing. That sounded totally like her mom.

"I kid you not. She said, 'Oh goody,' and then she said, 'I don't care what gender you date, but I wouldn't mind if they were Jewish.'"

I laughed. "M.O.T.," I said, then immediately had a pang about almost having been one. "Your mom's awesome."

"She is," Gab said. "But I'm so sad about Leila." She leaned on me a little. "I miss the way we used to be."

"But a lot of the time you two seem exactly how you used to be," I said.

"But it's always there. I feel it there, all the time."

I felt alienated from them in new ways — harder ways. I had been in the dark for years about important events between them. But what hurt more was seeing Gab's pain, and knowing she'd felt this way for a long time.

She hugged me. "You're the best, Jules. And I shouldn't have worried about telling you. I mean, you love Eli, and he's not even that nice."

I laughed. That was a true thing. I did love Eli. It was an imbalanced love, and I was okay with that.

"Thanks for letting me come over," she said, getting up. "I know you just wanted to go to bed. Thank you for saying yes."

"Of course."

"You always say yes," she said, and for a moment it looked like she might cry again. "It's one of the things I love most about you."

I smiled warmly at her. "I love you, too, Gab."

After she left, my mom came into my room. "Wow, it looks great in here!" She turned and tilted her head at the painting. "This looks pretty good with the light."

I turned and propped my head on my elbow. "It looks amazing."

She grinned, then sat on my bed and played with a lock of my hair — a gesture that, a few months ago, would have felt weird, awkward. "So what do you think of Casey?"

I smiled. "He seems like a good guy. It was really nice of him to help us move. And build my shelves."

She nodded.

"Are you thinking about . . ." I raised my eyebrows a few times.

She looked sort of sheepish. "Maybe. He invited me to Galena next weekend. Not just us," she rushed to add. "A group of us. Artists. Penelope Chavez has an exhibit in one of the galleries."

I nodded. "You gonna go?"

"What would you think if I did?"

I rolled my eyes. "Mom, you don't need my permission. But if you want it, you have it."

"You wouldn't mind?"

"Are you kidding? Think about it. Teenager with the house to herself for a whole weekend." I had to laugh at the alarmed expression that overtook her face. "I'm going to see Luke on Saturday," I reminded her. "So I won't even be home."

"Right." She bit her lip and glanced at me. "Maybe I'll go."

"Go! Don't be silly." I yawned and closed my eyes. "Could you brush my teeth for me? I'm too tired to get up."

She pulled me up, and I stumbled off toward the bathroom. The only toothpaste I could find was her weird fennel toothpaste. The taste reminded me of the absinthe we'd had that night we'd slept at Gab's, and I had a pang, thinking of all we had shared over the years, all the sleepovers and events and laughter and tears. We had grown up together, and now we were venturing out into the world. And I was happy about the changes ahead — hopeful and excited. But my heart hurt a little to realize that this part of our lives would soon be nothing more than memories.

Chapter 22

*S*aturday. Luke day. We were meeting at the house in Milwaukee to make the drive more manageable for me. Buddy, he told me, was visiting his sister in Arizona. It brought a flutter in my belly, the idea of our being alone, that I immediately tried to vanquish. Instead, I wondered for the umpteenth time if Buddy knew what had happened. Sometimes I was sure he must. Otherwise, why did he never reach out to me? He was grieving, yes, but it had been weeks. . . . Didn't he want to be in touch with me? Or was it just Mima who had missed me, who had wanted to know me?

Mom let me take the car, since she was off to Galena with her friends anyway. It only took about an hour to get there, a little over, and I was thrilled to see not only Luke's cute blue car in the driveway, but him sitting on the back of it, watching me as I pulled in.

When I climbed out of the car, we both hesitated. "Hey," I finally said, reaching out to give him a fairly quick friendly-but-not-too-friendly hug, which he returned at an equal level. His damp, freshly shampooed hair was cool against my cheek, and it smelled so goddamned good. *Ignore,* I coached myself. "You doing okay?" I asked softly.

He stepped back and shrugged. "One day at a time. How are you?"

I nodded. "I'm okay."

We went inside. "I realize you're probably starving," Luke said, closing the door behind me. He grinned. "So, do you want choice A or choice B?"

I smiled. "Do I even get to know what they are?" I followed him to the kitchen and stopped short when I saw the banquette, remembering the other time I'd walked in, and Mima was sitting there, trembling at the thrill of seeing me again.

"What is it?" Luke tilted his head, his brows furrowed. "Jules?"

I breathed, my hands pressed against my solar plexus. "I just . . ." I glanced at him, then turned my eyes to the floor. "I just was remembering the first time I saw Mima. She was sitting right there."

At the mention of her, his face changed, and I was

overcome with regret. "I'm sorry," I whispered. "I was just caught off-guard."

He took a deep breath, and then offered up a wobbly smile.

I felt terrible — I arrive and immediately upset him. "So what are these lunch options?" I ask, hoping to put us back on happier ground.

He raised his eyebrows. "Okay. Ready?"

I nodded. "Yes sir."

"We can either go out to lunch — I know a few places you'd totally lose your shit over. Or . . ." He smiled and pointed to a basket on the kitchen counter.

"*Iron Chef Ramen!*" He opened the basket and gestured toward it. "You have thirty minutes and you must use at least four ingredients in the basket!"

I started to laugh. "That's *Chopped,* not *Iron Chef.*"

"Whatever."

I looked from him to the basket and back. "Can I survey the ingredients before I decide?" I asked.

"Be my guest."

I peered into the basket. "Really, Luke? Jelly beans?"

He shrugged. "Creativity is the hallmark of a true Iron Chef."

"Mm-hm." I set the jelly beans on the counter and poked around in the basket. I pulled out the remaining ingredients: Ramen, of course. Spam. American cheese. An apple. An onion. Peanut butter. Oreos. Tomato paste. Tabasco sauce. Celery. "You've got to be kidding," I said, staring at my choices.

"Hey, if you're not up to the challenge, there's no shame in that," Luke needled.

I snorted. "Oh, I can rock this challenge. But . . ." I grinned mischievously at him. "You have to compete against me."

His jaw dropped. "You wouldn't."

I bounced a little. "You have to! Otherwise there's no challenge. C'mon, it'll be fun!"

He squinted at me. "You have a very twisted idea of fun," he muttered.

I laughed, but the word "twisted" caught at me. It was a reminder of what I'd done, what we were trying to move past.

If Luke realized how it hit me, he didn't show it. "Okay, fine. But when you have to taste my creation, you're going to be sorry."

"That seems certain."

I eyed the motley assortment of ingredients. "How do we decide who gets what?"

"By arm wrestling, of course."

I laughed again, but I felt an overwhelming rush of love. I struggled to contain the vastness of my feelings for him. I prayed it was just a matter of adjusting, that down the road I'd get used to how wonderful he was. Maybe things would get more real — maybe he'd even annoy me sometimes, like a sibling. I couldn't decide if that sounded depressing or like the greatest possible thing ever.

I pushed aside the feelings. "Rock, paper, scissors."

My paper beat his rock, so I went first, grabbing the Spam. Then we took turns choosing from the remaining ingredients, which was kind of pointless because he chose the worst ingredients each time. It didn't take me long to work out that if he couldn't beat me — which we both knew he couldn't — he would make me eat the most foul concoction imaginable.

Nonetheless, I took the battle seriously. I was glad he'd found something for us to focus on, something fun to do. I had been so nervous driving up, worried it would be awkward and terrible.

With my thirty minutes, I produced a spicy Spam and cheese ramen, topped with a chopped apple and celery salad. It was actually undeniably good.

I took the obligatory bite of Luke's purplish-gray overly sweet and oniony glop, topped with Oreo crumbs. "It is possible I've never tasted anything worse in my life," I told him, struggling to get the bite down.

He grinned. "I guess you win."

"I guess I do."

We took the winning ramen to the banquette and ate, the afternoon sun splashing in on us. "This is seriously good," Luke said, swirling cheesy noodles onto his fork. "Well, we can have Oreos for dessert. When you were little, you were a fool for Oreos." He glanced up at me, a teasing expression on his face. "All the tookies."

"Tell me more," I said softly. This was what we needed — to get back into that brother-sister frame of mind. "Tell me everything."

We watched more videos. Luke narrated hilariously, teased me mercilessly. It reminded me of Daniel and Gab. I wished Luke had a nickname for me, the way Daniel had dubbed Gab *Gumby*. I tried to remember to call Luke *Duke*. I wanted a past with him; I wanted inside jokes; I wanted shared memories. I wanted, more than anything, to lay the ground-work for a future between us.

But several clips in, there was Mima. And neither of us was prepared for it. At the start of the video, it was dark. She whispered to the camera, *This is what happens when I don't keep an eye on Luke after I put him to bed.* There was some rustling and then the camera lit dimly on Luke, in bed, sound asleep, his baby sister sitting up next to him, grinning.

What are you doing, Jules? Mima whispered on camera.

Little Jules shook her head hard, grinning.

Did Luke take you out of your crib? Mima whispered.

Little Jules shook her head, then nodded.

The camera zoomed in on Luke, asleep, mouth slightly ajar. Then back to me.

Say good night to Luke, Jules, Mima whispered.

Nigh-nigh, Duke, little Jules said softly, then reached up her arms to Mima.

Come here, you little monkey, she whispered, and the camera went dark.

"I'd forgotten," Luke said, his eyes welled with tears. "I'd forgotten she called you that. And seeing her healthy again . . ." Luke turned away and wiped his eyes. "I'm sorry."

"Don't be sorry," I said. "Don't apologize for grieving."

"It's just . . . When is it gonna get easier?"

"It will," I said softly, laying a tentative hand on his shoulder. I was nervous about touching him, but at this moment, it seemed cold not to. "It won't always be this raw."

He turned his bright eyes to me. "Promise?"

I nodded. "I promise."

I wanted to hug him, but I knew I had to be careful. The cues had to come from him.

"I forgot I used to steal you," he said, grinning weakly. "God, Jules. I've missed you so much."

My chest felt like it might burst with joy. I longed for the memories I could not retrieve, longed to remember things *with* him, but it was blessing enough to see them, to hear about them. And to hear him say he'd missed me . . . I didn't know if he meant he'd missed me his whole life, or if he meant since we last saw each other. I kind of hoped the latter, but I'd take either or both.

Out the bank of windows to the backyard, the sun sank

in the sky, filtering in blinding gold streams through all the glorious trees — a sight I would have seen a thousand times or more in a different version of my life.

This had almost been home. Almost.

After a moment, he said, "You should go soon, before it gets dark."

My heart sank, but I covered it with a smile. "We may be poor, but our car does have headlights."

He laughed. "Even so. I'll worry about you driving on the highway at night. And I have to get ready for dinner soon anyway."

I blinked. "Dinner?"

"Yeah, I have plans with Makayla."

My stomach dropped to my feet. "Oh . . ." I fumbled with what that might mean. *Don't ask, don't ask.* "Are you guys back together?"

He sighed. "It's complicated. We're not together, but . . . you know. It's a hard time. She loved my mom a lot, too." His expression softened, and I thought perhaps he was going to amend that to *our mom.* Instead, he said, "She's really been there for me these past weeks."

His words swirled in a confusing sting. "I would have been here for you," I said.

Only when the words were out did I realize how they sounded. They sounded petulant and weirdly competitive. Like I thought I might have had the role a lover had filled.

But he eyed me kindly, thankfully not hearing it that

way. "I know that. And I'm sorry again that I didn't handle that better, that I needed space."

It occurred to me that my actions might have pushed him and Makayla back together. That if it hadn't been for my kiss, I might have been the one comforting him at Mima's service. I might have been enough for him.

I stood up. "I have to go to the bathroom." I moved quickly across the house. I was starting to shake. I slipped into the tiny pink room and closed the door softly behind me.

What was wrong with me? I wanted to cry. It didn't matter if he dated or didn't date Makayla! I was supposed to be his sister, not his girlfriend. Why was I so fucking blind with jealousy?

I sat down on the closed toilet and held my face in my hands. I had to pull myself together. Could he tell I was upset? I hoped he saw my reactions as normal sibling stuff: hurt that he'd cut me out of his life, a desire to be included in moments that were important to him and to the family. Not twisted jealousy over things I could never have.

I stared at the floor through blurred eyes, willing myself to be okay, be normal. I took some toilet paper off the roll and blew my nose. When I reached over to toss out the tissue, a flash of red in the wastebasket caught my eye.

I hesitated long enough to wonder if I wanted to be the creepy girl who snooped through people's garbage. But apparently I did, because something about that flash of red was pulling at me.

I slid the wastebasket over and took a closer look. And then I recoiled.

The flash of red in the bottom of the wastebasket . . . it was a condom wrapper, poking out from a bundle of toilet paper.

My heart started to pound. I was pretty fucking sure it wasn't Buddy's, so that meant only one thing. Luke had had sex — probably quite recently. It had to have been Makayla. He wasn't exactly the casual hookup type, and he'd made it clear they'd been spending time together. But downstairs?? Had they been in such a hurry, so desperate for each other, that they couldn't make it up to his room? Oh my God, had they done it *on the couch,* right where we were just sitting?

I pushed the wastebasket back into place, my hands shaking. I tried to slow down the chaos in my head — the rapid fire of confusion and hurt and anxiety and jealousy that assembled into three clear words: *How could he?*

I knew my feelings were unjustified. I knew that Luke only wanted me as a sister, nothing more. But knowing that and seeing the evidence of his intimacy with someone else right in front of my face. . . . Those were two different things.

And suddenly I knew: I couldn't do this. I couldn't pretend I only felt sisterly about Luke, couldn't force myself to "get over" these feelings. I loved Luke in the wrong ways. I wanted him with all my heart, with all my being. I wanted him in all the ways — impossible ways. I couldn't bear the idea of seeing him with Makayla, or anyone else, for that matter. I wanted him to want me as much as I wanted him, in the *ways* I wanted him.

And he never would.

I'd been kidding myself, thinking I could somehow magically downgrade my feelings for him, pack the wrong ones away and keep the rest. I couldn't. I was totally, completely, stupidly in love with him.

And I had to get out of there.

I pulled myself together, washed my hands, and finally emerged. I found Luke in the kitchen, cleaning up from the ramen. *You should help clean up,* I thought guiltily. *You should be helpful and good.*

"I'm going to go," I said instead.

He glanced at me. "Hey. Are you okay?"

"Yeah!" I said it too fast, too loudly.

He walked over to me. "Jules? What's going on?"

Shit. If he was too gentle and kind and caring, I'd cry. I blinked rapidly and shook my head.

The concern on his face was plain. He would hug me if I let him. But I didn't want him to touch me like a brother. I wanted him to touch me like he touched her. Images sprang into my head — images I didn't want: Luke on the couch between Makayla's legs, pushing into her . . . his face in the throes of pleasure . . . calling out her name when he came. . . .

"Hey," he said softly. "What's wrong?"

God, he really did love me. I wanted that. I wanted to be important to him, wanted him to hurt when I was hurting. But I also wanted . . .

More.

I stepped back. "I'm sorry. This is just . . . harder than I expected."

He tilted his head. "You mean . . . Mom?"

I nodded, grateful for the face-saving excuse, though I felt guilty for latching on to it. "I just didn't realize how overwhelming this would be. And I'm really tired, and you're right, I should go before it gets too dark." I mustered up a smile. "Have a good time tonight. I'll talk to you soon."

I turned and beelined for the front door as he called out after me. But I couldn't stop, not even to let him say goodbye. If I stopped now, I'd dissolve into a giant puddle of tears, and he'd figure out how depraved and dishonest I was.

I flung myself into the car, trying futilely not to cry. I needed to drive, but my eyes were blurred with tears. I pulled out my phone, wondering who to reach out to. I glanced up when there was motion in my peripheral vision. A car had pulled into the driveway next to mine. Its driver regarded me curiously.

No. Just when you think things can't get any worse, the universe springs the unthinkable on you.

Makayla. She opened her door and climbed out. I turned my head away, but not before I managed to take her in. Her curly red hair spilling down from a messy updo. Her faded jeans and clingy white shirt. She was beautiful and slender and put-together and just completely unbearable. I hated her.

I started the car and jammed it into Reverse. It lurched as I stepped on the gas before the transmission had even registered the gear change. I backed into the street without even checking for traffic — thank God the street was clear, as getting into a fender bender at the foot of Luke's driveway in front of Makayla the Perfect would have killed me.

I made it maybe three blocks before I had to pull over. I couldn't see. I wasn't okay.

I parked on a side street and dug in the glove compartment for tissues and tried to pull myself together — at least for long enough to get myself home, where I could bury myself under the covers.

Just my luck — a minivan slowed and pulled into the driveway I was parked near, its inhabitants all eyeing me curiously. I turned my face away and grabbed my phone, pretending to be absorbed.

There was a message alert, and I didn't know if I could bear to look. I could just imagine what it might say: *Jules, Makayla said you were sobbing in the driveway, and then you snubbed her and took off like a bat out of hell.* He wouldn't say that, I knew. But he might pose a kinder, more concerned version.

But it wasn't from Luke. It was from Gab. It was a selfie of her and Leila, arm and arm, grinning. The message: *All is well.*

And just like that, the atomic world had returned to balance. Somehow, clearly, they had worked their shit out. I had wanted and needed this to happen, and I was relieved it had. And the timing of it . . . I wanted to see it as a sign that anything was fixable, no matter how broken it seemed — that maybe Luke and I could be okay, too. But Gab and Leila had a whole lifetime of love and trust to work from. Luke and I had fragmented, slippery little slivers of time.

I wrote back, *I am so, so glad, you guys. But, um. Something happened.*

Gab wrote, *What is it? Are you okay?*

I wrote, *No. Not okay. I am pulled over on a side street in Milwaukee, trying to stop crying.*

My phone rang immediately. I answered and blurted it all out without even saying hello. "And I know I'm supposed to be his sister and I know I shouldn't care if he does the dirty with Makayla fifty times a day and I know I'm fucked up, so you don't have to say it," I concluded with a rough hiccup.

"Oh my God, you poor thing," Gab said.

It was Leila's reaction that I worried about more, but when she said, "Oh, sweetie — that must be so hard," I cried with relief.

Gab instructed me on what to do. "Breathe slowly. Wipe

your eyes. When you're ready to drive, put your phone on speaker, and Lei and I will distract and entertain you all the way home."

"Not home," Leila said. "Gab's house. Just come straight to us, okay?"

I nodded. "Yes. Okay."

And I did. I drove carefully, focusing on the warmth and sureness of the voices I knew better than any others in all the world, returning to my nucleus. When I finally got there, they continued to hold me up, to get me through.

I also, at Gab's urging, had a long talk with her mom. She made me feel normal, validated. She helped me find all the truth I contained inside me. All the truth, and also the accountability and acceptance and goodness and hope.

There was nothing wrong with me, she assured me. It wasn't my fault I fell in love with Luke. Feelings are feelings, she said, and they're not right or wrong. They were inconvenient, though, and, yes, they posed a lot of challenges to the possibility of a future of any sort with Luke.

But after talking with her, I allowed myself to hope. I was still struggling to accept what could never be, but I had hopes for what maybe *could* be, in time. I considered my largely one-sided relationship with Eli, and how somehow that was enough for me. I thought of how I'd come to appreciate my mom, even though she was a far cry from perfect.

And Gab's and Leila's friendships were priceless to me. I had come to accept how it was with the three of us, that I'd never be an equal part. I knew fuck-all about chemistry, but I did remember learning this: *Almost all of the mass in an atom is made up from the protons and neutrons in the nucleus with a very small contribution from the orbiting electrons.*

Why doesn't the electron ultimately fall into the nucleus? We had talked about this in class — a discussion that quickly sailed over my head. So I don't know why it doesn't. It just doesn't. But if I had to be an electron, I could never want for a better nucleus than Gab and Leila. I would orbit them faithfully for the rest of my life, if they'd let me.

And so maybe with Luke, too, I could settle for less than everything. Because having a brother — a real brother — would be huge. It would be amazing.

Someday it would, just maybe, be enough.

Chapter 23

I plugged along, one day at a time, trying to get to that elusive better place. Gab's mom coached me through my first post-meltdown message to Luke. She helped me to strike the right tone, to connect as sincerely and honestly as I could without oversharing and burdening him with feelings that he didn't need to know about, feelings that I was working to let go of.

After that we kept in semi-regular contact, and he was good about reaching out if I'd been quiet. The steady, unchanging nature of his feelings for me, once a source of frustration, was now a lifeline. I was grateful.

So I tried to keep up the banter we were so good at — the easy, warm repartee we'd shared when I last saw him, the teasing and laughter over ramen. I tried to walk the line — enough contact to keep us connected, but not so much I spiraled into jealousy and desperation. It wasn't easy. But there was no other path forward.

On Mother's Day weekend, Casey reserved Mom for dinner and a movie Saturday night. On Sunday he would come for breakfast, and then we'd take Mom to the Art Institute. But with Saturday night free, I invited Gab and Leila for dinner.

I threw open the windows and puttered around in the kitchen all afternoon. It was the kind of day only May can pull off — softly breezy and fragrant. I splurged and made a creamy, lemony pasta with asparagus and shrimp. For dessert, I baked shortcakes and topped them with fresh strawberries and whipped cream. It made me happy, cooking and feeding people I loved. It affirmed solid, immutable things I was coming to know about myself — namely that food, friends, and home would always be important to me. And Gab's and Leila's enthusiasm and praise for my cooking filled my heart.

When we finished eating, we settled into the living room. The door to the screened porch was open, and slivers of warm light from the setting sun beamed in and made glowing puddles on the rug and hardwood floor. Leila was wearing shorts, and her legs-for-days never ceased to draw my envy. I thought of what had happened between Gab and her. Leila was such a sweet and beautiful creature. It wasn't hard to understand someone — anyone — being attracted to her. I imagined she'd fall in love in college, marry soon after, and have beautiful blond children who looked just like their mama. If she did, I hoped they'd call me Aunt Jules. And Gab, Aunt Gab.

Or maybe she'd become CEO of some amazing children's charity or something. Or maybe she'd surprise us all and become something we couldn't predict. I kind of liked that idea, too. Maybe I was learning to live with the unknowable. That would be useful. That would be good.

"Southern Comfort," Gab said, brandishing another unlikely-to-be-missed bottle of booze from her parents' cabinet and setting it on the coffee table.

"Make sure that leaves with you," I said to Gab. The last thing I needed was my mom coming home and finding me with empty bottles of the hard stuff. I supposed at some point she'd realize I have the occasional drink, but it wasn't on my agenda for Mother's Day weekend.

"I promise," Gab said. She cued up a Janis Joplin documentary on the TV. "Apparently SoCo was Janis's drink."

"Who's Janis Joplin?" Leila asked, settling on the floor in front of the TV.

"She was this amazing singer in the sixties." Gab fiddled with the remote. "She died at twenty-seven of an overdose. Booze and heroin. We will salute her tonight."

"Oh my God, Gab." Leila put her hands to her head. "Tell me you didn't get heroin."

"Oh hell no," Gab said. "Just weed."

I filled glasses with ice, and Gab poured inadvisable quantities of Southern Comfort into our glasses, topped with some ginger ale. I still worried about alcohol, but less than I used to. If I didn't drink or even think about it for weeks, that seemed promising. Maybe I could keep up this moderate approach through college and into adulthood. I'd probably be worrying and negotiating my rules for the rest of my life, but maybe I could make peace with that.

Gab started the documentary. We would end up turning it down and ignoring it anyway — we always did. Apart from in theaters, we always ended up talking over movies and then being surprised to see the ending credits rolling on the screen.

We talked about college — Gab and Leila would room together, of course. I wondered what it would be like, when they started making different friends and their circles expanded. They had just mended a pretty significant fracture . . . I imagined — hoped — that they would always be able to hold steady when there were cracks.

But now, here they were, joking about using the sock signal when they have bed guests in their dorm room. Gab gleefully recounted her sexperience with Byron, making fun of their awkward sexual moves the same way she used to mock her and Leila's basketball moves.

"Sex with men is grossly overrated." She raised her

eyebrows mischievously. "I have high hopes for women, though. Do you think Sammie Brock is a possibility or am I just dreaming?"

Leila's attempted smile was losing to a confused expression. "You like Sammie Brock?"

Gab's eyes flitted over both of us, then away. "I don't know. I think about her. It's probably just another passing crush. In the long parade of crushes." She stared into her glass. "Is that, like, weird for you to hear about?"

"Kind of," Leila said.

Gab's expression twisted. "I shouldn't have said anyth —"

"I mean," Leila interrupted, "I don't even know who you *like*," she said softly. "That's messed up."

Gab glanced up at Leila, and for a tense moment I didn't know if she was angry or hopeful. "Yeah, I guess it kind of is," she said quietly.

I exhaled. *Hopeful.*

Gab said, "After what happened . . . I don't know — I was afraid to bring up anything that reminded you of it. If it weren't for that, I would have told you."

"Gab," Leila said. "You can tell me." She scooted close to her. "You can tell me anything." She pulled her into a hug, and they held tight to each other. Proton and neutron.

Watching them, my heart was so full that I ached with it. When Gab opened her eyes and saw me, she laughed. "Lei. We made Jules cry."

Leila let go of Gab with one arm and gestured me over to join the hug, smiling. "Of course we did."

And that made the ache worse, and greater, the feeling that came from how well they knew me. I wrapped my arms around them both.

Chapter 24

I woke the next morning to the smell of real coffee. I followed my nose to the kitchen, where my mother was refolding the bag of coffee from Laroche's. "Happy Mother's Day," I said, hugging her.

She hugged me back. "I made you some tar," she said, stepping back and nodding at the coffee maker with a smile.

I laughed. "Bless you."

"What time should Casey come? Is ten still okay?" She pulled mugs out of the cabinet.

"Yup." I was making eggs in purgatory — poached in a spicy tomato sauce — and toasted sourdough bread and a fruit salad.

When the coffee was ready, we sat down at the table. "I have a Mother's Day gift for you," she said. She shrugged nervously. "If you want it."

"A Mother's Day gift for me?" I asked. "Isn't that backward?"

She smiled, then grew serious again. "I found Carol."

"Carol?"

"Ethan's mom." She held her hands tight around her mug.

I took a breath. "Oh. Is she still in Milwaukee?"

Mom nodded. "She's divorced now, though."

I nodded, trying to process what this might mean. Six months ago, Milwaukee meant nothing to me. Now, somehow, it was everything. "Did you talk to her?" I asked.

She shook her head. "I wanted to talk to you first. I'll do whatever you want."

"I want to meet her," I said. But upon saying the words, I immediately grew anxious. "But maybe not yet." I couldn't bear for another relationship with newfound family to go wrong.

She nodded. "Sure, no need to rush. Take your time."

"I will." And I would. This time I would proceed slowly. Carefully. Thoughtfully.

Casey arrived right on time, bearing a bouquet of white lilies. He wished my mom a happy Mother's Day and kissed her on the lips. We had breakfast on the screened porch, which was filled with the smell of the newly bloomed lilacs.

Then Casey drove us downtown to brave the crowds at the Art Institute.

"Does your daughter like the Art Institute?" I asked from the backseat.

"Allie loves all museums," Casey said. "She's a born nerd."

"I can't wait to meet her."

Casey glanced back with a smile. "She's excited to meet you, too."

As we worked our way down I-94, I thought of Luke. This would be his first Mother's Day without a mother. My heart ached for him.

I sent him a message: *Just wanted you to know you're in my thoughts today. I know it can't be easy. I'm thinking of her, too. *hugs**

Sending a similar message to Buddy was harder. I didn't know what he knew about me, what he thought about me. But I did it anyway.

Luke responded for both of them. *Thanks, Jules. We went to the cemetery and then out to brunch. We're going to watch the Cubs game this afternoon.*

I wrote, *I'm going by Wrigley Field right now. On our way to the Art Institute.*

He sent back a smiley. *Give the Thornes my regards.*

I sent a smiley back. *I will.*

And then I thought of Eli, who probably barely remembered Mother's Days with his mother. I messaged him, *Hey, is this a rough day for you?*

He wrote back a few minutes later, *IT IS AN AWESOME DAY.* He followed it with a photo of his acceptance letter from the summer program at University of Iowa.

I sent back congratulations and confetti.

He wrote, *A FEW MORE WEEKS AND I'M OUT OF HERE. PLUS, BONUS — LOOK WHAT IS IN THE CAFÉ.*

He sent a picture of an unreasonably attractive guy sitting at the window, reading and sipping coffee. Eli added, *PLEASE, JESUS, LET HIM BE GAY.*

I smiled. Oh, Eli. Apparently he was not at all bested by the day, which shouldn't have surprised me, given his general feelings about Hallmark holidays. I wrote back, *I'll send a prayer up, too.* And then I added, *I love you, fyi.*

He replied, *You're such a mom.* ☺

I laughed.

When we arrived at our destination, my mom threw me a bone and suggested we start in the basement.

This time I looked at every single Thorne miniature, with Mom and Casey at my side. Casey shared freely of his vast arsenal of history, geography, art, and minutiae. It wasn't hard to see where his daughter must get her nerdiness. I liked him an awful lot, although not as much as my mother liked him; she beamed at him like a smitten schoolgirl. Fortunately, he beamed back at her the same way.

I didn't even mind wandering around the painting exhibitions upstairs with them.

It was a good day.

Later that week, I graduated from high school. As we lined up, I heard girls saying things like, "Can you believe we're actually graduating?" And I thought to myself, *Well, yes. I can.* To me it was more like a "finally" than an "actually." I hadn't felt like a high-school kid in a long time — especially after all I'd been through that year. I was more than ready for "next." For once, I was the one who wasn't a huge emotional mess. I only welled up twice: when Gab's and Leila's names were called.

Summer blew in like a hurricane. My days at Tina's were dust-filled and unglamorous, but they were happy. Sometimes I would come home and find Casey cooking dinner. He planted herbs in pots in the small yard, and he often asked my opinions on which herbs to use in what dish, even though I suspected he knew more about cooking than I did by multiples. But it was clear that he was making an effort, and it meant a lot to me — more so for my mom's sake than mine. He wanted to be welcome. He wanted to fit in.

Mom was careful about how they were at home — he never slept over or anything — but there were changes. Hard not to notice that his name appeared in half her sentences. Also, she smiled more and zoned out a lot.

Gab had the summer job she'd been waiting her whole life for: a counselor at Camp Chi. She'd camped there as a kid, but she was never gone for more than two or three weeks. Now she'd be gone the entire summer. For me, it would be a taste of what was coming.

Eli was off in the cornfields of Iowa, making his novel more brilliant. I was glad he had something to offset the pain of Daisy's sudden passing. I had rushed to his side, just like I had when Jay died. I repeated my routine of comfort administration, rat removal, and cremation. I wrote Daisy's obituary on a napkin to match Jay's, and Eli framed them together. In the fall, he'd start over with new rats. But for now, his focus was Iowa. And even from afar, I fussed over him and he mostly ignored me. And that was okay.

Luke graduated from Lawrence, and it hurt my heart that Mima didn't live to see it. How sad Luke must have been on one of the most important days of his life. Buddy, too. I wished she could have been there. I wished I could have been there, too. In a universe where I hadn't fucked things up, I might have been. I messaged him my most heartfelt congratulations, and he thanked me. Very civil. Our correspondence now was less frequent, more moderated — a far cry from the days when I would wait with bated breath for my phone to vibrate with a new message, and then knock myself out to charm him with my cleverness in hopes of being irresistible. In hopes of being more to him than I ever could be.

But I knew now that what I wanted was impossible, knew that I had to learn to want less. If I wanted to hold on to him, I had to start letting him go.

Chapter 25

*O*ne weekend in late June, Casey invited my mom and me to meet his daughter. She was with him two weekends a month — longer in the summer and over holidays. Allie was a bespectacled eight-and-a-half-year-old with bangs and slightly buck teeth who asked a lot of questions and looked skeptical while evaluating the answers. The first thing she asked me was how many Harry Potter books had I read, and did I think they were overrated. I told her all of them, and not even a little. She smiled with her lips closed — probably self-conscious about her teeth — and said, "Okay, then." Like that settled it.

While Casey grilled fish in their tiny backyard and my mom made a salad, Allie showed me her bedroom, which had only a small portion of her prize possessions, since she lived at her mother's the majority of the time. But she did show me her rock collection, including her favorite pieces of pyrite, which, she explained, is commonly called "fool's gold" but is actually a sulfide mineral.

During dinner, I tried not to laugh out loud when she wanted to know which I liked better, sedimentary rocks or metamorphic rocks. Casey saved me by encouraging Allie to tell me about the differences, which she was only too happy to do. I was wildly and gloriously over my depth with her, but entranced with her intelligence and energy. She was geeky and bright and passionate about an amazing number of things. She was eight years old and already her own person. I was eighteen years old and still wanting everyone to like me. I could learn a lot from her.

One Saturday when Casey and my mom went to a gallery showing in Evanston, I babysat Allie and took her to her swim lesson at the Willow Grove pool. Her teacher was a cute, shy guy named Otis. He was a swimmer in college and, boy, did it show: his tanned body was a work of staggering beauty. I lounged under an umbrella in a sundress and dark glasses, watching Allie try to do what Otis was so patiently teaching her.

As I ogled Otis from behind the safety of my glasses, I couldn't help comparing him to Luke. Like Luke, Otis wasn't just hot, although he was definitely that. He was also adorable. Sweet. Someone I could imagine dating. But unlike Luke, Otis was not my sort-of brother. As with the guitar-playing hottie at Beloit, I felt a glimmer of hope at feeling that way about someone — someone who was not Luke.

When her lesson was over, Allie dragged Otis over to me. "Otis says I'm doing really good," she told me. "Tell her, Otis."

"Right!" He nodded and tipped his sunglasses up on his head. I'm pretty sure he was blushing. "Yeah, she's doing great." He had light brown eyes and a really sweet smile.

"So tell my dad, okay?" Allie said to me, making her eyes big.

I handed Allie her glasses, trying not to laugh. "I will tell him."

"Can I have money for a snow cone?" she asked, putting her glasses on.

I pulled a couple dollars out of my bag and handed them to her. She took off, her feet slapping wet footprints onto the concrete. Otis was still standing there, smiling at her, his arms crossed. The smell of sunscreen and chlorine emanated off him, not unpleasantly.

"She's a character, eh?" I smiled at him.

"Yeah." He grinned. "She's teaching me a lot."

I laughed, and he did, too. He had a great laugh.

He lifted his chin, spotting someone in the distance, then raised a hand in that direction. He turned back to me. "My next lesson is here. See you later?"

I nodded, although I had no idea if I'd see him later. I wouldn't have minded, though.

I watched him walk off.

He looked as good going as coming.

"This color is puce."

I looked up. Allie stood beside me, sucking on the top of her snow cone, making loud slurping noises. An anxious, sad feeling washed over me as I glanced at her snow cone, recalling the color of Luke's ridiculous ramen abomination.

"I asked for a mix of all the flavors," Allie explained. "That's why it's puce."

"How's it taste?"

"Good! Want to try it?"

"That's okay."

"It's the same price even if you get all the flavors. So it's a good value."

I smiled. I thought, *Enjoy the illusion of having it all, kid. Someday you'll discover that puce is not actually better than the color red or the taste of lemon.*

I hoped, for Allie's sake, that this lesson was a long time in coming.

She sat down next to me. "I saw Otis talking to you. Are you going to go out with him?"

"Ha. I don't think so."

"He's pretty cute." She side-eyed me like a know-it-all.

"Yeah, he's not hard to look at."

She laughed and slapped her leg. "Not hard to look at! That's funny. Did you make that up?"

"No." I laughed.

"I wonder if he's smart," she said, gnawing on the ice with her front teeth. "Brains are more important than looks. Do you think he has a girlfriend?"

I leaned back on the chaise. "Probably."

"Do you have a boyfriend?"

I only hesitated for a moment. "No."

"Do you think your mom will marry my dad?"

Her question jarred me. I didn't know much about her mother — I didn't even know if she had remarried. I knew she and Casey divorced when Allie was just two.

"I don't know," I said. "Do you?"

She nodded. "I hope so."

I couldn't help smiling. "You do? Why?"

She tipped the snow cone and slurped the liquid. "He's always in a really good mood now. He likes her a lot."

"Do you like her?" I asked, tilting my head.

She nodded. "She's really nice. She cleans the kitchen and she talks him into letting me have Cocoa Puffs."

I laughed. I guessed my mom was trying with Allie like Casey was trying with me.

"Plus her name sounds like mine. Abby and Allie."

"That's true!"

She grinned at me. Her teeth were turning puce. "And also, then you'd be my sister!"

Something shifted in my chest. I sat back in my lounge

chair, watching her. She tipped the snow cone back, drinking the liquid, some of which spilled down her chin. "Oops," she mumbled, dabbing at it with her towel.

I couldn't help smiling at her. She was way ahead of me, thinking about our parents marrying, but the idea of a sister . . . I had never considered something like this. I could be a big sister. And Allie — she was so special. I could make sure she knew how special she was. I could send her letters from college. I could introduce her to all my friends as my sister. And she would look up to me. I would love her, and she'd love me back.

"That could be pretty cool," I said, reaching over to flick an ant off her leg. "Being your sister."

"Yeah. Hey, Jules?" she said without looking up from her snow cone.

"Hey, Allie?"

"Can you make that macaroni-and-cheese ramen-noodle thing?"

I laughed. "Again?" I had made it for her before her lesson, just a few hours ago.

She nodded. "It's so good. I never knew you could do so much stuff with ramen noodles. How'd you learn that?"

"I don't know. Trial and error, mostly." I looked away. It was impossible not to think about Luke when I thought of ramen.

"Well, you're an awesome cook."

Iron Chef Ramen.

I lowered my sunglasses before Allie could see me tearing up.

Gab's remark about not being a good correspondent proved prophetic, because by mid-July I'd only heard from her a few times. I actually heard more frequently from Eli as the weeks wore on. He had met someone at a writing workshop, and he sometimes sent me random brief texts about how hot/smart/cute/talented this guy was. I hoped he was falling madly in love. But I hoped even more that he wouldn't get his heart broken. I worried about that, especially when he sent this message:

Jules? If anything ever happens to me, I want you to write my obituary. You have to promise. Make it really good, okay?

I was so alarmed that I wrote back: *WE ARE NOT TALKING ABOUT YOUR DEATH AND YOU'D BETTER NOT DIE ANYTIME SOON OR I WILL FUCKING KILL YOU. ARE YOU OKAY?*

And he wrote back, *Never better, Drools, no worries. Swearsies. Just thinking about the (very very very) faraway future. And wanting to make sure you'd be the one to write it.*

It was so dumb, but tears stung my eyes, although whether it was more the idea of his dying someday or the idea that he wanted me to write the obituary, I wasn't even sure. I wrote, *I promise.*

And then came something truly unexpected. On a rainy day at the end of July, I found a package at the front

349

door when I got home from work. The return address was Milwaukee. Luke's house. My stomach clenched up instantly — I had no idea what it might be.

I was covered in dust from unpacking countless boxes of old books at Tina's, so I paused to wash up before getting out a knife and cutting through the brown tape that sealed the box closed.

At the very top of the box, there was a folded note. From Buddy.

Dear Jules,

I hope this note finds you well.

In this box are things Sarah wanted you to have. She set them aside in the weeks before she passed and asked me to get them to you. Mostly they are family heirlooms, passed down to Sarah from her mother or grandmother. She labeled them so you'd know what they are, where they came from, that sort of thing. After meeting you, she was more certain than ever that these things would mean something to you, and I can't tell you how much that pleased her. There are, she said, some things a woman wants to pass on to her daughter. These are those things.

I paused to blink back tears. Just when I had begun to accept that maybe I didn't mean as much to this family as I'd hoped . . . this.

I read the rest of his note:

Sarah always felt you were a gift. Knowing you're okay brought closure that she'd always needed. Seeing you again meant the world to her. To both of us. To all of us. Thank you for that.

I wish this note were coming to you sooner, and I hope you'll forgive me. Although Sarah's passing wasn't unexpected, it was somehow no less a shock. Growing old together was always the plan, and I'm still struggling to understand a life without her.

Please keep in touch, and perhaps soon we can see one another again. Luke tells me you're going to Beloit. I think that's wonderful. Perhaps sometime I could visit you, maybe take you out to lunch?

With much love,

Buddy

I set the paper down and cried. The note itself was so overwhelming that I needed a moment before I explored the contents of the box.

That she felt I was a gift . . . *she* was the gift. *They* were the gift. How lucky I had been — in so many countless, immeasurable ways. And how close I'd come to losing everything. I still had Buddy, and with each day that passed, I hoped I could still have Luke, too — and not the fantasy Luke, but the real one. The lasting one.

When I had steadied myself, I began going through the contents of the box, entranced by the treasures within. I never imagined family heirlooms being passed down to me, but here they were. Mima's mother's jewelry. Candlesticks from Poland. A brass mortar and pestle from Russia. Some handwritten Jewish recipes with words I didn't even know. *Kreplach. Gribenes. Schmaltz.*

I couldn't wait to learn what they were.

In the very bottom of the box, wrapped in layers and layers of tissue, I discovered an old, darkened silver mezuzah. Warmth tingled through me as I removed it with trembling hands. In Mima's spidery pen, a note wrapped around it said, *From the Belarus home of Leon Faigen, my maternal grandfather.*

I pressed it to my heart. A world was opening up to me — a world I hadn't quite felt was really mine to claim. But if Mima had mothered me, even only for a while, and wanted to pass down to me these precious family heirlooms, then perhaps I was entitled to some small sliver of that history?

I sat on my bed, my chest so full I didn't know how to bear it. Finally, I picked up my phone and sent a photo of my new treasures to Gab. I wrote, *Look what Mima left me. #MOT*

Relentless heat pushed July into August, when Leila went to France with her family. Around the same time, my mom got a painting — the one I had been thinking of as *The Fucked-Up Sky* — into a juried art competition. Casey was beside himself with pride. He brought sparkling cider over to celebrate and surprised her with an invitation to a weekend away in New York, where there was a gallery walk. She glanced at me, hesitating. I laughed and shook my head, like *You don't have to check with me, silly. Go to New York.*

But her first thoughts were of me. Somehow I had become the center of her universe.

Also in New York now was Luke. Bard had offered him a fellowship, and he didn't hesitate.

I had begun to accept that Luke and I would never be Gab and Daniel; I understood that now. And it wasn't just because I'd crossed a line with Luke. The reason Gab and Daniel were Gab and Daniel was that they grew up together. They shared parents; they shared relatives; they shared memories. And, yes, they shared genes, but it was their sprawling, detailed history that truly made them siblings. Luke and I would never have that.

But I would always hope for — work toward — the possibility of our being *something.* I wasn't over him, not by a long stretch, but my love for him was real. I hoped that, in time, that love would reconfigure itself into something good, something workable. Something sustainable and enduring.

Love was worth fighting for.

Chapter 26

*L*ate one steamy mid-August evening, I sat on the screened porch, drinking crimson hibiscus iced tea and drafting an e-mail I'd been mentally composing for months. The call of crickets rose high and loud, and the heavy scent of late summer roses drifted up as I read what I'd written.

> *Dear Carol,*
>
> *I understand that you would be open to meeting me, and I would like that very much. I'd be happy to drive up to Milwaukee, or if you'd prefer you could come see us in Maplebrook. I'm free the next couple of weekends, and then I'll be at Beloit as a new student, which also isn't too*

terribly far from you. Let me know what might work?

Looking forward to meeting you!

Love,

Jules

With a deep breath, I set it in motion. I watched until the "sending" alert changed to "sent," marveling at the way the fraction of a moment has the potential to change a life forever.

A warm breeze lifted my hair as I set my phone down. Fireflies flickered over the grass, winking in and out as twilight edged toward dusk. I sipped my iced tea, then picked up my yearbook. In the waning light, I again paged through the senior baby pictures, endlessly fascinated by trying to guess who was who. Gab I would have known anywhere, despite the eye patch and costume. Even as a toddler pirate, she had the countenance of someone who knew she owned the room.

Leila's picture was tougher to look at. We don't know how old she was — maybe a year? A little younger? — but her expression had a blankness that caused a terrible squeeze in my heart.

The photo of me, nearby on the same page, stood in sharp relief. A silly, giggling, chubby, overjoyed child. Each time I looked at it, I felt at once enormous gratitude and unbearable sorrow. I loved the photo, loved how happy I looked, loved that it captured a time that had almost been lost to me, a time that I knew informed who I was today. But I couldn't look at it without thinking of my mother, and what that day, that time, must have been like for her. And of course Mima, the woman who had stepped in and saved my life when it most needed saving. Gratitude and sorrow. Rich and sweet and bitter.

As I set the yearbook down, my phone alerted me to a message. I picked it up from the table and glanced at the screen, eager to see if it was an email from Carol.

But it was a text from Luke.

My heart did its familiar dance, but instead of trying to repress my natural reaction, I opened myself to it, trying to observe it as honestly and clearly as I could — something I learned from Gab's mom. And while there was an undercurrent of that old, inappropriate excitement — I was only human, after all — the dominant feeling was purer than that. It was similar to the pleasure I felt in getting a rare message from Gab at summer camp or a postcard from Leila from Provence. Or a text from Eli about his workshop or boyfriend. It was the happiness I felt in knowing that people I loved were thinking of me.

His message was a photo — a messy kitchen counter with a few packages of ramen noodles and various other items. He wrote, *Apparently I'm no better at shopping and cooking in NY than I was in WI. Any ideas here? I have a couple pans. And a fork. And running water.*

I couldn't help smiling. I enlarged the photo to get a

better look. Eggs. American cheese. Sour cream and onion potato chips. Deli ham. Oh, Luke . . . He was such a bachelor. But this actually had prospects.

OH AND MEASURING CUPS. I HAVE MEASURING CUPS.

Progress! I wrote.

Baby steps, he replied.

Yes. Baby steps. I wrote: *Do you have a small pan with a lid?*

He sent a photo of exactly the right pan — small and deep enough to be able to cover an egg with noodles.

I wrote, *Perfect. I might be able to finesse a creamy ham and cheese ramen with a poached egg and potato chip topping, but after all, I am an Iron Chef. But you? I don't know . . .*

He wrote back: *Oh come on. Give me a chance. I've learned a lot. Like not to add jelly beans.*

I laughed out loud. We had inside jokes — not as many as Gab and Daniel, but it was something. And maybe, in time, we'd have more.

Okay, I wrote. *But you have to do EXACTLY AS I SAY. Step one: FOLLOW THE DIRECTIONS ON THE PACKAGE EXACTLY. YES, USE THE FLAVOR PACKET. AND A TIMER. USE A TIMER. Step two: while it simmers, crack an egg into a small bowl. Slice two pieces of cheese and two pieces of ham into strips the width of a black piano key.*

Luke: *THANK YOU FOR CONVERTING THE RECIPE INTO UNITS I UNDERSTAND.*

Me: *I HAVE LEARNED THINGS, TOO.*

Understatement of the century.

Me: *Step three: when timer goes off, add ham and cheese and stir until cheese melts. Step four: carefully drop egg in and use a fork to cover it with noodles. Step five: cover and turn off heat and wait four minutes. Step six: transfer to bowl and crush some potato chips over the top. Step seven: EAT.*

He wrote, **cracks knuckles* I'M GOING IN. STAY TUNED FOR PHOTO.*

A warm feeling spread through my chest.

Happiness. Hope.

I looked out at the evening sky as the day gave up the ghost. A last bit of coral glowed at the horizon as the sun disappeared. Soon the velvet sky would glimmer with stars.

When Luke messaged the photo of his dinner, it looked exactly as it was supposed to. *It's so good!* he wrote. *Finally got something right.*

I wrote, *Excellent work, Ramen-san.*

I learned from the best, he replied.

I sent a smiley.

The first stars twinkled against the dark sky. I leaned back and breathed in the soft night air, rich with the exquisite smell of the roses. Soon their blooms would fade, and then they'd be gone, and summer with them. That familiar ache of loss washed over me, but rather than sinking into gloom, I paused to examine the feeling, that tendency of mine to lament what *isn't*. I tried to observe it without judgment, the way Gab's mom had taught me.

Things bloom and then they die, yes. But so many things happen in between, some of them staggeringly beautiful in their own right: The glorious foliage of fall. The pristine, crystalline beauty of winter. And didn't I start this year longing for the particular heady wonders of spring?

Why was it so easy to lose sight of what I had? The truth was, I wouldn't trade any of it.

Perhaps the secret of contentedness lay in being attentive to what *is* rather than what is not. Being fully present in each season, each moment, appreciating what treasures it offers — and trusting that other treasures, maybe even unexpected ones, could be waiting around the corner.

I reached for my phone. *You still there?*

Yes, he wrote. *I'm right here.*

Acknowledgments

I owe such a debt of gratitude to my family: Noah, Zach, and Gabe, thank you for unwavering support and all manner of help. Gabe, you are my story oracle. Thank you for your invaluable reads and feedback — and for bringing Eli to life in *A Perfect Wedding*! Unforgettable.

Kaylan Adair, my brilliant, beloved editor, you are a dream. Thank you for your devotion to my work and for the immeasurable ways you make me better. Working with you is a gift and a joy.

Huge thanks go to Mary Lee Donovan, Pam Consolazio, and the entire team at Candlewick. I couldn't feel luckier.

Molly and John Cusick, thank you from the bottom of my heart for all you've done for me.

Marieke Nijkamp, fierce warrior and earth angel, I can't thank you enough for your incomparable vision, brilliance, and good-heartedness.

Rachel Solomon, I cannot remember how many early versions you read of this novel, but I thank you for all of your spot-on feedback and also for all the fun we had!

Susan Bickford, you were such a wonderful help and guide when I was navigating this story! Thank you for the years of support and friendship.

To my beautiful ogre Tena Russ, endless thanks for finding my title and fielding all my painting questions — and for all the years of life-affirming spicy lunches.

To Ashley Herring Blake, much gratitude for a very thoughtful read that led to some important changes. I am endlessly appreciative of all your generosity and goodness.

Helen Wiley, thank you for being so freaking smart, for your clear eye and weirdly deep well of information, and for your kind heart.

To Stephanie Kuehn and Stacey Lee, thank you for thoughtfully fielding questions of great specificity and importance.

So much love to all you amazing book bloggers, librarians, and readers. Thank you for all you do.

Rafe Posey, aka Pet, my steadfast friend and brilliant critique partner, thank you for always "getting" me, for always having all the nouns, and for always being yar in the pursuit of fish. (It is your CHIEF CONCERN.) I wouldn't trade you for anything. You are a wonder and a treasure and you *still* amaze me every day.

To Audrey Coulthurst, aka Maud, the most amazing writing spouse/coauthor/promo person/tech assistant/support system/eating companion/cocktail cohort/friend anyone ever had, there aren't enough pages in this entire book to express how grateful I am to you. Thank you for every laugh, every inappropriate unrepeatable, every MM, every good oyster, every bad idea, every fiery chile, every fix, every entrusted feeling, every encouragement, every morning tweet, every bizarre action, every translation, every coffee spew, every hatched plan. Thank you for being mine.

And finally, for various reasons, much gratitude to: Dahlia Adler, Jessica Bayless, Bonnie Blackburn, Mia Drelich, Kathleen Glasgow, Jessica Golub, Karen Hattrup, Emily Henry, Leofranc Holford-Strevens, Brian Katcher, Kerry Kletter, Katie Locke, Adriana Mather, Mark O'Brien, Caleb Roehrig, Deanna Roy, Rachel Simon, Kali Wallace, Sybil Ward, Elissa Whiteman, and Jeff Zentner.